cold case murder in kingfisher falls

Book Three

the charlotte dean mysteries

Phillipa Nefri Clark

cold case murder in kingfisher falls

an important note...

This book was previously published with the title **Deadly Secrets.** The book has a new title and cover and has been re-edited following rights reversion.

This series is set in Australia and written in Aussie/British English for an authentic experience.

Like to discover more about Charlotte, other titles, and Phillipa's world? Visit Phillipa's website where you can join her newsletter. www.phillipaclark.com.

For Charlotte and every person who overcomes their past to face the future with hope

chapter
one

The top of the falls offered a bleak outlook so early in the morning. It was the beginning of Charlotte's first winter in Kingfisher Falls. A swirling wind collected the chill from the river, and shivering, she gathered the scarf around her neck. Heavy mist covered the pool below, rising to the lookout in the distance. The tallest trees poked through the swirling whiteness, peppering it with strange shapes.

She'd stood here for a while—since what passed for dawn. This spot beside the top of the waterfall still called her. And rather than the trek down difficult terrain then up a long and tricky set of broken steps, Charlotte had discovered a new path back to her home.

Since finding the back gate in her garden, hidden behind overgrown vines on the fence, she'd uncovered lots of new tracks and trails in the bushland behind the bookshop. One wound through the corner of the forest to meet the river. Much quicker and less exhausting than the climb from the bottom of the falls. And as safe as any other trail around Kingfisher Falls.

She turned for home. This path was pretty with early sunlight filtering through the canopy of ghost gums to

sparkle on the slow running water. She passed the turn off to
the main road. Home was a fast-five-minute walk. But it was
through dense bushland once the river veered away. And
when the undergrowth closed in, as always, a shiver went up
Charlotte's spine.

There are no monsters in here!

Since her first view of this sprawling tract of bush a few
months ago, something kept Charlotte from venturing too
far in. She'd teased herself about the silly reaction more than
once, yet the fear lingered, and she hurried.

An internet search of the area once showed her the reach
of the land. Many hectares of native trees and bushes but
little in the way of walking tracks, except around the perimeter. According to signage around the land, it was owned by
the Kingfisher Falls Shire Council and it wasn't designated as
anything other than shire land. Not as a park, or recreation
area. Few locals used it, although Charlotte sometimes came
across people walking their dogs.

The trees cleared as the path joined a wide, rutted track.
A few hundred metres further and the back of the bookshop
came into view. Charlotte stopped for a moment, her attention on the window from her upstairs apartment overlooking the bushland. In the months she'd lived there, she'd
never seen the bushland from the room thanks to a
wardrobe blocking the window. Today this would change.
Trev was dropping by to help her move it. With a smile,
Charlotte got going, letting herself into the garden through
the back gate and locking it.

————

After a shower and coffee, Charlotte went food shopping. If
Trev was kind enough to give her a hand, then she'd make
lunch for him. Not the most confident cook, she'd taken a

couple of lessons over autumn with Doug, chef and part owner of the local Italian restaurant, Italia. Doug, along with his wife, Esther, who owned a women's clothes shop in town were her friends now.

She browsed the delicatessen department, frowning as she deciphered the scrawl of her handwriting when she'd made a list before her walk.

Never write until after coffee, Charlie.

What she planned was a simple pizza made from scratch, topped with a handful of ingredients. One was bocconcini cheese.

"What would you like, love?" On the other side of the counter, Maryanne slid on a pair of gloves. "Your usual chilli stuffed olives?"

"Not what I had in mind, but yes, please, and then—"

"Excuse me! I was waiting."

Charlotte and Maryanne turned to the woman who'd interrupted. She hadn't been there a moment ago. With unruly long red hair and a voluminous, bright purple skirt touching the ground, she would have been hard to miss.

"Please, go ahead. I'm still browsing." Charlotte smiled at Maryanne, then the other woman, who didn't even meet her eyes.

Harmony Montgomery. She'd moved into town earlier in the year and opened a shop down the street and around the corner from the bookshop. *Harmony's House of Mystique.* A fortune teller, or something of the kind. Not something of interest to Charlotte. Their paths hadn't crossed until now, although Harmony made her presence felt around town by stopping people on the streets to give them a card to redeem for a free reading.

It was an ongoing debate between Charlotte and her boss, Rosie, who was curious. "Don't waste your money." Charlotte had cautioned more than once.

"But the first one is free."

"Then don't waste your time."

"Just a bit of fun." Rosie would grumble.

Charlotte knew sooner or later Rosie would end up doing what she wanted, but it grated on her nerves. She was facts based and struggled with the idea of what she considered fake promises.

Maryanne handed a wrapped parcel to Harmony with a friendly, "Is there something else?"

The other woman shook her head as she almost snatched the parcel and walked away. But then she did an abrupt about face and reached a card over the counter with something like a smile forced on her face. "How rude I must sound. Please, accept a free reading at your convenience."

This time she left and once she was out of sight, Charlotte glanced at Maryanne, who turned the card in her fingers before tucking it into a pocket and changing her gloves.

"I'm sure you were first Charlotte, so sorry about that."

"It really doesn't worry me."

"She's a little bit...full on. Must be her connection with the other side. Now, olives."

————

There'd been no point discussing Harmony Montgomery further, not when Maryanne's beliefs differed from hers. Personal beliefs were tricky. One of the biggest obstacles for a psychiatrist to overcome.

Which you no longer are.

Not entirely true. As long as she paid her dues and complied with the requirements, she was a psychiatrist. So far, she'd hung onto it. Afraid to let it go. But afraid to live it again. Charlotte pounded the pizza dough. She loved the bookshop. Thump. And intended to buy it when Rosie was ready to sell. Thump. Thump.

Charlotte covered the dough and left it on a side table behind glass where the sun would warm it enough to do its thing. She made a coffee and took it out to the balcony.

The day was pleasant now. Kingfisher Falls had enjoyed a long autumn and how beautiful a season it was. The last of the leaved deciduous trees decorated the valley and hills with gold and red and purple. Although the evenings came faster and were cooler, the days still offered enough warmth to enjoy the outside.

Elbows on the railing, Charlotte held her cup between her palms and watched the street below. Not much happened on Sundays. Traffic in the shape of cars and pedestrians wandered to the local churches, or cafés, or both. Families window shopped as they headed to the parks. A peaceful and sleepy day.

Since the events earlier in the year, the town had resumed its normal routine. No murders, or attempted kidnapping. No old ladies with evil intent, or younger ones, for that matter. Her little town was again a sweet and safe haven. If only she could sort herself out. The conflict inside was more than whether to keep her licence. It revolved around her mother's illness and a nagging worry of her own future health.

It mattered now. More than ever, thanks to a man named Trevor Sibbritt.

chapter
two

Trev climbed the stairs to Charlotte's door two at a time.

He waited a moment before knocking, running a hand through his short hair, and taking off his sunglasses. Then, he tapped.

The door swung inward. "Hey." Charlie held it open as he entered, then closed it behind them both.

He sniffed the air and his mouth watered. Whatever was cooking was good. Garlic and basil wafted his way and his stomach rumbled. Quietly, he hoped.

"Thanks so much for helping with this." Charlotte disappeared around the corner and he left his sunglasses on the counter and followed. She was in the bedroom at the back of the apartment. The room was large and under furnished with only a narrow old bed along one wall, and the wardrobe —his target—blocking the window.

"It's a big piece of furniture."

"So, I'll ask someone stronger?" She grinned.

"Hysterical. I just don't want you hurt."

"Then grab an end."

The apartment was once the home of the family who built the building and ran the downstairs as a bakery until

Trev's parents bought it and turned it into the bookshop. Since then, there'd been various tenants renting the apartment, but this wardrobe was old and probably an original piece left behind with the sale.

And heavy. It took them ten minutes to move it. Bit by bit. More push than lift. But once the wardrobe was against the wall, he joined Charlotte at the liberated window. Panting. A bit.

Covered in grime and spiderwebs, the window still flooded the room with daylight. Charlotte brushed a web aside and worked on the lock without success. "Darn. Would you have a go and I'll get a brush and pan."

By the time she returned with an assortment of cleaners, the window was wide open. It slid up and Trev blew dust out of the runners, wishing he hadn't at the cloud of particles. "Think I made it worse."

"I'll do a proper clean in here later but will just move some of these." She began sweeping away the long-abandoned webs. "Then we can see out without them sticking to us."

"Like this?" Trev extracted a cobweb from a strand of her hair. "Not a big issue for me as such."

Charlotte stopped sweeping, her head tilting as she ran her eyes over his head. "Nothing could hide in such short hair."

"What smells so good?"

Her eyes widened and she sniffed the air. "Oh, I'd better turn the oven off." And she was gone again.

Trev finished cleaning around the window frame and gazed around the room. It needed some love. Some cracks filled and new paint would go a long way. Updated furniture. The old bed was in poor condition beneath a large cardboard box. He'd noticed it before.

The only other time he'd been in here in years was to

look at a corkboard Charlotte hid, one with her list of clues around the death of Octavia Morris. And his mood wasn't good then.

A pile of Christmas cards sat on top of whatever else was in there. He picked up the top one. A beautiful handmade card.

"Oh. Um, here, I'll put that away." Charlotte hurried in and took the card from his fingers. Her face was rigid with the serious, slightly anxious expression he'd come to recognise. This box was related to her past. She slid the card away and folded the flaps over the contents.

"So, is lunch burnt?"

"Come and find out."

————

Charlotte waited for Trev to bite into a slice of pizza, holding her breath as he chewed, not giving anything away. They sat on the balcony with iced tea and the pizza between them. She wasn't going to eat until he gave her a hint of its palatability.

He swallowed. "Did you lace this with something?"

"Sure. I always poison people I invite over."

"Because you're not eating it." He nodded to her plate. "Getting bored without any murder mysteries to solve, so creating your own?"

"By murdering the new police officer in town. Who happens to be the adored son of the woman I work for and love to bits." Charlotte picked up a slice. "Where would I hide your body?"

"In the woods. And this is fantastic." Trev took another bite and winked.

It wasn't bad. The crust might have been a fraction thinner

but tasted good. And the toppings were yum. Bocconcini, semi dried tomatoes, garlic, and basil from the garden. Yes, her own herbs were coming along as well as a selection of vegetables. Next time, she'd create something more ambitious and use more of her home grown produce. Next time.

"What's the smile for?" Trev asked.

Being happy? Knowing you live here in Kingfisher Falls now? And you like my pizza.

"Nothing really."

The sparkle in Trev's eyes told her he didn't believe her.

———

"I can't understand why anyone would deliberately cover this view!" Charlotte finished cleaning the window in the back bedroom and tossed her cloth into the bucket of soapy water. "It makes no sense."

"Stopped trying to work out why people do things a long time ago." Trev leaned out of the window to peer down. "Garden looks pretty. Lots of vegies growing."

Charlotte joined him. "Carrots. Lettuce in two varieties. I'll put rocket in. Some beetroot. And look at the basil and rosemary!"

"Always enjoyed my garden in Rivers End." Trev stepped back. "Hope it gives the next incumbent some pleasure."

"I'm sure Rosie is happy to share her garden with you."

"And I'm enjoying being home. But it'll be good to find my own place again."

"You could buy Octavia's mansion." Charlotte kept her face straight. "Or there is Glenys Lane's place. I hear that's going on the market to pay her legal fees."

"Bit too spooky up there for me. Actually, both are too creepy. Good thing you're not a real estate agent." He glanced at his watch. "Sorry. Speaking of Mum, we have a shopping date. Apparently, I need new sheets and blankets."

He headed for the door, giving Charlotte a much-needed moment to control a sudden rush of heat to her face. She'd once slept at Rosie's in the room always kept ready for Trev's visits. The sheets were fresh, yet his scent had lingered on the soft cotton.

In your mind!

"Where are you shopping?" She pulled herself together and followed. "Can't imagine there's too many places close by."

"She has her heart set on Highpoint. There's a place there she likes. And it is about a forty-minute drive, so I'd better get a move on. Unless you'd like to come along?"

"Tempting. Thanks, but I might give the bedroom a full clean and get an idea of how to jazz it up a bit. For the next shopping trip."

Trev opened his arms and Charlotte snuggled against him for a moment. "Thanks for helping me."

"Pleasure. And lunch was lovely, Charlie." He released her and reached for his sunglasses. "Enjoy cleaning."

———

"Sure. Love to clean. Best. Thing. Ever." Charlotte pushed the bucket away and closed the wardrobe door. Whoever once lived here might never have cleaned the inside of this heavy timber unit. But now it was done and after two hours working non-stop, so was Charlotte.

She lowered the window across to close it and locked it with a bit of pressure. The view from up here, high above the track behind the fence, was straight into the bushland. There were gaps she'd not noticed. Sunlight on the trees gave an impression of a path of sorts with a trail of colourful flowers alongside.

Charlotte put her cleaning gear away and considered making a coffee. But the path intrigued her and she was longing to stretch her legs.

A few minutes later, she unlocked the gate. Standing in the middle of the track for a moment, she looked back to the window then across to where she remembered the path beginning. At first there was nothing to mark it. Only the usual dense undergrowth and the familiar sensation of trepidation. But then it opened to a narrow but defined trail.

To where?

Under her feet, the path was dirt and wide enough for one. Flowers grew in scattered clumps on either side. Daisies. Or at least, daisy-like flowers in purple. It was almost as though they'd been sown along here because Charlotte hadn't come across them on any of her other walks, nor, as she looked side to side, were there any further off the path. She took some photos. Perhaps Rosie would know what variety these were.

After a few minutes the path disappeared and Charlotte stopped. Behind, there was nothing to indicate a whole town was close by. A little shudder rippled across her shoulders and she clenched her hands.

"It is quiet. Isolated. Nothing more." The sound of her voice offered little comfort. The path may have ended, but the flowers continued off at a sharp angle. Charlotte followed them, skirting bushes and stepping over logs. A clearing opened. A long-fallen gum tree rested to one side. Tree ferns softened the perimeter. Somewhere close by, the river gurgled.

This was a peaceful place. Beautiful in its solitary way. Cool. Restful.

Between two tall trees, the flowers massed to form a long, purple rectangle of sorts.

Charlotte's stomach tensed. At one end of the mass, there were other flowers against a rock. But in a wreath. A fresh wreath.

This was a grave.

chapter
three

Charlotte scanned the area around her. The flowers in the wreath looked so fresh. What if the person who'd laid them was close?

How old was the grave? Assuming it was a grave and not a prop for a photo shoot or some prank.

It is a grave.

All was quiet. Not even birdsong reached her ears. She dialled Trev, keeping one eye on the way she'd walked in.

"I hope you are calling with a reason for me to stop shopping." Trev answered. Shopping mall music played in the background and a child screamed.

Rosie's voice echoed through the phone. "Don't believe him. He is having a wonderful time, darling."

"Hi Rosie."

"Charlie says hi. You finish browsing, Mum, and I'll be right back." A moment later, the music quietened a little. "Sorry. Found an exit. What's up?"

"I went for a bit of a walk."

"Ri…ght."

How to explain?

"I closed the window upstairs and saw a path. One with flowers. So, I followed it and now I'm here."

There was a pause from Trev. He must be reconsidering his decision to answer the phone.

"Anyway, there is a point. And I don't know what to do but I imagine phoning a police officer about a grave is a good start."

"Sorry? I know it's a bit noisy here, but I thought you said a grave."

"Oh, didn't I say that first?"

"Charlotte, what grave?"

"The one in the forest. Under some tree ferns." Somehow it was important he knew something relevant.

"Tell me you are okay."

"Of course. And it isn't a new grave so don't think you need to hurry home. It might be years old. Or not a grave at all, but it is covered with flowers and a new wreath. Here, I'll send you a photo."

Perhaps she should have led with an image. Her words weren't working, and Charlotte recognised the effect of adrenaline on her system. She zoomed in on the grave and took a couple of shots, then sent them to Trev.

"The flowers in the wreath look so fresh. There's lavender and roses and—"

"Charlotte stop for a sec."

She took a long breath, imagining Trev checking the photos. He'd tell her it wasn't real. To go home and have a coffee and a lie down.

"I know you won't touch anything."

"No. And I'm a distance away." Charlotte said.

"Can you find your way back there? For that matter, can you find your way out?"

"Yes. And yes."

"Then leave now. Go back into the apartment and wait

for a uniformed officer to arrive. I'll make a call and leave once I find Mum." The music grew louder again. "Text me once you are home."

"Okay, but if anyone is in this grave, they're beyond immediate help and I can—"

"You can start walking. Send me your location and get walking. Now, please."

Charlotte grinned at his authoritative tone. "I'm leaving. Tell Rosie I'm sorry."

Once Trev hung up, Charlotte sent him her location and spent another few minutes taking more photos. She climbed on a tree stump and did some panorama shots. The light through the trees was pretty but fading. Her phone dinged.

Are you home yet?

"Are you?" She typed back.

On my way.

And got going.

Once the grave was out of sight, she panicked and retraced her steps to find it. From then on she took photos every few metres. Trev might be driving now so couldn't keep an eye on her location, but a sense of urgency drove her to follow his instructions.

I mustn't forget the path.

But she was back on the flower trail and ahead, the main track beckoned. Soon she was running, and she didn't know why and then sunlight filled her eyes and she was out of the bush. She sprinted to the back fence and flung the gate open. Panting, she turned and memorised the way in again. Then shut the gate and locked it.

———

"I appreciate it, Bryce." Trev disconnected the call from his steering wheel. Detective Bryce Davis might not be his first choice to go to Charlotte, but someone had to, and he was still so far away.

"Darling, everything is fine."

"Charlotte is probably still taking photographs from every imaginable angle. Why does she even do that?"

From the corner of his eye, Trev was aware of how stressed his mother was getting. She might sound relaxed and supportive, but her hands gripped his phone and her face was set.

Think, Trevor.

If…and it was a biggie, *if* it was a grave, then whose? Kingfisher Falls might have more than its share of corrupt politicians and peculiar criminals, but murder? Apart from Octavia Morris' recent death—solved—he couldn't recall another crime of this calibre.

He reached his hand over to cover Rosie's. "She's okay. She just doesn't listen well."

Rosie laughed. And he joined in.

His phoned beeped and Rosie checked the message. "She's in the apartment. The third bedroom to be precise. And watching from the window *in case*."

"In case?"

"You know Charlie."

"Can you elaborate, Mum?" Trev wished he had the patrol car. Why was he so concerned about getting home quickly was a mystery. Charlie hadn't seen a murder, or been stalked, or any one of the number of things she attracted to herself. Yet every sense drove him to touch the accelerator a bit more often and worry. Worry every minute.

"She likes to record things. I imagine there is a reason, which she might not even understand. But she photographs anything and everything."

What kind of reason?

Charlie had a difficult childhood. And a tough adulthood.

Were her terrible experiences with two former clients enough to drive her to cover herself with a record of some sort?

"What happens next, dear?"

"I'll go and take a look. Seeing as Bryce is around, he can give me a hand determining whether there's a body there. If so, we'll call in the medical examiner."

"Are we turning into Midsomer Murders? First Octavia… oh!" Rosie turned to Trev. "Do you think Glenys killed more people?"

"Apart from her husband and Octavia? Is anyone else missing?"

"Pity Jonas and the Murdoch brothers aren't," she muttered.

"Mum." Trev had to smile.

"I know, I know. There haven't been many odd occurrences in our town. Not for a long time. The only one I remember disappearing was the young lass who ran away. Before Dad and I bought the building. Do you recall?"

"Not really. What happened?" Trev overtook a car and accelerated as the speed limit increased.

"She was the middle child of the Ackerman family who owned my building. Her brother was a few years older and not interested in taking over the business. I remember overhearing an unfortunate argument between her and her mother when they didn't see me come into what was then the bakery. She wanted to marry some boy she'd fallen for but was only seventeen. Her mother was furious. Said he was too old and she too young."

"And then?"

"One day she left. Packed up and moved. The family were tight lipped, but it seemed she'd had enough and wanted to live her own life. The building went on the market soon after, I recall. So, not exactly an exciting murder mystery."

"You know, there's nothing at all exciting about murder."

"Of course not, dear."

Trev snuck a glance at his mother. She was calm now, and the little smile on her lips was disconcerting. He'd asked himself another time whether Charlie was a bad influence on his mother or was it the other way around.

Bad as each other.

And he loved every minute of being with them.

chapter
four

Charlotte alternated between the window in the bedroom and the balcony overlooking the street, checking her phone every few minutes. Trev must be getting close. He'd take Rosie home first... or would she insist on accompanying him? Poor Rosie, dragged away from enjoying a rare shopping trip.

On her way from bedroom to balcony, she stopped and closed her eyes. The adrenaline still coursed through her, making her chest tight and emotions unstable. She took measured breaths to the bottom of her lungs and opened her eyes a little at a time. Better.

This wasn't one of the book club ladies lying dead in front of her. No blood on the rug in the perfect room wiped clean by the killer. She didn't have to deal with ex Leading Senior Constable Sid Browne. He was no longer a police officer and Trev would take seriously any input from Charlotte, not brush it aside.

Once he was here, she'd show him the grave. Or whatever it was.

You know what it is.

Much as Charlotte wanted her find to be nothing more

than a teenager's prank, or even a tribute to a lost one, her instincts said otherwise. The size and shape were a giveaway. The level of the ground dropped beneath the flowers. Whichever poor soul was buried there was long decomposed.

Back at the railing on the balcony, Charlotte checked the street. No Trev. But a familiar car drew up below. The man who stepped out looked straight up and grinned. "Not enough trouble going on in town these days?"

"Very funny. I'll meet you downstairs."

Before Bryce had time to reply, Charlotte grabbed her phone and keys, locked the door and ran down the steps. He'd been one of the detectives involved in solving the murder a few months ago and helping her when things got nasty, but they'd had a rocky start.

He waited in the driveway with his arms crossed. "Detective."

"Detective." She grinned at the nickname he'd given her earlier in the year.

"Believe you need supervision."

"What on earth did Trevor tell you?"

"Not to let you go into the bush with a shovel. Actually, do you have one?"

"Of course. But you're not going to just dig up a potential crime scene. Are you?" She put her hands on her hips. He wasn't getting near the garage until she knew what he had planned. "Sid Browne wanted to walk all over Octavia's house and I'm not about to let—"

"Chill. I'm teasing."

"We'll need your shovel, Charlie." Trev hurried down the driveway. "Hi, Bryce, thanks for getting here so fast."

The men shook hands.

Charlotte bit her bottom lip. If Trev wanted the shovel, presumably he knew how to avoid damaging evidence. She wasn't a police officer, let alone a forensics expert. But it bothered her.

Let them do their job.

"Are you happy to show us the way?" Trev asked her.

"Do you really need the shovel?"

"Best to take it with us. Or I can go get one from home."

Bryce wandered away to make a phone call. Charlotte headed for the garage and opened the roller door.

"Charlie?"

She took the shovel from a hook and held it out.

Trev stepped close to her as he took it. He looked worried. "I don't know what's under those flowers and it may be a deceased pet or someone's treasured memories. Or a body. But the weather has most likely destroyed any trace evidence and neither Bryce nor I will make things worse."

A small sigh escaped Charlotte's lips and her shoulders untensed a little. "Okay."

"Sure?"

"Sure."

———

Charlotte retraced her steps, Trev close behind and Bryce a little further back, taking his time and watching everything. Or at least it appeared that way when she'd glanced at him.

"Why are there daisies here?" She pointed them out to Trev. "I don't think they are anywhere else in the area and they are so obvious along this path."

"Good question. Are they what got your attention?"

"Yes. From the window in the back bedroom, these are clear when the sunlight touches them. So now I'm thinking somebody deliberately covered the window."

"Hold the thought. There's a lot to do before we decide if this needs more than a look."

"Hang on a sec. Not sure which way." Charlotte referred to one of her earlier photos and pointed. "Oh. This way."

With a sense of déjà vu, Charlotte swept aside a low branch. The grave was there.

"Stay put, please."

Much as she wanted to go closer, Charlotte wasn't about to argue. Not in front of Bryce, who brushed past to follow Trev. She planted herself on a fallen log to watch.

Trev and Bryce took their time viewing the spot from different angles, nobody speaking. Bryce slipped gloves on and squatted at one end. Trev took photographs and Charlotte snapped more as Bryce lifted the wreath.

He placed it to one side. "Fresh. Can smell the flowers."

"And more of those daisies." Trev gestured to the planted mass. "Let me get some more photos. The way they're planted looks deliberate."

Bryce waited until Trev lowered his phone, then used his fingers to remove dirt from a small section. First a handful of flowers. A scoop of dark soil. Then more. Charlotte crept closer as Trev peered over Bryce's shoulder.

"Take more please. See this? I'll clear a fraction more...is that better?"

"Yup." Trev's voice was gruff as he captured image after image. "Done."

Bryce straightened.

Charlotte got a glimpse into the hole. A bone.

"Didn't Trev tell you to stay over there?" Bryce said. He glanced at Trev. "Human?"

"Charlotte?" Trev asked.

She dropped onto her haunches. "Metacarpal, possibly a thumb from the shape. Short of digging up more, that's my best estimate."

"And we're not the ones to disturb this anymore." Trev

held out a hand to Charlotte and she took it, standing and holding onto him for a moment.

Silence fell as they all stared at the wreath. The comfort of Trev's hand filled a bit of the empty space in her heart which had opened up since finding the grave. For once, she wished her instincts weren't so good.

He squeezed her fingers and released them. "What now, Bryce?"

"I'll go make some calls. Get a crime unit out here and arrange a parameter for Crime Scene Services. Doubt if much will happen given how close we are to nightfall."

"Charlie, you go with Bryce."

"I'd rather stay. If I'm allowed."

Bryce laughed as he headed out of the clearing. "Why would anything stop you?"

Charlotte waited until he was gone. "He always assumes the worst of me."

"He rates you highly, Charlotte. Otherwise you'd have been sent back to the main track once we knew the right direction." Trev leaned against the fallen tree. "Thank you for handling this so well. Recognising what you'd found and contacting me."

Eyes drawn to the flowers covering the grave, Charlotte joined Trev. "She's been there for a long time."

"She?"

"I think. How sad for her to be here all alone for so many years. Nobody knowing where she was. Nobody able to grieve for her." Charlotte blinked back a prickle of tears at the back of her eyes.

"Someone knew she was here." Trev pointed to the wreath. "Even if those flowers self-sowed over the body, the wreath didn't put itself there."

"And recently. Is that why you're staying until help arrives?"

"Now we know what this is, my job is to prevent the area being tampered with. This clearing won't be left alone until CSS say so. Could be days."

"I'll bring you coffee. And food."

"Coffee would be nice. But there'll be a rotation on watch." Trev put an arm around Charlotte's shoulders and held her against him for a moment. "Mum wanted to see if you'd like to come by for dinner tonight. And you should. Even if I'm here."

His arm was nice. Safe. She was always safe around him. "I will. But I hope you're not here all night."

"I'll know more once Bryce gets back. Go home, Charlie."

"Are you sure?"

"Much as I enjoy being alone with you in this otherwise picturesque place...yes. And keep your phone out and your eyes open." He brushed his lips against her cheek and then released her.

She was cold now. It happened every time he held her and then let her go.

"I'll walk with you to the path."

"I'm fine. You protect her." Charlotte stretched. "At least now she'll get a proper burial. Eventually. Whoever she is."

chapter
five

"What a terrible discovery." Rosie poured two glass of gin and tonic over ice. "But what made you look there in the first place? Shall we sit outside while its warm enough? Here you go, darling."

"Thanks." Charlotte took both glasses and followed Rosie's wheelchair to the outdoor dining table. Once Rosie settled at one end, Charlotte handed one glass over and sat to her right. The first sip was welcome. More than she expected. She let it reach her stomach and warm it before remembering Rosie's question.

"It was a trick of the light, I guess. Sunshine on the bushland at the right moment and there they were, a trail of flowers."

"What kind of flowers? Where were you?"

"Oh. Trev helped me move the wardrobe and the window offers a wonderful view of the forest behind the bookshop. I was closing the window after cleaning in there. And they are a daisy. I think. Here, I took some pics."

"Of course you did." Rosie's lips curled upward.

"Well, you know I do." Charlotte scrolled until she found

a couple taken well away from the clearing. "Along the path there are clumps of these." She turned the phone.

Rosie used her finger and thumb to enlarge the image. "Definitely an aster of some kind. If you bring me one, I might know which, if it matters."

Does it? Who knows, so soon in the investigation.

"I recognise the look on your face. You may not be so free to do your sleuthing thing with Trev around." Rosie held her hand out to Mellow, one of her cats, who'd wandered out of the house. Mellow jumped onto her lap with a purr. "But at least I'll spend less time worrying about what you are up to."

"Me? I'm always safe, Rosie."

The disbelief on Rosie's face was enough to make Charlotte laugh.

"Shall I count how many times you've put yourself into danger in the few months you've lived in Kingfisher Falls?"

"No. You really don't need to go to the trouble. Dinner smells good."

"It should. You were telling me about seeing the flowers."

Charlotte gave Rosie an edited version of events up to leaving Trev alone in the clearing. "Eventually, I took coffee back to Trev and Bryce and they were still waiting for some unit to arrive. It was getting dark and Trev insisted on walking me almost all the way home again."

"Good for him."

"I'm quite able to walk along a path, Rosie." Charlotte finished her drink, not quite believing herself. Independent as she was, his presence in the twilight had been welcome. Whoever left the wreath may be around. Watching. And not have good intentions. She'd gone straight to the back bedroom and waved to him where he'd waited at the edge of the forest.

"Except now we might have another killer on the loose.

And you, darling, are too special to put at risk." Rosie put her hand over Charlotte's. "I might give dinner a quick stir."

"Oh, let me. And I'll refresh these if you like." She took both glasses to the kitchen. In the oven was a large ceramic pot. Charlotte lifted it out, surprised at its weight and when she removed the lid, delectable scents of earthy herbs and vegetables rose with the steam. Her stomach rumbled in response as she stirred.

"Can you flick the rice cooker on?" Rosie called.

After stirring, Charlotte returned the pot to the oven and checked the rice cooker was ready to start. Once that was on, she made new drinks and re-joined Rosie. "What is in dinner? It looks and smells fantastic."

Rosie beamed. "One of my originals. We used to eat this at least once a week and the boys named it a beansarrole. Graeme and Trev would devour it after a cricket match, yet it is so simple. Root vegetables and the more variety the better. A whole garlic head. Bay leaves from the tree out the back. A bunch of thyme and sprinkle of cumin seeds. Tomatoes. And red kidney beans or chickpeas, or even lentils. Whatever I have on hand. Top with natural yoghurt."

"I can't wait."

"To homemade meals and good company." Rosie raised her glass.

"And not having to wait too long." Charlotte grinned.

Clink.

————

Trev slumped against the wall outside the front door, searching his pockets for keys. He had an hour to shower, eat and return to the clearing to sit and watch all night.

Watch over a lost soul.

Laughter drifted from outside and he smiled. On a day

like this, hearing his mother and his—whatever Charlotte was—laugh, was better than winning the lottery. A reminder of what he had. The happiness in his life. Unlike the poor person, or remains of a person, in the forest.

He gave up on the keys. A growl at his feet made him glance down. "Mister Mayhem. Why aren't you with your sister?" Mayhem's tail snaked from side to side with displeasure and he glared at Trev.

Trev tapped on the door.

Charlotte opened it, the welcome on her face warming his heart. Then, her eyes dropped to the annoyed cat and she raised her eyebrows. "Please, both of you, come on in." She stepped back and Mayhem stalked past her without acknowledging she existed.

"Perfect timing, darling. Dinner will be ten minutes." Rosie wheeled down the hallway, Mellow on her lap. "You are staying?"

"Have to be back in about an hour. I might shower before dinner if there's time?"

"Go. We're having beansarrole."

"Best news all day." He kissed her cheek. "Back soon."

A hot shower and change into uniform later, Trev followed his nose to the kitchen. His mother was instructing Charlotte on the fine art of plating dinner and both were giggling. Really giggling. Perhaps the empty glasses on the counter contributed. He watched unnoticed, aware he was smiling and unable to do anything but enjoy their interaction.

Last year he'd brought Charlotte to meet his mother on a day trip up from Rivers End. The women hit it off from the first moment and before he knew what happened, the person he longed to know better had left to work for the one he knew best. He'd held onto the promise of a future, never knowing how to help it happen. But it was Charlotte with her fierce sense of right and wrong who'd set the wheels in motion without realising.

"Then a dollop...no, that's not a dollop." Rosie took the spoon Charlotte held and extracted a big scoop of creamy yoghurt from a tub. "That, darling, is a dollop."

"She's right." Trev announced his presence. "Now, shall I take these outside?"

———

Charlotte kept sneaking looks at Trev. There was something in his expression, in his eyes, she wasn't used to seeing and it worried her. On the surface everything was normal. He kept a tight rein on what was bubbling beneath his normal relaxed self. He was a naturally calm person. She'd been with him in moments of extreme pressure and he'd always maintained a sense of cool control. This discovery of hers had rattled him.

"Do you think it is better with the inclusion of the turnip?" Rosie was focussed on her meal, spearing pieces of vegetable with her fork and scrutinising them. "I wasn't sure, but some grew this year and I thought—"

"Mum, I love it." As though to prove it, Trev filled his mouth.

"Oh. Okay then. They are baby turnips so taste quite sweet. I think."

"Rosie, this is beyond delicious. And now I know how to make it, I shall practice once a week until it is perfect." Charlotte sipped from a glass of wine Trev had poured earlier for her and for Rosie. He was on his second glass of water.

"Good. Good. Anyway, Trevor you can't surely be out there all night?" Rosie's tone gave away her concern. "Not alone."

"Not alone, Mum. But we need to ensure there's no chance of the site being interfered with. We're armed with everything. Tarps in case it rains. There are floodlights set up. We even have plenty of food and coffee."

Rosie grunted. "You call that food? Why don't I send the leftovers with you?"

"Because I'm not at school." Trev smiled and leaned across to kiss Rosie's forehead. "Thank you though. But I've been at this for a while now."

"How many skeletons did you find in Rivers End?" Rosie wagged her fork at Trev. "None, I would imagine. No, it is Kingfisher Falls turning us all into investigators."

Charlotte's eyes darted from Rosie to Trev, who in turn, watched Charlotte.

"What?" She ventured.

He glanced at his watch. "I need to head back. We'll do a statement tomorrow, okay? About what you found and so on."

"Of course."

And?

"I know you're curious and like solving puzzles, but you need to be patient. Let everyone do their job."

"I am patient."

Even Rosie laughed.

chapter
six

Long after Trev left and she'd helped Rosie wash up, Charlotte brooded on the assumption that she'd rush in and interfere with a police investigation. She walked home after hugging Rosie goodnight, stroking Mellow's soft fur and being hissed at for daring to glance in Mayhem's direction.

She knew not to intrude. In the past, there'd been good reason for her to take notice of clues and keep notes. If she hadn't, would criminals such as Glenys Lane, Veronica Wheemor and Bernie Cooper be in the judicial system? Not to mention the young thugs whose rampage through Kingfisher Falls stealing Christmas trees frightened half the town last year. Even Sid Browne might still lord over the community as resident police officer, instead of fair and responsible Leading Senior Constable Trevor Sibbritt.

Thanks for the help, Charlie. We'll erect a statue in your honour.

There was more activity on the streets than usual for late on a Sunday night. Word spread fast here. People were curious about the heightened police presence on the parcel of bushland. Cars drove along, their occupants watchful.

Charlotte stopped outside the florist. Is this where the

wreath originated? Autumn colours filled the window, rather than the roses and lavender of the wreath. Wasn't lavender more a summer flower? She made a note on her phone to check.

"I know you are curious and like solving puzzles." Trev's words echoed in her head.

It was true. And she couldn't bear injustice. Where was the harm in keeping track of thoughts and ideas? It wasn't as though she was going to run her own investigation. She took some photos of the window. She might drop in during lunch tomorrow. To browse for some ideas for decorating her balcony a bit more.

She waited at the kerb for a police car to turn and drive toward one of the entrances to the bushland. Trev was overseeing the operation until Crime Scene Services arrived in daylight. He and Bryce had already taken a lot of photographs before Bryce left for the evening. Kingfisher Falls might never have had so many police here at one time.

Upstairs, Charlotte made a cup of tea and took it to the back bedroom. Tea was her night time go-to when thoughts kept her from sleeping. Leaving the light off, she perched on the windowsill after sliding the window open. Trev's police car was parked a bit further along the track from the flower trail and was the only unit in sight. There must be another way into the clearing. Far within the canopy of trees, fingers of light generated an eerie glow. Voices drifted on the breeze.

Charlotte finished her tea, yawning as the events of the day caught up. She wanted to be awake by dawn to keep an eye on things.

―――――

It was far earlier than dawn when she woke. For a few moments she tried to go back to sleep but her mind was already spinning with thoughts.

If the person in the grave was a local, why did nobody know they'd gone missing? She'd asked Rosie about it.

"I don't recall there ever being a missing person alert. And being such a small community, surely I would have known?" Rosie had frowned as she'd tried to remember. "Perhaps they were a traveller, and nobody knew they were here?"

Or they'd been from another place and buried here. Until an approximate year of death was established, how would the police even begin to look?

Charlotte wrapped herself in her dressing gown and returned to the other bedroom. Somewhere out there, Trev was probably drinking yet another coffee and wishing for his bed. But he'd not rest until he handed over the scene.

A light moved through the trees toward the glow. It disappeared. Most likely an officer checking the parameter. Then, it reappeared again close to the flower trail. Stationary for a few minutes, then moving a bit at a time.

Leaving the room for a moment, Charlotte grabbed her phone. Back at the window she tried using the camera to zoom in, but between the darkness and dense bush, nothing showed but a blur. Which she photographed anyway. The stop-start continued and Charlotte texted Trev.

Morning. Is one of your team going up and down the flower trail?

Less than thirty seconds later her phone rang.

"Where are you?" Trev's voice dripped exhaustion.

"At the window. I woke early."

"What can you see?"

"Looks like a torch. At first it was heading your way then it went off. Now it is moving then stopping all the time."

"And you think it is along that path?"

"Or close. I take it this isn't one of your team?"

"Team of two and we're both here. I'll take a look."

"Well, be careful. It might be the killer."

"Thanks, Charlie."

"Sorry."

He chuckled and hung up.

What if it was the killer? What if whoever buried the woman was a local and wanted to see what was going on?

Charlotte opened the window enough to peer out. The air was cool but not cold. She kept her phone close and listened. Only the occasional night bird cut through the quiet.

The light went off.

What on earth was going on down there?

chapter
seven

They don't belong here.

Cops all over the clearing. Hands touching the sacred site. Filthy boots clomping over it. Not once in all these years had anyone looked. Soon, everyone will know.

Why now?

Precious flowers are uprooted. Tossed aside as if garbage for disposal. The glare of floodlights transforms the soft grass into nothing more than ugly green carpet and the flowers into an unwashed blanket.

It is time to retreat. Not be seen. Not yet. The flashlight flicks off again. Bad batteries. A shake and it lights up. Each step away from the clearing stabs at the hole inside.

I cannot bear this. What will happen?

The light fades and extinguishes. It doesn't matter. The way is well known. But someone follows.

Another path, little more than a line of dirt. This leads away from the path to the river. Longer. And more risk of exposure. Best to wait a while. Wait here in the shadows of the trees where the track is visible should anyone approach.

Dawn soon. The buildings opposite the track are silhouettes. And somebody stands at the window of one.

It is a woman at the window, and she stares toward the path to the clearing. To where a cop emerges, his hand raised to wave. The woman waves back. Was it her? Did she walk through the forbidden forest?

The woman is the one who ruined everything.

And like the others, she will pay.

chapter
eight

Exhaustion went on the backburner when Charlotte texted. Trev's first thought was she'd gone against everything he'd asked and ventured into the bushland. Pre-dawn—in his experience—was a dangerous time. More risk of crime. Or running across a snake or into a deadly spider web.

Hearing her voice and reassurance she was safe at home was a relief. There was enough to worry about without thinking she might be up to her sleuthing ways. He grinned. She belonged in a forensics crimes unit. He'd told her once, back in Rivers End, how amazing her experience as a psychiatrist would be combined with a crime unit.

After their phone call, he left the constable who'd joined him last night to watch the clearing. He trusted Charlotte. If she said there was a light, there was. He took his time, only using his flashlight to check he was on the right track a couple of times. Perhaps somebody should have stayed at the entrance to the flowered path, but staffing was short.

He paused for a moment, using his ears instead of eyes. A flutter of wings carried a bird too close to him from the far end of the path. He ducked. Too early for birds. But no other sounds.

Trev continue to where the path met the wider track. His eyes scanned the sides of the bush, past his patrol car, along the fences, up to the other end. Not a movement. Charlotte had once mentioned this parcel of land was quiet in an odd way and after spending a night in the middle of it, he was inclined to agree.

Charlotte was at the window and he raised a hand. She waved in return and it touched him how concerned she was about his wellbeing. He tapped her number into his phone and waited until she answered to turn back along the path.

"What did you find?"

"Nothing apart from a startled bird flying at me."

"What startled it?"

What indeed.

"I'll have another look around in daylight, once I hand over."

"The light went off after we spoke. Well, it did flicker on for a few seconds then nothing so perhaps they heard you approaching."

"Charlie, why are you awake so early? There's another hour until dawn."

"Too much excitement. Wrong word. You know what I mean."

He did. Yet another crime in a town known for its sleepy atmosphere. This was an old crime though.

"Are you going to try to sleep again?" Trev turned the flashlight on again after almost tripping over a tree root. "I'll come and see you when I'm done here."

"Maybe." Her voice wasn't convincing. "I might make some tea and read for a bit."

"Not a thriller I hope."

She laughed. "Might leave those for the moment. Are you back at the...um, clearing?"

Trev rounded the last of the bushes and nodded to the

constable, who'd stood at his approach. "Yep. I'll see you in a little while."

"Stay safe." She disconnected the call.

For you, always.

————

Sleeping was out of the question. Something bad was going on. Already had gone on. With not one shred of evidence or knowledge of the identity of the person in the shallow forest grave, Charlotte knew in her gut this crime was committed locally. And the killer was still at large.

It might have been an accident.

One covered up by a friend, or family? Someone scared of being blamed. This didn't explain why no missing person came to mind with Rosie.

Charlotte found herself playing with the flaps of the box on the bed. Since it arrived last year, she'd barely touched the box. Sent from Lakeview Care in Queensland, it was filled with items her mother considered precious. Angelica had insisted she have them. And now her mother's mental health was at an all-time low, Charlotte needed to visit her. Soon.

She opened the flaps and scooped the Christmas cards up. Beneath them were letters tied with string. Those she also took then hesitated and put them back in the box. Instead, she picked up a photo album, a small one-photo-per-page type. There was a sense of familiarity when she held it, yet she didn't remember it. Like so much of her early years.

In the kitchen, Charlotte changed her mind about tea and started the coffee maker she'd bought not long ago, then stared at the Christmas cards and photo album now on the counter. She already knew what the cards said. Each was signed the same way.

Merry Christmas, sweetie. You are loved. Z.

They were dated. One a year between her second and eleventh birthdays. Angelica knew who Z was, teasing Charlotte for not remembering, but then her mother's mind had slipped back to wherever it disappeared to. No explanation. No clues.

But the photo album stirred up uneasy feelings. Her mother kept things for a reason but usually known only to herself. She'd once kept a smooth pebble she'd taken from a beach, displaying it on the mantlepiece and forbidding Charlotte to touch it. As a young child, the pretty stone intrigued Charlotte but she knew better than to disobey. One day she returned from school to find the pebble thrown into the bin.

She sighed, putting her coffee down and opened the white vinyl cover of the album. The first photograph was a view. Black and white, it was a simple picture of a park. A family sat on a picnic blanket in the distance. There was a fountain. Nothing familiar.

Turning the page, she had two more photographs to look at. The one on the left was Angelica. Young and smiling. Not a care in the world. Except her hands were clenched together against her chest in a pose Charlotte knew all too well. Her mother's way of controlling herself, at least until things got too much. She might be in her late teens or early twenties here.

Opposite was an image of a house. Charlotte lurched back, and her hand went to her heart as recognition flooded into her mind. White paint peeled off weatherboards. An unkempt garden. Broken steps up to a small porch where Angelica sat on a chair holding a toddler-aged Charlotte. Standing at her side was a short, lean man with blonde hair.

"Dad." She whispered, touching his face.

This was the house she grew up in. A broken house.

Like us.

Her fingers trembled as she slid the photo from its sleeve

and turned it over. There was a date. Her second birthday. And words. *The birthday girl with her parents. Smile!*

"But…" Charlotte reached for the closest Christmas card and opened it. Heart pounding in her ears, she compared the handwriting. Whoever wrote on the back of the photo also wrote on the cards. Did Z take the photo?

The first Christmas card was dated only a few months after this photograph was taken. If Z was at the house for her second birthday, then where had they gone? Was this a relative never spoken of? Angelica was certain Charlotte knew who it was. She replaced the photograph, her eyes going back to the younger image of her mother.

"You should never have had me."

Charlotte clenched her hands as she stepped away from the counter, then she raised them to inspect. She was doing what her mother did. She forced them to open. And then the tears came.

chapter
nine

A persistent tap on the door shook Charlotte out of the part-sleep, part-daze she'd fallen into. She scrambled off the sofa, almost tripping over shoes she'd left ready to put on for work. Dressed for the day ahead, makeup and hair in place, she'd sat down for a moment to regroup. Charlotte checked her watch. A moment plus an hour.

"Only me, Charlie." Trev called just as she reached the door.

She drew her breath in, all the way to the bottom of her lungs, and exhaled as she swung the door open. "Nobody else would risk seeing me this early."

"I don't know anyone else I'd show this tired face to." Trev was leaning against the door jam. "Are you okay?"

"Come in. Of course. Coffee?"

"You know all the right things to say." Trev closed the door behind himself and pulled a stool out at the counter. "How long until you go downstairs?"

"Half an hour. Enough time to get you at least two coffees and breakfast. Well, if you trust me to cook some." Charlotte busied herself with the coffee machine. "Espresso?"

"Perfect. I'll pass on breakfast though and it is nothing to do with your cooking."

"Sure."

"Charlie."

"Do you know, the time young Lachie Woodland came to visit, he gave me some wonderful ideas for breakfast…mushrooms in butter, eggs, tomatoes—"

Trev groaned. "Stop. I'm hungry. But I have to meet Bryce and Katrina at the station soon."

Charlotte brought two coffees to the counter. "Sorry. I was just teasing."

"Raincheck?"

She nodded and blew on her coffee before taking a tentative sip. She put the cup down. "What happens now? Do you have any idea who she is?"

"No. Not even if it's a 'he'. Crime Scene Services have arrived. They've taken over for now." Steam rose from Trev's cup and he closed his eyes, breathing it in with a 'mmm'.

"They'll be careful? Look after her?" Charlotte bit her lip at the emotion in her tone.

Trev opened his eyes, and gazed straight into hers. His were calm, caring. "They will take great care. It will take hours. Longer. Every step will be recorded by video and camera. The area will remain a crime scene until the medical examiner says otherwise."

The sense of relief surprised Charlotte. "Good. But surely you won't be spending every night out there?"

Now, he smiled. "Getting too old for that. No, shouldn't need to. The police tape will remain and probably a couple of constables will get some extra hours for the first couple of nights, but we'll see. This is an… unusual situation."

"Will the detectives get more involved?" Charlotte finally drank some coffee, realising she'd barely touched the one from earlier. She'd not eaten either but if Trev wasn't staying for breakfast, she wasn't going to worry about it.

"I'm hoping they have some time to help me, actually. Lots of door knocking ahead. All the properties backing onto the bushland, apart from you of course. I might need to get details of the previous tenants here though."

"Well, if the wardrobe wasn't across the window then, they'd have had a great view."

Charlotte and Trev's mouths both dropped open.

As one, they picked up their coffee cups and headed to the back bedroom.

———

"I wonder who moved it in the first place. Maybe Mum knows." Trev stared at the offending wardrobe. "Mum and Dad bought the place before her accident. So, she's been up here plenty of times."

Charlotte's mind wandered. Rosie hadn't visited upstairs in years. Not since her husband died and Trev went off to his own life. But she wanted to visit, and Charlotte longed to return some of the hospitality Rosie showered on her.

"Trev?"

"What's up?"

"I'd like Rosie to come for dinner. And you. And Lewis."

Trev blinked. His head must be on the case and here she was, changing the subject.

"She hasn't been to the apartment for many years. The stairs are so steep, and—"

"I can carry her up. What a lovely gesture and she will enjoy seeing the balcony." He squeezed her hand and curled his fingers through hers. "Let me know when. Well, once we know what's going on here, anyway."

His eyes moved to the track behind the fence as a medical

examiner's vehicle pulled up near the path. A uniformed officer jogged to meet the car.

"Somebody has to know who she is." Charlotte finished her coffee. "How do I help?"

"You stay patient." Trev turned his back on the window and smiled. "As you can see, the appropriate authorities are involved. We don't know anything except there is a body in a shallow grave. One that's been there for quite a while. So, we wait."

"And once you have some information?"

"Are you certain you don't want to become a forensic psychiatrist?"

"Oh. I remember you mentioning that once before. And tempting as it sounds, I've fallen for the bookshop."

Trev still had her hand and he drew it to his lips. "For the... bookshop." His lips touched her fingers.

A tingle rushed up her spine and her breath caught.

"That's what you've fallen for?" With every word he moved closer.

You want me to answer?

Words had no hope of passing her lips. She was lost in his eyes.

His phone rang.

He sighed and released her fingers with a low, "Sorry."

Me too.

He got as far as the door to answer, stopped and turned back. "Appreciate it. On my way." Then hung up. "Katrina's bringing coffee seeing as there's still no decent machine in the station."

"You're going now?"

"Better." He gazed at the box on the bed. The flaps were open and some of the Christmas cards had slipped out, exposing the photo album. "I'm always here if you want to talk, Charlie."

This wasn't his problem. And he couldn't know how bad things once were. She had no place for pity. Afraid she'd already shown too much of herself, Charlotte shrugged. "Nothing to talk about. But thanks."

"Okay. I'll see you later."

She followed him to the kitchen, where he insisted on washing his coffee cup. A moment later the door closed behind him and she leaned her forehead against it. If only things were simpler.

chapter
ten

The bookshop was busier than expected for a Monday morning but most of the customers were as interested in discussing the recent events as buying books. Speculation rippled through the town if the comments were anything to go by.

"Do the police know if it really is a body. A human body?" Bronnie, who worked at Italia, rested her elbows on the counter as Rosie rang up her sale. "Maybe it's a prank. You know, a pretend skeleton put there to scare someone."

"I'm sure the medical examiner will work it out," Rosie said.

"But, how strange would it be if it is for real? All these murders in our little town! I hope there isn't a serial killer about."

"I'm sure there isn't."

Charlotte wasn't at all sure but what was the point of worrying anyone?

Bronnie left and Esther hurried in.

"Can't stay but wanted to be certain you are okay, Charlie."

"Me?"

"We know you found the…um…the place."

Small town gossip.

Charlotte had spoken to nobody apart from Trev and Rosie. Trev wouldn't discuss it with anyone not in law enforcement.

Esther glanced at Rosie. "Anyway, I left Doug watching the shop so might go back before he sells somebody a green skirt with an orange top." With that she was gone again, and Rosie busied herself with the computer.

"Rosie Sibbritt?"

"I said nothing."

"To anybody? Even Lewis?"

Rosie turned with an apologetic smile. "I had to tell him. It is possible he might have mentioned it to Esther. But I'm sure that's all."

"It probably doesn't matter. I know hardly anything so unless someone remembers some incident or person disappearing, we need patience. As Trev insists." Charlotte grumbled.

"Did you see him this morning?" Rosie's eyes brightened.

"At which point of the morning? I saw him from a distance at about four when he investigated an odd light moving around near the clearing."

Rosie's mouth dropped open.

"Nothing came of it. He looked around then waved at me and rang to tell me to go back to bed."

"He's a good boy. And then?"

"Then he stopped by for coffee once he handed over to the crime scene police. He was exhausted."

"Hopefully by now he's gone home to have a sleep. I wonder if he's eating enough?"

Charlotte laughed. "Rosie, stop worrying. Were you like this when he was living in Rivers End?"

"At first, yes." Rosie nodded. "I missed him like crazy and

likely drove him to drink with all my phone calls. You're right. I shouldn't worry." A broad smile filled her face. "I'll let you do the worrying."

"Rosie!" Charlotte grabbed an armful of books to put out, afraid Rosie would see the heat in her face. Since he'd kissed her fingers, she had all sorts of thoughts spinning around her head, none which she wanted to share with Trevor's own mother. She slid books into their places then noticed they were upside down.

"I'll stop." Rosie had followed her to the corner of the bookshop. "If I've upset you enough to make you do that, then I promise not to say anything."

Charlotte got onto her knees to fix the books. "No. You go ahead and tease all you want. I didn't get much sleep and have a lot to think about."

"I can't imagine how you felt yesterday, finding the grave." Rosie patted Charlotte's shoulder. "You've always said something about the forest made you uneasy."

"Silly imagination."

"Or a sixth sense." A woman spoke from nearby.

Rosie jumped and Charlotte climbed to her feet and turned. "I'm sorry, we normally hear the doorbell..." her voice trailed off as she recognised the woman. Harmony Montgomery. "How may I help you?"

"I'm after a book, but I couldn't help overhearing you."

I need to check who's around before I speak.

Recovered from her surprise, Rosie rotated her wheelchair to smile at Harmony. Charlotte didn't know if they'd met, only how interested Rosie was in doing a reading. By the expression on her friend's face, Rosie was pleased to see Harmony.

"Which book can I help with?" Charlotte had no intention of discussing what Harmony overheard. It was neither the woman's business, nor Charlotte's information to share.

"One about the region. I'm new here and interested in learning about its history."

"Well, let me help. I'm Rosie." Hand outstretched, Rosie nodded. "We used to carry a wonderful pictorial book, but they are no longer... available."

She exchanged a glance with Charlotte. No longer available was quite true, with most of them incinerated by Glenys.

"Is there an alternative?"

"I have a couple of ideas if you'd like to head over to the far corner with me." Rosie wheeled away with Harmony, still talking.

Charlotte sighed and returned to the counter. There were orders to place, so she opened the screen and copied over the list Rosie made earlier.

"Oh, I would love to do that!" Rosie's voice lifted in excitement. "When would you like me to be there?"

As the women approached the counter Charlotte put on her best smile. The one reserved for difficult customers. Harmony clutched a couple of books against a multi coloured waistcoat buttoned over a white blouse. Around her neck were several loops of beads, some with pendants shaped as the sun, moon, stars and flowers, and large gold hoops on her ears. Her skirt was the same purple one from the supermarket yesterday.

Charlotte stood and reached for the books to scan. "I'll pop these through for you. Very nice. I have the Macedon Ranges book upstairs."

"You live upstairs?" Harmony gazed around the bookshop. "You've turned it into a lovely shop, Rosie. Inviting."

Rosie was still on the other side of the counter with Harmony. "Lots of work, but worth every bit. My husband completely remodelled the downstairs. He'd be proud to see how successful the bookshop is after all these years."

Harmony gave a card to Rosie. "There's my details so ring when you want to visit. And as you can see, one of my specialties is after-life communications. If you wished to speak to him."

Charlotte opened her mouth to warn Rosie but shut it again. They could talk later. Alone. As it was, Rosie's eyes had misted up and the smile on her face was wistful.

"There you go, Harmony. Would you prefer to pay by cash or card?"

"Only ever cash." Harmony opened a purse. "Perhaps you'd like a free consultation as well? We could explore your feelings about the forest you mentioned." She handed over some money. "Get to the reason you are uneasy about it."

Charlotte got change and a receipt. "There you are. Thanks for the offer. But as a psychiatrist I have considerable skill in uncovering the root cause of most responses, including my own. There's a certain science behind it."

When Harmony's lips pursed, Charlotte knew she'd hit a nerve. She mentally kicked herself. The woman was a customer and new to town. And she could feel Rosie's eyes on her.

Collecting her books, Harmony stared at Charlotte. It wasn't hostile, but Charlotte's stomach fluttered at the intensity. Then, Harmony smiled. "There's science behind everything, I believe. Even magic. And seeing beyond this world. A psychiatrist? How intriguing."

After another few words with Rosie, she left, and Charlotte flopped onto the stool. Rosie wheeled around to join her.

"I know, I know. I'm sorry I was rude."

"You don't believe in clairvoyants," Rosie said.

"No. And I've seen too many people hurt. Disappointed and misled. I don't want you to be next."

Rosie played with the card from Harmony. "I'm curious.

Nothing more. And besides, it gives me a chance to get to know a new resident and have a good look inside that shop of hers! All Lewis talks about is what might be behind those curtains."

"Then maybe Lewis should visit her," Charlotte said.

"He doesn't believe in her any more than you do. But he does like to know what's going on in town. I should ask him about any missing people. With all his years running the local tour bus, he'd surely have heard if there was ever a mysterious disappearance."

"Except Trevor doesn't want anyone interfering." Charlotte stood and stretched. "I need coffee so might run over the road and get us some?"

"Yes please. And Charlie? I won't tell Trev if you don't."

chapter
eleven

The corner café was busy, so Charlotte ordered the coffees and said she'd be back. She peeked into Lewis' shop to make sure he was alone, and seeing him up a ladder at the back of the shop, she ducked in.

"Isn't this where we met?" She asked.

He looked down at her with a wide smile. "My darling girl. Yes, I believe I was stocking this precise shelf when you wandered in requiring a gift for a certain special lady."

Before Christmas, with no idea what Rosie might like, Charlotte had ventured into Lewis' beautiful homewares shop. He'd agreed a new teapot was in order and been a welcome friendly face in a town she barely knew. Now, as Rosie's suitor—as Lewis liked to call himself—he had become a firm friend to Charlotte.

As he climbed down, Lewis chatted about the weather. On the floor, he pushed the ladder across so it wasn't in the way and peered at Charlotte over his glasses. "Are you here for business or pleasure?"

"I'm here on a whim. Two reasons. First, I want to invite you to dinner in the apartment soon. With Trevor and Rosie.

He's offered to carry her up the stairs, so she'll finally get to see the place again."

"Wonderful! Oh, she will be delighted! And when will this be?"

Charlotte followed him to the counter of the shop where he took a tissue and patted his forehead. "Not certain. Perhaps next Saturday? Then if we're late, it won't matter so much the next day."

"Yes. Good thinking. We can be rowdy out on your balcony. Drink champagne and sing." He grinned and Charlotte's heart melted. He was the sweetest of men and once Rosie worked past the feelings of disloyalty to her deceased husband, she'd have the happiest of lives with him.

"It will depend a bit on what's going on. Trevor may be caught up with the investigation so we might need to be flexible."

Lewis leaned on the counter. "What a shock for you, my dear. Are you alright?"

"Thank you, yes. I'm glad I found her because nobody should be left alone for so long."

"Her?"

"My gut instinct. Nothing more." Why was the feeling so strong? "If I'm not careful, I'll start believing Harmony."

"Harmony?"

"She thinks I have a sixth sense. Overheard Rosie and I talking about the forest."

He snorted. "At the best, she is misguided."

"Anyway, I do have a second reason for visiting. Rosie will ask you the same thing but if I ask first and Trevor finds out, then she won't get in trouble."

"But you will?"

Charlotte shook her head. "Not really. He hasn't said not to ask questions, just to be more patient. But I'm curious whether you remember any missing person from the area? Even a long time ago."

Lewis pulled out a stool and perched on it, his expression thoughtful. "No actual missing persons case comes to mind. Not where an investigation happened. But people do move on and sometimes, their leaving is sudden."

"Any names you can recall?"

He nodded, more to himself than Charlotte. "The young lass from the bakery, from the apartment you now call home. She was here one day and gone the next with not a word to anyone."

"Didn't her family look for her?"

"They were an odd lot. Been in town for decades but never a real part of the community. Kept to themselves. Talk was she had a boyfriend her parents disapproved of, so we all assumed she'd run off with him."

"Anyone else?"

"Only other one is even stranger. Terrance Murdoch's own wife packed up and left a few years back. He was beside himself. Told everyone who'd listen how happy they'd been until she received an anonymous phone call filled with lies and malice about him."

Sounds promising.

"What kind of lies?"

"He wouldn't go as far as to tell us. And he refused to say where she'd gone. But all her belongings disappeared—some to the tip. Presumably he sent the rest to her. So, it is not a missing persons case at all."

"Has anyone in town ever heard from her again?" Charlotte's interest grew. Terrance was a sneaky man with few morals, in her opinion.

"Not to my knowledge. Have you asked dear Rosie?"

"I will. Speaking of Rosie, I told her I was getting coffee

so perhaps I need to go. Before she reports me as a missing person."

————

Charlotte hurried out of the café with two coffees in a tray, almost running straight into Trev. He stepped aside just in time. "Attempting to assault a police officer?"

"Why aren't you in bed?"

The second the words passed her lips, heat flushed from her neck to the top of her skull. What was wrong with her? First losing the ability to form words and now coming up with unsuitable ones. She forced herself to meet his eyes. And wished she hadn't.

The corners of his eyes crinkled with mirth and something else. Recognition of her discomfort or amusement at her inability to behave in an appropriate manner? Either were bad.

Stop overthinking it.

But she'd never experienced such...reactions. Not to anyone.

Trev leaned in and whispered, "Stop overthinking it."

"Since when could you read minds?"

"Secret talent."

"Do you want a coffee? I can run back in—"

He took the coffee tray from her. "I'm coffee-ed out. But I'll walk with you."

They crossed the road as though the silly moment never happened. Thank goodness.

"Why are you in such a rush?"

"I told Rosie I'd be right back and was longer than expected."

"They look busy in there."

"Yeah. They are."

She knew he was curious. Wanted more of an answer.

"So, any more news?" Time to change his focus.

"Nothing of note. The crime unit have a long day ahead of them. Soil samples, even plant samples. CSS have all manner of tests they run to identify how long a body has been buried based on the effects on the environment around it."

"And any theories who it is?"

They stopped just before the bookshop as though both knew to keep the conversation private.

Trev's expression was suspicious. How had she become so bad at keeping anything from him? "Give."

"Sorry?"

"What is your theory, Charlie? And what is it based on?"

She glanced around. The pavement was deserted. "Fine. I do have a couple of suggestions. I mean, assuming there isn't a wallet or some other identification with the body."

"I'm listening."

"There's been two women from the town disappear without much, if any explanation. One came from the family who owned the bakery right here. Before they sold to your parents. The other is the wife of Terrance."

"Murdoch? How do you know this?"

"Um. Yeah, anyway, she allegedly received a phone call accusing Terrance of something and so she packed up and left him."

There was the slightest smile forming on Trev's lips. "Did he report her missing?"

"Now, I'm not a police officer so not privy to those things. Although Rosie might know more."

"Rosie might know what?" On cue, Rosie appeared out of the bookshop. "And why are you talking out here? Is this a secret meeting?"

"No, Mum. Just listening to Charlie's theories."

"Then listen inside." She turned. "I thought *you'd* disappeared, Charlie."

"I had an errand to run while I waited for the coffee. Sorry about that." Charlotte and Trev followed Rosie inside. "Here's yours."

"Have you slept yet?" Rosie eyed Trev. "Not by the look of you."

"Thanks."

"Mothers tell the truth." Rosie put her coffee into the cup holder on her chair, then folded her arms. "What does Rosie know?"

"Charlotte is picking up gossip from around town."

"Hey!" Gossip, indeed.

"She thought you may recall some details about Terrance Murdoch's wife."

Rosie's eyes widened. "Is that who you think is...you know."

"Mother."

"Okay, okay. But if you want some more information, you need to wait until after work. Your dad kept some notes about Bryony Murdoch, and I'll have to find them. Which means you, young man, need to get some sleep so Charlie can come over after work and help."

chapter
twelve

Watching them wastes time. But how else to learn what they know? Look at them.

Leading Senior Constable Trevor Sibbritt.

Rose Sibbritt.

Charlotte Dean. Doctor Charlotte Dean. The interloper who thinks she's better than everyone. Better educated. Smarter.

First, they gathered at the shop. Huddled around their secrets. Laughing so loud the sound crosses the road.

He left. Those women stayed at their work, so he was the one to follow. Was he returning to the forest? Or back to the police station to meet the detectives.

Neither. His mother's home. Better than staying with the doctor. Much better she is alone in her upstairs rooms. One way in and out. Easy to observe her comings and goings.

And now she arrives at Rose's doorstep. They are all here. As long as they stay a while, there is a chance to find what was left behind. What is kept locked away.

chapter
thirteen

"Your father had no time for idle gossip, as you would recall."
Rosie opened the timber filing cabinet Trev had bought her
earlier in the year. They were in the small room she used as
an office. "His journalism was about truth. Hard hitting
pieces exposing injustice, or heart-wrenching reunions
against the odds. He didn't like fluff, as he called it."

Trev remembered long discussions over the dinner table.
Dad outraged in his quiet way by tabloids chasing celebrities
or sensationalising crimes. His insistence of holding the
press to a higher standard. It rubbed off on him, no doubt.

Rosie flicked through files she and Charlie had created to
catalogue the work of Graeme's life. "Once he settled here in
Kingfisher Falls, he took to the life of the country journalist
with the same passion as his overseas assignments. And he
learned to balance his distaste for what he'd call fluff, with
the community's love of it."

"What kind of things?" Charlotte perched on the edge of
the desk, sipping a gin and tonic. She'd changed into a long
dress and her hair fell around her shoulders. Trev wanted to
take her photograph and preserve this moment. She was so
pretty. And clever. And good-hearted.

"You know you're staring at me."

Trev blinked. "Impossible." At least she had a twinkle in her eyes. "Dad wrote pieces on everything from the impact of environmental change on small communities through to the ingredients of the winning cake from the local show. It was the latter kind he liked the least, but always treated the people he interviewed with respect and kindness."

"Perfect description." Rosie pulled a file out and peeked inside. "This one. Shall we go outside to look through it? I'm a bit selfish about enjoying the last of the nice weather."

Outside, the cats occupied the seats along the wall. It took all of a minute for Mellow to climb onto Rosie's lap, but Mayhem ignored their existence. Trev opened a beer.

"To give Charlie a bit of backstory, Bryony Murdoch was far too young for Terrance, in my opinion. She was nineteen when they married and he was well into his forties. Nothing wrong with the age difference as such, but she moved from interstate to marry him and they'd met twice."

"Do you remember where they met, Mum?"

"I think at a conference he and Kevin attended when they had their conveyance firm. She worked at the hotel where it was held and it all happened fast. Quite a nice girl, Bryony. Always a smile. She used to do a few hours a week at the pub, but I don't remember a lot else."

From the file, Rosie extracted a copy of a newspaper. "Graeme wrote an article after she'd gone. It wasn't about her, not specifically."

Trev found the article. Titled *Where do they go?*, it was about people leaving their homes, not under suspicious circumstances, but never to be seen by their loved ones again. He scanned the columns, his heart a little heavy as he recognised his father's trademark manner of writing. "He mentions Bryony Murdoch…and Vi Ackerman."

"That's the name of the people we bought from. Vi was

the lass who vanished." Rosie was animated. "He wanted to raise awareness for the effect it had on families."

Charlotte stood and looked over Trev's shoulder, a strand of her hair dropping forward to touch his neck. He found himself rereading a section as her scent did odd things to his concentration. He tried again. "So... Dad also mentions there was no police investigation into either disappearance because neither person was reported missing by family or loved ones."

"Why write the article then? No offense to him." Charlotte took her seat and sipped the last of her drink.

"None ever taken, darling," Rosie said. "It wasn't an in-depth investigation into those two people but a look at what happens to those left behind. And most of the article was about people in other towns because the Ackermans were long gone and Terrance did nothing but complain about being abandoned. Graeme told me Terrance said he'd done everything for Bryony, and she was a selfish... well, I won't repeat that bit."

Trev finished reading and passed the paper to Charlotte. "Another drink?"

"Please."

Rosie held her glass out with a smile as he stood. "And me."

When he returned, Rosie was flicking through hand-written notes. His father's handwriting. He'd like to spend some time going through the old files. Just to be close to Dad again for a while.

"Bryony was last seen on the fourteenth of June in 2002. She stopped at the bridal shop to speak to the owner, Concetta Bongiovanni—there's a person I've not seen in years—who was her closest friend in town."

"What bridal shop?" Charlotte looked puzzled. "Am I missing a secret mall?"

"Closed a few years back." Rosie continued, "According to Graeme's notes, she'd had a phone call which upset her and decided to leave Terrance and the town." Her finger followed the writing. "Concetta offered her a place to stay but Bryony was insistent. She had packed a small suitcase and was wearing a dress but had forgotten her coat."

Trev frowned. "June? Although we're having unusually warm weather now, it is normally quite cold. Or was it in her car?"

"No, dear. Terrance kept one car and she walked everywhere. According to this she was getting a lift to the railway station, being that bit further out and all, and going back to her family. She left without letting Concetta help and was never heard from again."

Charlotte nibbled her bottom lip, a sure sign to Trev of her feelings churning. He slid his hand to hers beneath the table and she grabbed his fingers like a lifeline.

Rosie put everything back in the file with a sigh. "Sounds as though the poor woman wanted to leave quickly. I was aware she'd left but couldn't really blame her."

"How old was she?" Charlotte's voice sounded shaky.

"Twenty-five or so." Trev answered.

"Young. So young to disappear." Charlotte released Trev's hand and nestled the glass between hers. "Do we know if she made it safely to her family, wherever they are?"

The doorbell rang and Mayhem growled from his chair.

"That'll be dinner." Rosie pushed herself back from the table.

Trev stood. "I'll go. Food sounds brilliant." He was starving and only realised it this minute. He'd ordered from Italia when he knew Charlie was coming over, not wanting to put Rosie out again and knowing she wouldn't let him cook without fussing. Once he had his own place, he'd cook for both of them all the time. When he could find somewhere.

chapter
fourteen

Over dinner, Charlotte directed the conversation back to Bryony Murdoch. Thinking about it was unsettling but she wasn't prepared to let it go. She needed to know what happened to the young woman in such a mismatched marriage.

"Did Graeme ever find out what happened to her?" she asked Rosie.

"I'm not certain he looked. After all, he was researching the impact on those left, not those who did the leaving. Trev, will you be able to find her?"

Trev had just taken a mouthful of pasta and everyone waited as he finished it. From the way he was eating, Charlotte wondered if it was his first meal of the day. Lots of coffee, but maybe no time for food.

"Sorry. By the way, this is delicious." He put down his fork. "We're getting ahead of ourselves tonight. I understand Bryony sounds like someone at risk of harm and maybe she was, but the crime scene officers only took the remains away a short time ago. I have no information yet on any evidence uncovered or any defining features."

"But even if it isn't Bryony's body, shouldn't we look for her?"

"I'll have a talk to Terrance. See if he can provide more details. If nothing else, what's happening now is a good reason to look behind the scenes a bit. I don't mind rattling his cage." He picked up his fork and slid more pasta on. "Mum, do you know where Mrs Bongiovanni lives these days? I remember her. Nice lady with a big smile."

Rosie grinned. "Good memory, dear. She did like you and always had some treat tucked away for when you'd drop by on your paper run. "The smile faded. "It's been years. She always said she'd retire to the beach and her grandson had a place around Torquay, I think. Would you like me to look for her?"

"Not yet. But I'll keep it in mind."

"Then what about Vi Ackerman?" Charlotte ventured, playing with the stem of her wine glass. Rosie had insisted they share a bottle, even though it was a Monday night. Italian food needs red wine, she'd said.

Over his own glass, Trev's eyes were hard to read. He must be tired of her sleuthing, but this was more. Something about the discovery of the grave with its covering of flowers alarmed Charlotte in a way she'd not experienced. Was alarmed the right word? Perhaps not. Unsettled. Frightened even. To think of what happened…

"I can't answer about Vi Ackerman." Trev creased his forehead. "I don't remember her or what happened."

"You were only twelve or so. We bought the bakery within a year of Vi leaving and you had your thirteenth birthday party the week before we opened the bookshop. She was an older teen so you wouldn't have come across her at school. Only at the bakery perhaps." Rosie bit into a piece of garlic bread.

"But she wasn't even an adult when she left?" Charlotte

asked, then grinned at Rosie's expression as she chewed her bread. "Sorry, I'll keep talking while you eat. She must have had friends who worried about her. Had she finished high school? Or was something going on at home which drove her away."

"What kind of something?" Trev refilled the glasses.

Charlotte shrugged and sipped.

"The Ackerman parents weren't very sociable, but nor did I ever see or hear anything to suggest they weren't loving to their children." Rosie said. "They belonged to a fringe religion which discouraged personal interactions with people not of their beliefs."

"How many children?"

"My goodness, Charlie, you are full of questions! And making me remember long forgotten facts."

Trev was amused. Charlotte snuck a look at him as he watched his mother with a slight smile. As always, the love and commitment between them tugged at her heart. Such devotion was alien in her own experience. The love between parent and child of any age was something she observed but never felt.

"There were three. Yes, pretty sure I'm correct." Rosie announced. "An older boy, possibly a year or two more than Vi but do not ask me his name! And a young child, a little girl I believe. Quite a bit younger. And I think I've used up all my brain power for one night so how about we move into the living room now we've all finished. Time for a coffee."

A little later Trev and Charlotte wandered out to the street, after Rosie kissed her cheek and told her son not to hurry back. Charlotte didn't even bother responding. Rosie could tease all she wanted but neither she nor Trev were about to bite.

They reached the end of the street and turned the corner. "She means well," Trev said.

"No, she doesn't. She wants a wedding and is quite happy to keep pushing until her dreams come true. But I do love her."

"And what do you want?"

"To not talk about this right now." Charlotte sped up a little. "I'm fine to walk home alone if you'd prefer to get some much-needed sleep."

Trev caught up and captured her hand. "I'll sleep soon enough."

She slowed again and they strolled toward town.

"Speaking of weddings, what do you remember about the bridal shop? And Concetta Bongiovanni."

"You remembered her name."

"I love the way her name sounds when I say it. Con-sh-e-tta Bon-gee-o-varni. Did anyone call her Connie?"

"They did. My memories are of a silver-haired lady who peppered her English with Italian and kept a box of Italian chocolates behind the counter. I'd drop the weekly paper in on Saturday mornings and she'd beckon me over and let me choose one."

The smile on Trev's face said it all. A childhood memory intense enough to recall after all those years.

"Can you still taste the chocolate?"

"I can. And smell the flowers she kept on a long glass table."

"What kind of flowers."

Trev glanced at her. "Why do you ask?"

"Curious. Do you remember?"

"No. I recall the scent, but not the flowers. I was a kid then."

They crossed the road past the roundabout.

"Where was the bridal shop?"

"On the corner. There." Trev pointed to the one opposite, which was now a jewellery shop. "Years of delivering local papers ingrained every shop of the time into my head."

Charlotte stopped and stared over the road. The building —like much of the town—was old, but in a charming way. "Kind of reminds me of George's jewellery shop." George was the last of a long line of jewellers back in Rivers End, a true gentleman still working in his seventh decade to create works of beauty.

"A bit. But nothing matches what George makes. You've seen the engagement and wedding rings he designed for Thomas and Martha fifty years ago? And those for Christie and Martin?"

She had. Works of art crafted by passion.

They kept walking. Trev's hand was warm around hers. It was nice. She'd never had a boyfriend as such. No young man to walk her home or hold her hand.

You're too old for a boyfriend.

As though Trev sensed her ponderings, he released her hand and put his arm around her shoulders. After the slightest hesitation, she slid her arm around his waist and snuggled close to his body. Never too old for a boyfriend.

Past the bookshop they turned into the driveway. Almost at the stairs, Charlotte blinked as one of the motion-sensor lights came on. "I always forget that is so bright."

"Much better now you have the lights. And once winter is really here, you'll appreciate them even more."

At the bottom of the stairs, Trev put both arms around Charlotte to look at her. "Want me to check the apartment is safe?"

"No. I want you to go home and finally get some sleep. Last night must have been exhausting."

"I'm tired. Brain doesn't want to settle, but once my head hits the pillow I'll sleep. And you need to rest tonight." He kissed her forehead. "There are still officers at the crime scene, so everything is well under control. Detective Dean is safe to sleep."

"Okay. She will try." Charlotte smiled up at him. Under the artificial lights his face was lined with exhaustion. She pushed away a ridiculous urge to smooth the lines. "Goodnight, then."

He didn't respond apart from a tightening of his arms around her.

"Do you need me to walk you home? This could be a long night," she said.

The corner of his lips curled and he touched them to hers. "I'm going. But go lock yourself in first."

When he dropped his arms, Charlotte wished them back but before she had a chance to do anything rash, she hurried up the stairs. After unlocking the door, she glanced down. "See you tomorrow?"

"Count on it."

She locked herself inside, unable to stop the silly grin somehow plastered on her face.

chapter
fifteen

Dreams haunted Charlotte's sleep. Images of brides drifting through the forest as though carried on a breeze, their faces covered by veils. She chased one then another, reaching out to touch them, to ask their name, but never fast enough. One led her to the clearing and circled the grave, which was flowerless. The bride laid her bouquet on it. As she straightened, she began to remove her veil...

Charlotte sat bolt upright, the covers falling away and her heart beating fast.

Light crept through the part open curtains. Early morning. She forced herself to take deep breaths until the panic subsided.

A dog barked close by, and then another. Excited barks. Charlotte slipped into her dressing gown and padded to the third bedroom, rubbing her eyes. A police car and a crime unit vehicle were parked near the flower trail. A man and woman walked along the main track with their dogs. Labradors, tails wagging in delight as they took turns carrying a long stick. A uniformed police officer emerged from the forest to speak to the couple. They called the dogs to them and attached leads before heading back the way they'd come.

How long would the area remain a crime scene? Cordoned off in parts to protect it from unauthorised activity and the risk of interfering with evidence.

Like two playful dogs trampling over the clearing.

Charlotte yawned. She wanted a shower and coffee.

Half an hour later she sat on the balcony, forcing herself to stay out of the third bedroom. Being at the window all the time wasn't getting anything done. At least out here with a hot coffee between her hands, she could think, rather than speculate.

The brides in her dreams fascinated her. Dreams always meant something, and she had a particular interest in their relationship to the waking mind. The brides disappearing before being caught represented her inability to connect the few pieces of the puzzle together. Without better information—who was in the grave for a start—she couldn't begin to construct a profile of the killer.

If she was murdered.

Another piece of missing information. Although the likelihood was whoever buried the body killed her, there was a chance it was an accident. Or even someone stumbling upon a deceased person and being too afraid to report it.

Would Henry do such a thing? Henry had helped cover up other crimes, too afraid to speak out and risk being blamed. He was out on bail now, awaiting a trial date for his part in being an accessory after the fact. Charlotte reached for her phone to call Trev to ask if he thought it worth speaking to Henry. But she put it down before dialling. It wasn't even seven and he deserved to sleep.

Then there was the final bride in the dream. She had deliberately laid down her bouquet and been aware Charlotte was there. And she wanted to be seen.

"Are you the victim?"

Charlotte knew she'd dream of her again. Until she solved this, the bride would insist on her attention. But why a bride? Was this because of the discussion last night? Of the bridal shop and a young woman running from a marriage?

It was more. Last night, as she and Trev stood near the roundabout, something tapped in the back of her mind. Something about a bridal shop, or brides. A dress.

Charlotte stood so fast her coffee spilled.

———

The storeroom at the back of the garage was as dusty and dark as Charlotte remembered. She'd intended to empty it out over summer, but between local crimes to help solve and her job, as well as spending time with Trev more recently, it was forgotten. And Rosie had offered to help, but again, other priorities arose.

The room was as wide as the garage and narrow with just enough space for a row of shelves all the way along the back and to move around. At the far end was a pile of boxes piled onto each other. All manner of old objects, boxes, suitcases and knick-knacks filled the shelves.

According to Rosie, most of the storeroom's contents came from the original owners of the building, the Ackerman family. And some from tenants during the years Graeme was alive. When Charlotte moved in last year, the apartment was long vacant.

Charlotte knew why she was here. Her hands found the clips on either side of the old cane chest and opened them. Before lifting the lid, she paused, aware her heart raced. Since the first time she'd looked in here, months ago, she'd known there was a sadness attached to the items inside. If she was right…

She replaced the clips. Not here. Trev needed to see this. This might be evidence. The trunk was awkward to carry because of its size and heavy enough to make Charlotte put it down twice. At the bottom of the stairs she made a decision, and instead, carried the trunk inside the bookshop. If Rosie objected, she'd ask Trev to help her take it upstairs to open. She pushed it beneath the counter in the kitchen.

Back upstairs, she'd missed a call from Trev, so turned the coffee machine on again as she dialled.

"Did I wake you?"

"Me? I was going to call before seven and thought I'd let you sleep. I was downstairs."

"I admit I've only been awake a few minutes." Trev sounded tired. "Did you sleep okay?"

"Sure, if chasing veiled brides around a forest counts. Don't ask. I'm making my second coffee."

"I can smell coffee. Mum's rattling around in the kitchen so I'm about to see if I can help make breakfast. Anyway, reason for the early call is we've had a tip the media are on their way up. More officers will arrive over the next hour to handle the area, but you needed to know."

"I'm not a fan of media."

"Agree. They have a purpose but poking around in the early part of an investigation isn't one of them. The crime unit are working overtime to clear the area, but they have at least another full day ahead."

Charlotte wandered into the back bedroom. "And the last thing they need is having cameras pushed in their faces."

"I'll make sure that doesn't happen. I'd better get moving."

"See you later."

If Trev was caught up wrangling media all day, she might have to delay opening the trunk. No point if he wasn't there. Kingfisher Falls didn't need an influx of reporters.

The sky was grey. Charlotte checked the weather on her phone. Possibility of rain. Bad for the crime unit but good when it came to an annoying media mob.

chapter
sixteen

"Of course it can stay here," Rosie peered at the chest beneath the counter, "but only if you promise I can see what's inside once Trev's here."

"You really don't know?"

"Only what you've mentioned before. I'm not certain if it belonged to the Ackerman family, or one of the tenants. And because Graeme never mentioned the contents, it must have already been packed when he moved it."

Charlotte refilled their water bottles from the filtered jug they kept in the fridge. "Do you remember how long ago the bridal shop closed?"

"Let me think. Thanks, darling, let's go back to the front counter." Rosie took her bottle and wheeled ahead. "About eight or nine years. Connie was ready to retire and had the best closing down sale! All those lucky brides getting huge discounts from such beautiful gowns. The final day, when she dropped the remaining stock to half-price, there was a line outside the shop an hour before she opened." Rosie laughed.

"Were there so many brides-to-be?"

"They came from Melbourne and all over. Connie's

dresses were quite special. Each one unique. And you are going to let me see inside?"

"Yes. Sorry, as soon as Trevor is about and has time. Unless he thinks it is yet another of my silly ideas." Charlotte sat next to Rosie and opened her water bottle.

Rosie turned to face Charlotte. Her expression was serious. "He doesn't think that way. Not of you, not ever. Don't you realise how much Trev respects you? Not only as a woman, but as a psychiatrist. He might tease you about sleuthing, but he is in law enforcement so can't exactly encourage it."

"Oh."

"Oh, indeed. My son admires your spirit and bravery. It might alarm him when you are in danger, and it certainly alarms me."

"I'm sorry. I never intend for bad things to happen."

"Then stay away from dangerous people. Quite simple."

Someone wandered in and Rosie immediately greeted them, going around the counter. Charlotte absorbed her words. Trev respected her. Admired her. Stay away from dangerous people.

Trouble had a way of finding Charlotte. Minding her own business in Rivers End, a vengeful ex-patient followed her from Brisbane and caused havoc. Since arriving in Kingfisher Falls, how many people had tried to cause harm around her? Enough to count on a hand. Or two.

Speaking of trouble. Charlotte couldn't believe her eyes when Sid Browne pulled up across the road. No longer in the patrol car—which had undergone repairs and detailing since Trev took over—he drove a battered old station wagon.

Rosie returned with the customer and put through the sale, chatting about the weather and chance of rain, before saying goodbye. As soon as the customer left, Charlotte patted her arm. "Look."

Sid had the window down and stared at the bookshop. It was unlikely he could see them so far behind the glass, but a shiver ran the length of Charlotte's spine.

"What the heck is he doing here?"

"I thought he and Marguerite moved. Or were selling or something," Charlotte said. "Since he lost his job, and the one disciplinary hearing I attended as a witness, he's been out of sight."

"Well, he can go back to being out of sight! Why is he parked there? This is like his behaviour around Christmas, always hassling us. I might phone Trev."

"He's kind of busy right now, Rosie. Unless Sid steps inside, let's ignore him. Best way of dealing with bullies." Charlotte wanted nothing more than to stride over the road and confront the man. She'd done it before and wasn't afraid to stand up to him again. He'd responded to his dismissal from the police force with accusations of being set up, but then disappeared from the town he'd lived in with his wife for many years.

Rosie nodded, but put her mobile phone on the arm of her wheelchair. Charlotte slid her own into a pocket. "Come on, we were going to do an inventory check in the children's area."

———

Talk among customers turned from the body in the forest to the convoy of media vehicles parked around the forest. Charlotte longed to look over the fence, but the customers came in non-stop and Rosie had a lunch time appointment.

As she'd collected her handbag and hat, Rosie was quiet.

"Meeting Lewis?" Charlotte asked as she took Rosie's place at the computer to update the inventory they'd counted.

"Not today. I may be a few minutes late, so apologies in advance."

"Um... you own the shop and don't need to ever apologise, so don't worry at all. I've got plenty to keep me busy."

It was only after Rosie left that Charlotte worked it out. She was going to Harmony's House of Mystique for her reading. If she'd realised, she might have suggested some ways Rosie could avoid being taken advantage of. Which sounded patronising. Charlotte sighed. Rosie was an adult and able to see through whatever nonsense Harmony spouted.

Inventory updated and a few customers later, she checked the time a bit surprised that is was well over the hour that Rosie expected to be gone. After years of running the shop either alone or with a young assistant, Rosie had rarely taken a proper lunch break until Charlotte came along. Most days now, she spent lunch time with Lewis, who was happy to close his own shop to share a bite with the woman he adored.

Sid was still across the road. Cigarette smoke wafted through his open window and he flicked the butt onto the road. That was enough for Charlotte. She stepped onto the pavement, hands on hips, and stared at him.

"Pick it up."

"Or what?" He still knew how to sneer. "Gonna make me?"

She took the phone from her pocket and scrolled to an app. "Nope. Going to take a photograph and send the details to the EPA." She took the photo, ensuring his face was visible.

"You go right ahead, Doctor."

Charlotte walked far enough down the road to take another photo, this time of the whole vehicle, including licence plate. Back outside the shop, she tapped the details into the online form. "Hey, Sid, just to make things easier, what is your address now?"

He snorted, wound up his window, and started the motor. After revving the engine, he pulled out and drove off, the exhaust spewing smoke everywhere. Charlotte took a photograph of that as well. "You forgot your butt."

"Charlie, what on earth?" Rosie approached. "What did we discuss about staying away from dangerous people?"

"Sid isn't dangerous. If he was, he'd have pushed me over the cliff, not helped me up. But he is a pest and I've sent a report to the EPA for littering from a car. And now I shall pick up his disgusting butt."

"Here. Take a tissue. Can't be too careful." Rosie dug a clean tissue from her bag and a card fell out.

Charlotte scooped it up. "An appointment with Harmony. Another one?"

"Stop judging me, Charlotte." There was an unfamiliar sharpness in Rosie's voice. "Yes, another one." She wheeled into the bookshop.

After retrieving the cigarette butt and tossing it into a bin, Charlotte followed Rosie, working on a suitable response. Upsetting her was not the intention, not ever.

chapter
seventeen

Rosie insisted Charlotte take a lunch break, more, Charlotte suspected, to delay any discussion about Harmony, than to ensure she was fed.

She *was* hungry and at last able to run upstairs to see what was happening behind the fence. From her fridge she grabbed a tub of yoghurt, then hurried to the third bedroom. In the past week she'd spent more time in here than all the months since moving in.

The scene from the window was bizarre. She slid the glass across, pulled up a stool she'd brought in earlier, and opened the tub. Almost as good as popcorn and a movie.

An assortment of media cars and vans lined either side of the track behind the fence. At least three news channels plus a couple of digital newspapers and a national print newspaper were represented, according to signage on vehicles. Set up a bit further along, a marquee was a hive of activity and Charlotte noticed people leaving with plates. A catering tent.

At the entrance to the flower trail, two uniformed police ignored the attempts of a reporter to get their attention. He was accompanied by a camera crew and pushed a microphone at one officer. Trev emerged from the forest and stepped between the reporter and the officer. Arms crossed, legs braced apart, he spoke to the reporter for a moment. His face—from this distance—was calm but serious.

"You tell them!" Charlotte muttered.

The microphone was lowered, and the camera crew waved off but the reporter persisted with Trev. It made no difference. Trev spoke again and this time the reporter turned away. He motioned for the camera crew and set up a few metres away.

A small group of people had gathered to watch. Locals, from the look of them. But how interesting that Terrance and Kevin Murdoch were amongst them. And Jonas Carmichael. The men stood a bit back, deep in conversation, then Jonas left the group and by-passed the camera crew to approach Trev.

What I'd give to hear this.

Jonas gestured at the media and Trev nodded. But then, Jonas turned his attention to the flower trail and took a step. Trev's arm shot out as a barrier to prevent an unwanted intrusion. Jonas halted but his body language was angry. Affronted. He barked something at Trev before spinning around and stalking back to the others, pulling a phone from a pocket and dialling as he strode.

The yoghurt was finished. Charlotte closed the window and checked the time. She'd been gone for long enough.

———

Rosie smiled when Charlotte appeared with two coffees she'd collected from the corner café. And a small bag of Rosie's secret vice. Miniature pastries from the bakery. One peek inside and the smile broadened.

"Thank you, darling. You can offend me more often if saying sorry is this delicious."

"I'll refrain from discussing my thoughts on Harmony. But I am sorry I overstepped. And may I have one?"

After tearing the bag open, Rosie placed it between them. "I need to say sorry for snapping at you. So, we will share."

Once Rosie made her first choice, Charlotte extracted a tiny éclair. "I was concerned for you. Nothing more." She popped it in her mouth and closed her eyes with a soft "Mm" as cream, chocolate and choux pastry squished together in a delectable explosion of sweetness.

"Charlie, I know Harmony is probably just very good at reading people and may well follow a formula to get people to believe her, but she's also insightful. Surprisingly so."

"I'm listening." If Rosie wanted to talk about the reading, Charlotte was interested in her experience.

Rosie took a long sip of coffee, her expression thoughtful. "She's been in Kingfisher Falls for what, a couple of months. Yet she knew the bookshop was once a bakery. She said she saw flour around me and the smell of fresh bread. Now, that is common knowledge, so it didn't impress me. But darling, she knew I used to dive!"

"Wouldn't it be easy enough to find out? And I'm playing devil's advocate, but if she knew you were coming to see her, she could prepare. Ask casual questions about your accident, for example."

"Ask who?"

Charlotte shrugged. "Other traders. Or an online search."

"Hadn't thought of that." Rosie chose another pastry, holding it aloft as she spoke. "She said I yearn to… smell the sea." Her eyes were unnaturally bright, and she put down the pastry. "To feel the ocean breeze on my face."

"And you do. I can see the longing in your face, Rosie." Charlotte took her hand. "And if Harmony telling you this encourages you to go visit the coast, then it was worth it." She reached for a box of tissues. "I'll take you if you want."

"The thing is-" Rosie took a tissue as a tear streaked her makeup. "I was certain I'd never visit the sea again. Only from a distance like in Melbourne. You can see Port Phillip Bay from some areas. But to taste the salt on my lips from the open sea, after all this time?"

"Didn't Lewis suggest a short break a while ago?"

Rosie nodded.

"Did he have a destination in mind?"

After dabbing her eyes, Rosie nodded again. "I do believe I refused, not because of the timing, but where he suggested. It was down on the Bellarine Peninsula. He wanted to book two rooms right on the beach."

Trev once told Charlotte his mother refused to go near the sea after her accident. Not even to visit him in the seaside town he'd called home for so long. He thought it must remind her of what she'd lost. The use of her legs. Charlotte thought otherwise. She released Rosie's hand and rubbed her shoulder instead.

"You do know it is okay to love him?"

Rosie's eyes shot to Charlotte's.

"Lewis is your future, if you feel that way about him of course. Your life with Graeme was wonderful, amazing. And those precious memories will remain in your heart, just as Graeme will." Charlotte smiled. "Not many people get to love two special men. And be loved back. Be fearless, Rosie. You deserve it."

With each word, Rosie visibly relaxed. If this was the burden she'd carried so long, then it was time to give herself permission to move on with her life.

Are you listening to yourself, Charlie?

With a small sigh, Rosie retrieved her pastry. "Why are you here, Charlie?"

"In Kingfisher Falls?"

"In the bookshop. You are an incredible psychiatrist." The pastry made it to Rosie's mouth at last.

"I'm good with pep talks. Which makes me good at selling books. And books are my number one love, so it makes sense to me." Books were much easier to deal with. They didn't stalk you or make complaints.

A movement near the door caught Charlotte's attention and she looked across. It was Trev, standing just inside the doorway. Something deep in his eyes, resignation or sadness, she couldn't be certain which, made her think back to what she'd just said. Had he heard her say books were her number one love?

chapter
eighteen

Dreadful timing. Walking in on what was a private moment between Mum and Charlotte was bad enough. But did Charlie mean it? Did she rate her love of books and the bookshop above any feelings for him? All this rushed through Trev's mind before he could sort his logic. Because an arrow had pierced his heart.

Pull yourself together. This is tiredness at play.

"Sorry, am I intruding?" He should have followed an earlier urge to go home for a quick nap.

Charlotte glanced down. She knew he'd heard, otherwise she'd have smiled at him.

"Never. Do you want some coffee?" Rosie wheeled around the counter with her arms open. "I can offer instant."

He leaned down for a hug. She'd been crying. "What's wrong, Mum?"

"I had a little moment. Missing your father a bit. Nothing more."

"I miss him too."

There wasn't a day he didn't think of Dad. No son could be luckier than him to know a father like Graeme Sibbritt. Kind, compassionate, and fair. Always fair.

"One day I hope someone thinks I'm even a tenth the man he was." Trev wanted the words back the minute he spoke. Too personal. As he straightened, his eyes sought Charlie. Her head was tilted, listening and watching, but what went on behind those gorgeous eyes was anyone's guess.

"Well, you are. And more." Rosie headed behind the counter. "What's the latest, son?"

"Media everywhere." He leaned his arms on the counter. "I expect them to be a pain, but not our local councillors."

"Jonas," Charlotte said.

"And you know this, how?"

She grinned and all of a sudden, his world was right again. Exhaustion and lack of food was messing with his head.

"Window. Third bedroom. Lunchtime."

"Oh, that's where you ran off to! I thought I'd upset you with my overreaction."

Trev looked from Charlotte to his mother. Was overreacting contiguous or hereditary?

"Never. I was curious after all the customers talking about it." Charlotte's eyes moved back to his. "Have you eaten lately?"

On cue, his stomach rumbled, and they all laughed.

"I'll get something next but wanted to check in. Jonas wants to look at the clearing. Thinks he can go into a crime scene because he's running for mayor."

"He's doing what?" Rosie's jaw dropped.

"I thought you knew everything going on in town, Mum."

"Clearly not. Nobody will vote for him. Apart from his cronies."

Unless he was the only runner. Stranger things had happened before but Trev agreed. Jonas Carmichael had one foot on the wrong side of good. Nothing he had proof of, not yet, but his association with criminals such as Veronica

Wheemor and Sid Browne shadowed any good he might otherwise do.

"Speaking of his cronies…" Charlotte glanced at Rosie, then back to Trev, "a certain ex Leading Constable showed his face earlier."

Trev straightened, looking out to the street by instinct. "Sid was here? Where and why? What did he say? Was he threatening?"

"Dear, calm down. He sat in a car over the street for a while and watched the shop."

Calm was the furthest thing from his mind. Sid Browne was nothing but trouble. Always was. And his wife, Marguerite with her accusations and lies over many years. Sid being removed from the police force was a day he cherished.

"Trevor? You appear rather angry. He didn't do anything." Charlotte stood and touched his arm.

"I'd like to…" He drew in a breath and focussed on the feel of Charlotte's hand. "Tell me what happened."

Charlotte used the tone he recognised as "Doctor Dean". Reassuring, firm in a no-nonsense way. And rarely used on him. "As Rosie said, he sat in some old beat-up station wagon for ages but when he tossed his smoking cigarette butt on the street I did pop over and request he pick it up."

Request? A bubble of mirth rose in Trev's throat as he imagined what really happened. Charlotte storming over and demanding he collect his litter. He felt his lips twitch. "Go on."

"Silly man refused so I took some photos and reported him to the EPA on their app. Simple. I did tell him what I was doing. He drove away."

"Charlotte."

"Trevor." There was laughter in her eyes and she patted

his arm then removed her hand to answer the phone when it rang. "Sorry."

I'm sorry. I like you touching me.

Charlotte turned the phone over to Rosie after a brief chat. "Lewis for you."

"Oh, lovely." Rosie took the phone and wheeled off to the corner of the shop.

"Now she's busy, I need to let you know something." Charlotte lowered her voice and leaned closer over the counter. "She went to see that Harmony earlier, for a reading. That is what's really upset her because the woman mentioned Rosie longing to be near the ocean and it all led to a conversation with me about her missing your father and being allowed to move on."

"You made her cry?"

"No. I helped her stop crying, Trevor. And you're missing the point. Two points."

"I got both points. But I like teasing you."

Her expression softened a bit. "Not nice. What are the points." The doctor tone was back, which mixed with a flicker of irritation in her eyes tempted him to close the difference between them and kiss her. Perhaps not the time.

"I've asked Mum to visit me in Rivers End since I moved there. Being near the sea has been a problem since her accident. A reminder of what she lost."

"And a bit more. It reminds her of your father."

Which made sense. His parents adored their regular adventures out at sea around Australia and overseas. It was their time together.

He nodded. "I get it. So, what is the answer?"

"Point two. Moving on."

"Lewis?" Trev glanced over when Rosie laughed at something Lewis said on the other end of the phone. He'd known Lewis his whole life, and his wife when she was still alive.

Good people. Friends with his parents. Kind to his mother when his father died.

"He asked her to have a holiday with him. Some months ago. At the time she said she was too busy to leave. But she told me just now he wanted to take her to the sea."

A dull ache rolled into Trev's heart. How lonely she must have been all this time, and thinking she had to hold onto the past when there was a bright and happy future waiting for her. He swallowed hard as he looked back to Charlotte. The gentleness in her eyes told him she understood.

Rosie finished her conversation and headed their way.

"I had a thought this morning." Charlotte announced, obviously to cover their discussion. "And it led to me retrieving something from the storeroom behind the garage."

"What kind of thought?" He was almost afraid to ask.

"More of a dream. But it reminded me of something I'd seen before which may... or may not, have relevance to the disappearance of Vi Ackerman."

"And Charlie brought it into the kitchen for when you have time to look," Rosie added. "But you need to eat so later is fine."

Charlotte and his mother exchanged a glance he didn't understand. This thought of Charlie's must be important. At least to the two of them. What was another ten minutes without food?

chapter
nineteen

Charlotte was disappointed when Trev's phone rang. They were in the kitchen, about to remove the lid of the cane trunk. He'd apologised and dashed outside to answer. She wandered back to the counter where Rosie looked up in surprise.

"He's on the phone."

"Well, while he is, I should tell you about my chat with Lewis."

"I'm all ears."

"We're having dinner tonight at India Gate House. And I told him I'd like to talk about… well, maybe having a little break together sometime."

"Wonderful! What did he say?" Charlotte pulled out her stool and sat.

"That he'd better start collecting travel brochures." Rosie's smile was beautiful. Their earlier talk had made a difference. Perhaps Harmony helped. Either way it was a huge step from the woman who wanted to go forward but had no idea what held her back.

You do know your stuff, Charlie.

"Best news in days."

"Could use some good news." Trev hurried from the back of the shop, sliding his phone into a pocket, his expression grim. "Weather's turning. Crime unit is finishing up but need more hands so I'll look at the trunk later."

"Is there anything I can do to help?" Charlotte stood. "Even just carry stuff or hold umbrellas."

"Thank you. But no."

"Here's a key to the back gate. Bit faster."

He took her spare key, nodded, and disappeared toward the back door. Charlotte dropped onto her stool with a plaintive, "I can be useful."

"And he knows. But it's a police matter, darling."

"Hm."

"So, what did you see from upstairs? At lunchtime?" Rosie asked.

"Oh yes. We never got around to that. Lots of media down there with vans and a catering tent, believe it or not. And locals in a huddle to one side. Onlookers for the most part, but the Murdochs and Jonas were there as well. And he got in Trev's face at one point."

"Can guess who came off best there."

"Yes. Jonas was furious when Trev wouldn't let him onto the flower trail."

Rosie peered over her glasses. "You've called it that before. Flower trail. Is it really so filled with those flowers?"

Charlotte dug out her phone. "I know I showed you a close up, but I have some I took on the way out. This one... yes, is within sight of the main track and taken facing the back of the bookshop." She handed over her phone on an image. "To me, they are a border. Pretty purple flowers lining either side of what is, admittedly, a narrow path."

Zooming in, and then out again, Rosie squinted at the image. "I'd love to see in person."

"Might wait until everyone clears off."

"Yes. But you are right, darling. These don't look self-sown at all. Too well spaced and kept clear of the path itself. And you mentioned there are more. On the grave." She looked up and handed the phone back.

"Like a blanket of purple. And that is what caught my attention. Something wasn't right about it." Nothing was. Charlotte tapped her fingers on the counter, thinking. Whoever planted these knew about the grave.

"Tell. Come on, I can see the cogs turning."

"If they're not self-sown, then a person deliberately planted them. On the path and the grave. Why? What is it about this flower that matters? And why even do it? Was it the killer, guilty and wanting to create something pretty in a bizarre repentance? Or another party who knew something and was unable to go to the authorities. A bit like… " She trailed off, not wanting to speculate aloud.

"A bit like Henry?"

"You're good at this." Charlotte offered a quick smile. "Yes, like Henry. His fear, and other limitations prevented him talking about his knowledge of certain crimes. This might be another one he knew about. And I think Trev needs to explore this theory if nothing else."

"I'd love a sample of the flower. Not that I'm an expert, but if I don't recognise it, we could check with Darcy."

What a good idea. Even if they didn't need Darcy's opinion, Charlotte hadn't visited the Christmas Tree Farm for a few weeks and missed seeing the Woodland family. If nothing else, it was time to return the tree she kept in a pot near the bottom of the stairs. Time for it to be planted somewhere and allowed to grow to its full potential. She smiled to herself.

"Mind if I tag along?" Rosie grinned. "Harmony's psychic ability is rubbing off on me because I can tell you are planning to visit them now."

"This is true. Well, the bit about my plans. And of course, you can come with me. I think we are overdue to cuddle Sophie."

"Sophie Charlotte Woodland," Rosie corrected. "Your gorgeous little namesake."

"What if I call Abbie and see when it suits? Well, once I can get to the path to collect a sample. Then we'll go for a drive and take my pine tree along."

"Can't wait to hear what young Lachie has to say about it."

At the ripe age of eight, Lachie was wise beyond his years. His take on the world was interesting and at times amusing. He and Charlotte had a running joke about her tree being half alien. Yes, it was time to visit their friends.

————

Rosie headed home a little early to prepare for her dinner date. By the time Charlotte closed the bookshop, heavy clouds had darkened the sky. She locked up and headed for the stairs.

Behind her, someone rattled the back gate and she froze.

"Locked." A female voice.

"Then nobody will disturb us."

Was that Jonas?

Charlotte crossed the small garden and stopped her side of the gate, listening. The gate was locked so Trev must have come back through at some point.

"We'll do this with your back to the bushland. Take a few steps back. Yeah. Give us a minute please."

The female voice continued but too quiet to hear her words, interspersed with an unknown male voice. An area lit up the dullness. A spotlight? Were they about to interview Jonas? Charlotte's hand went to the lock on the gate.

"Thank you, Mr Carmichael? We'll do a countdown. Ready?"

"For you. Always."

Oh, for goodness sake!

"Four, three, two, one... we are joined this evening by local councillor Jonas Carmichael. Mr Carmichael, the discovery of a body buried deep within the bushland here has sent shock waves through your town. What was your reaction on hearing of this awful crime?"

Charlotte lowered her hand.

"Of course, I'm in shock as is the community. To think one of our own may have fallen victim to foul play is... distressing."

"Yet this isn't the first time Kingfisher Falls has housed a killer. As recently as the beginning of this year, an elderly woman was brutally murdered by someone she trusted. One has to ask what the level of law enforcement was then, and now?"

Charlotte placed one foot on the lower cross beam of the fence as Jonas continued.

"I have asked the same question with little explanation. It is true our previous resident officer has been replaced but it remains to be seen whether the new incumbent is an improvement or not. He certainly won't co-operate with you, or by assisting my enquiries as future mayor."

That was more than enough for Charlotte. Hands on the top of the fence, she raised herself, so both feet were on the beam and her head was over the top and staring straight at a startled Jonas. She didn't speak, just gazed back.

The reporter followed Jonas' line of sight and gestured for the camera to follow her as she hurried to the fence and poked her microphone close to Charlotte.

"You have a bird's eye view of the bushland, Mrs... ?"

"Please turn that camera off me," Charlotte spoke firmly.

With a quick, "cut" to the camera operator, the reporter took a step back to better see Charlotte. "I'd like to interview you, Miss, Mrs... ? Would you mind coming to this side of the fence? It would be good to have the perspective of someone living so close to all of this."

"Her name is Charlotte Dean." Jonas approached, sounding miffed. "*Doctor* Charlotte Dean."

"Even better! What is your expert opinion on this tragedy?"

"She's an ex-psychiatrist so I wouldn't be wasting the last of the light on her."

The reporter ignored him. "I'd really love to chat to you away from here, Doctor. I imagine you have an excellent view of what's going on from your flat."

"I do. My only interest in speaking with you is to remind you, the media, of your obligations."

Eyebrows raised; the reporter took another step back. "Which are?"

"To let the police do their job. And not burden an under-standably worried local community with misleading commentary about the quote, level of law enforcement, unquote."

"I see. Anything else I need to remember?"

The sarcasm didn't improve Charlotte's opinion of the woman.

"Perhaps go to better sources for information than someone who has a vested interest." She glanced at Jonas who had a smirk plastered on his face. Her heart sank. "An interest in free publicity." Hopefully clarification would avoid threats of a slander suit.

"Does this mean you won't give me an interview?"

There was a tone of smugness in the reporter's voice and a movement from the camera operator told Charlotte why. He had a phone recording the conversation.

"I'd like that deleted thanks. I asked not to be recorded."

"No. You asked for that camera to be turned off. It was. Now, I'm happy for us to start over with a proper interview and that footage will be sacrificed."

"I want a copy. She slandered me." Jonas said.

Charlotte climbed down. She leaned against the fence with her hands clenched.

"Doctor Dean! We can sort something out."

"She isn't a real doctor. She plays at it when it suits her, like checking people are dead and finding bodies." Jonas must have got close to the fence because his voice lowered as if he was talking to her through the timber. "You've interfered one time too many. Got you now."

chapter
twenty

When someone knocked on Charlotte's door an hour later, she stood at the kitchen counter and willed them to leave. A storm was closing in and thunder rolled across the hills in the distance. Another knock.

Go away.

Her phone rang. Trev. She snatched it up.

"Hi." Even to her ears, her voice was strained.

"Hi yourself. Care to share a bottle of wine with a weary man?"

Nope. Not now. Not when she'd probably got herself in trouble and maybe even him.

"Don't you want to go eat or sleep or do paperwork?"

There was a long pause. Maybe the word 'sleep' triggered him into a nap on the spot. "Probably, but I'd prefer to spend a little time with you."

"Oh. Um. I left town."

He chuckled and there was a tap on the door.

"You might as well open it. Otherwise I'll sit on the top step and drink from the bottle."

Charlotte hung up. She'd have one glass with him, share some small talk, and then send him off before he worked out she was upset. Big smile on her face, she swung the door wide. He held up a bottle of wine.

"Seems I arrived home a second ago. Please come in."

He did and headed to the kitchen. She closed and locked the door after a quick look outside. All appeared quiet.

"I found a portal and it takes me from one part of the world to another in milliseconds."

"What did you do?" Trev found two glasses and opened the bottle.

"Excuse me?"

He glanced up between pouring with a grin. "You don't want to answer the door despite my offering here. Something is up. New clue?"

Trev's presence overwhelmed her. His strength and steadiness. His belief in her no matter what she did. Her whole life she'd managed. Been in control of everything around herself. But she was so, so weary of holding the world at bay. Tears prickled behind her eyes and all she wanted was his arms around her. Her mouth quivered trying to stop the emotions surge through her.

"Sweetie? Oh, Charlie." He put the bottle down and then he was there, in front of her, his face filled with concern. "You're crying. What happened? Are you—"

She threw herself against him and burst into tears. His arms folded around her and she was safe. His warmth seeped into her body which was colder than she'd known. Cold from fear and fighting her flight response since her gate was rattled.

The sobs subsided as she regained control. His heartbeat against her ear was fast. He was worried. It wasn't fair because she'd involved him in something he wasn't even aware of. And now she had to tell him. Before everything collapsed on her again. She reached in her pocket for a tissue, not quite ready to leave the sanctuary of Trevor's embrace.

As though he knew, he shuffled them both to the sofa and somehow, she was on his lap, her head on his shoulder.

"Where's that tissue?" The gruffness in his voice revealed his concern. Charlotte found a clean tissue. He dabbed beneath each eye, his face close to hers. "Think we'll need a few more. There's a whole lot of tears on those cheeks."

"I'm sorry," she whispered.

"For letting me comfort you when distressed?"

"No…never for that. For losing control. Not being strong. Making a scene—"

His lips touched hers in a gentle kiss.

This stopped her talking and breathing. For a moment. Then as if nothing happened, he adjusted them both so she was upright. His hand brushed a strand of hair from her face.

"Care to tell me what's going on?"

"I'd rather not but I will. Any chance of opening the wine first?"

"For courage?" Trev grinned. "Hop up and I'll pour you a glass of bravery."

She took off for the bathroom while he opened the wine. After splashing her face with water, she glanced at herself in the mirror. Little to show for the tears. But her eyes were serious as she reached for a way to explain what happened with the reporter.

Tell it as it was.

Not at all sure this would work, Charlotte shook her head at her reflection and made her way to the kitchen. Trev was pouring the white wine and glanced up. "Where would you like to sit?"

"Balcony. Even with the storm coming." She opened the sliding door and Trev followed her out with the wine. "But once the storm hits, I'm back in there."

"Why do they scare you?"

"Loud. Unpredictable. Uncontrollable."

Trev handed her a glass as he joined her at the table. "To overcoming fears." He toasted.

"Sounds like a plan. Cheers."

The first sip of wine was smooth and warmed her stomach in seconds. Storm or not, she didn't know how long they'd be out here. He might leave the minute she told him what happened. She frowned. This was the old thought process. Not the new one she worked so hard to embrace.

"I won't be cross."

She stopped staring at the wine glass and looked at Trev. "How do you know?"

"Just do. So, what, or who, made you cry?"

The quiet insistence in his voice and on his face reassured her. Another sip and she cleared her throat.

"Okay. I think I made myself cry because a situation happened and despite my intentions, it would have been better to leave it alone."

"Go on."

Before she could back out, Charlotte told Trev everything. From the moment the gate rattled to the final words from Jonas. All the time, Trev watched her, his fingers playing with the stem of his glass but not a drop of wine passing his lips. Lips which tightened at the implied threat from Jonas. When she was done, Charlotte sat back.

"Jonas Carmichael is a grandstander, Charlie. He wants attention and running for mayor will make him even greedier for it. Threatening you over what are quite innocent statements won't help his cause, so I'd not lose sleep over it."

Now, he drank a mouthful, eyes never leaving Charlotte's. His confidence helped. Someone running for mayor who also had a lawsuit against one of his potential constituents wasn't a good look.

"You don't need to protect me, Charlie."

No, she didn't. But protecting those she... cared about,

was ingrained in her soul. Her thing. Keeping her mother safe taught her to look out for everyone else. Except herself.

"I'm sorry."

"And you don't need to apologise for caring." His hand covered hers. "I love your fierce spirit and readiness to jump in when you see unfairness in the world. You've done it for Mum more than once, and for the Woodlands and others. You should be proud of who you are."

"You're not annoyed with me?"

"Nope."

"Or frustrated because I won't stay quiet?"

He shook his head.

Oh.

They sat for a while in silence, apart from the occasional rumble of distant thunder. Trev was unique. From the first time they met, he'd seen through her to the core of who she was. Better than she did. And he liked her. Genuinely liked her.

"When did you last eat?" she asked.

"One of the Kyneton officers snuck into the media tent and grabbed a couple of plates of food. But that was hours ago."

Charlotte pushed her chair out. "Well, we need some food then."

As if agreed upon, she picked up her glass and went inside.

chapter
twenty-one

While Charlotte prepped the ingredients for an omelette, Trev went downstairs to collect the cane trunk. He let himself into the bookshop with her key and scooped the trunk up, a little surprised by its weight. After resetting the alarm and locking the door, he hurried to the stairs, rain-drops hitting his head.

Charlotte held the door ajar for him and he turned side-ways to fit the trunk through at the same time. "This is what you found in the storeroom?"

"Yes, last year. Put it anywhere. Do you want to eat first?"

He lowered it onto the floor in the living room. "Starving."

Something smelled good.

"Need a hand?"

She was back in the kitchen, all traces of her earlier distress hidden behind a smile. "Um, yes, if you can set the table. Do you want to eat in or out?"

"Rain's here but the storm is miles away. What would you prefer?"

"You choose." Charlotte turned on the stove. "I've got

some long slices of bread in the oven with some herb butter on. Thought the eggs can go on top."

Nothing had ever sounded better. Trev collected cutlery, salt and pepper, and the bottle of wine. The balcony still appealed so he set things up out there. Charlotte had transformed the old area into a welcoming place to enjoy. Her latest addition was a herb garden. He returned for their empty glasses.

"Did you use your own herbs on the bread?"

"I did! Doing some cooking classes with Doug changed my fear of trying new recipes. It is fun and the ones I mess up still are edible. I've used dill and basil, because I love basil with everything, and added some garlic but that was from a jar unfortunately." She checked the bread and nodded.

Trev leaned against the counter. The woman in the kitchen was bouncing with happiness and it filled his heart. When she'd sobbed in his arms, his own heart was broken. She should never cry. Charlie deserved every good thing in life.

"You okay?" She put plates on the counter. "Looking a bit pensive there."

"I'm very okay."

A moment later, she laid a long slice of herby, buttery bread on each plate, then slid fluffy omelette onto each. With a flourish, she added a sprig of parsley. "Perfect! Well, the flavour remains to be seen, but it looks nice."

On the table, under lamp light, the plates were pretty. Charlotte took some photos. "You may eat now." She grinned as she sat opposite and put her phone away.

He didn't need a second invitation. Creamy, cheesy eggs matched the herb bread with perfection. And somehow, breakfast for dinner suited the crisp white wine and the backdrop of rainfall. Contentment tiptoed into his heart.

They talked between bites and sips. There was laughter and pauses. Stolen glances and smiles.

All too soon, the delectable meal was finished. He laid his cutlery on the plate.

"This? Anytime you intend making it, please call me."

Charlotte smiled with her eyes and that was enough for now.

A long rattle of thunder followed a sharp blaze of light. She jumped then bit her lip.

"What if we open this trunk of yours?"

In minutes they were inside, the table emptied and more wine poured. The sliding door remained open, allowing the fresh smell of rain to fill the living room. Charlotte cleared the coffee table and Trev relocated the trunk there.

"Tell me what you know about this?" He waited as Charlotte did her usual thing of taking photos from every angle. "I'll ask Mum later, but I guess the two of you have discussed it."

"At length." She put the phone on the arm of the sofa. "I believe this was left by the family who sold the building to your parents. The Ackerman family. It is possible though it might be from tenants. Rosie doesn't remember which, only that your Dad packed items away from them both."

"What drew you to open this, of everything out in the storeroom?"

Charlotte half-smiled. "You'll think I'm silly."

"Doubt it."

"It reminded me a little of Martha's trunk in Rivers End. I know hers is an antique crafted in England from timber but it was the feeling of discovery. What might be inside? I'd expected old tea towels or something. But instead… " The smile turned sad.

Trev unclipped the clasps and lifted the lid right off. This he leaned against the coffee table. Red silk shimmered under the overhead light. He slipped on a pair of gloves. "I know you've handled some of the items but this will reduce any further contamination should CSS need a look."

The silk was folded across the top of the trunk. As Trev lifted it by its corners, a sweet scent filled the air. He exposed the next layer. Something was familiar. Not the silk, nor the teddy bear lying beside what appeared to be new baby clothes. And not the white lace of the wedding dress folded beneath them.

He sniffed the air, then dropped to his knees to inhale rose and lavender from the items within the trunk. His mouth tasted chocolate. Dark, Italian chocolate and the voice of Concetta Bongiovanni rang in his ears. *Il tuo premio*. Your reward. Every Saturday for two years.

"Trevor?"

Charlotte regarded him with puzzled eyes. He must look odd, kneeling on her floor and sniffing an old trunk. Trev scrambled to his feet. "I know where this dress is from. Well, I think I do."

"The bridal shop? I recall you saying you remembered the flowers in there, and the taste of Italian chocolate. Why are you smiling?"

"I really, really want a piece right now."

"Memory association. So, the lavender and rose is what you remember from the bridal shop?"

"I delivered the paper there for two years. Connie loved her flowers."

"She might remember this dress." Charlotte reached for it but pulled her hands back before making contact. "Are you going to see what else is there?"

"I might lay the top upside-down on the floor to place each item on in order and if you'd care to photograph it all?"

"Knew my need to record everything would come in handy." Charlotte grabbed her phone. "Go for it."

First, Trev slid his hands under the teddy bear and lifted it so Charlotte had access to both sides. "While it looks old, it also appears new. If that makes sense. No sign of wear or use. Typical mass merchant teddy I think." This went onto the lid. Next were the baby clothes. "Newborn size. New and unworn, by my estimate. And another readily available brand."

"How do you know so much about baby stuff?"

"I do have friends with children." Trev grinned at Charlotte. "Been to a few baby showers and can find my way around a nursery department of a shop."

A slow flush brightened her cheeks, which he thought adorable.

"Not certain about lifting this dress. And before you ask, I have no experience with wedding dresses other than taking the paper to the bridal shop. But I would imagine they are normally folded and wrapped a certain way to protect them?"

"Asking the wrong person. But yes, I agree simply folding it like this one may not be ideal. Same as any long dress." Charlotte leaned closer. "Seeing as you have the gloves, is that a pin at the back?"

Trev raised the bodice of the dress to look at the back. Sure enough, a tiny safety pin in a discreet piece of lace held a thin string. With a tag. He met Charlotte's eyes. She was every bit as curious as he was.

"Photos first."

She obliged and then got even closer as he turned the tag. "Connie's Brides."

Trev liked facts. It was the backbone of his job. But his gut said otherwise right now. How Charlie knew was beyond him, but she was right in believing this dress, the trunk, were connected to the shallow grave.

"What else is in here?" Charlotte was oblivious to his pondering.

"I'll lift this as carefully as possible." He managed to keep the wedding dress folded more or less as they found it, lowering it onto the items on the lid.

"Are these old school books?" Charlotte knelt now and took photographs. "Looks like workbooks and a year book. And newspapers."

"I'm not prepared to take these out. This one here-" he pointed to a scruffy exercise book. "Look at the name."

Charlotte narrowed her eyes to read the scrawl. "Vi Ackerman. And that's a diary under it. I can see the corner enough to recognise it. Had one similar as a teen."

"So, either this is a random box of items, or belonged to Vi. And what would a seventeen-year-old want with a wedding dress? For that matter, afford one like this."

"Trev... more than that. The baby clothes. And the teddy bear." Her voice broke a little and he reached across to squeeze her forearm. "Something terrible happened. I don't believe she upped and left. Not for one minute. I think Vi Ackerman is the person I found."

chapter
twenty-two

Trevor left near midnight, and minutes later, the storm came. He messaged her to say he'd made it home in time, and to send her an emoji of a penguin for some reason—which made her smile—and then she sat in the third bedroom with the window open.

All the lights were off in the apartment. Charlotte cradled a glass with a dribble of wine in it, the last of the bottle shared with Trev over dinner. As tired as she was, thinking of the simple meal and company kept her too alert for sleep. The mystery of the cane trunk had deepened but now there was something to investigate, even if Vi was not the poor soul from the forest.

Except, you are.

Charlotte gazed through the rain. Every time lightning flashed, the flower trail lit up. All the media were gone. The police were gone. Only strands of police tape flapped about in the gusts of wind. The remains from the shallow grave were in safe hands at last. In a day or two, the identity might be discovered. Or at least, the approximate age of the body and date range of how long she'd been there.

Tomorrow morning, she intended to collect some

discreet samples of the flowers for Rosie. It might be for nothing. But somebody planted those flowers and Charlotte wasn't about to let go of the mystery.

A long, forked flash lit the sky and Charlotte covered her ears. The boom that followed was long and close. She stood to slide the glass across. More lightning. A movement caught her attention.

Was someone on the track below? Surely her eyes were mistaken from the after effects of the sudden light. She waited as the rain increased. Just as she was ready to turn away, another fork from the sky, this with a green tinge telling her it was too close for comfort. And there, at the entrance of the flower trail, a person.

All she saw was a raincoat and wide brimmed hat pulled down to the collar before whoever was out there ran out of sight. Toward the grave site.

Charlotte took off for the back door. Stopped and threw on her red trench coat. Stopped again and found a flashlight and her keys. Then was down the stairs, careful as they became slippery toward the bottom. In a few seconds she'd reached the back gate and unlocked it, then slid the latch across, her fingers struggling to grip the steel.

Once open, she stepped through, waiting for lightning. When it came, there was no sign of the person. They must be along the trail. Who and why? Was it the person who planted the flowers?

She sprinted over the track and worked her way along the trees to where the flower trail began. With her flashlight, Charlotte sought the narrow path. It was the footprints which showed her the way. Deep steps in the mud.

Need my phone.

No point going back. Charlotte flashed light along the flower trail. Empty.

The rain bucketed down, soaking through her hair, and

streaming down her face. She pulled her collar up and water trickled down her back. This was a terrible idea. But if she found the person…

Charlotte took a few steps in and the canopy enfolded her. Thunder growled overhead and she shuddered.

Be brave. This is important.

Whoever was out in this weather needed help. If they were grieving an old loss and too afraid to show themselves, she could become a conduit between them and authorities. Or was this a reporter? Charlotte gripped her flashlight and sploshed across the muddy ground, her feet already wet through. Surely the lack of a police presence didn't signal a free for all?

The flashlight went out.

"Bother." Charlotte shook it to no avail. As best she could, she followed the path, stopping often to wait for the sky to light up and guide her.

Ahead, the area which she'd previously navigated around to reach the clearing was open. The bushes cut down and pushed to one side. No doubt so the authorities had better access than clambering over and around thorny plants.

Police tape still surrounded much of the clearing. Around the site of the shallow grave, extra pickets and tape made it clear the area was not to be breached. Charlotte halted against the thick trunk of an old tree, hoping for some relief from the rain. Within the cordoned area, a shadowy figure squatted beside a pile of dirt. Flowers were scattered through the dirt—what once was a blanket over long buried remains.

Charlotte was torn. Nobody should be in that space. Although the crime scene services team were gone, by leaving police tape they'd signalled it was out of bounds. She needed to stop this person interfering with the ground and surrounds. And if they were in grief, she'd get them to shelter and call for help.

As she stepped forward, lightning overhead turned the clearing into day and the person lifted their face to the sky.

With a gasp, Charlotte retreated to the trunk and flattened herself against the furthest side. This was the last person she wanted to run into out here. Her heart pounded and her fingers tightened into balls. She had to wait it out. Let him leave.

Why was he here? What possible reason could he have for breaching police tape and inspecting the site of a grave? He had to know the victim.

Charlotte snuck a glance around the tree and flung herself back. He approached. Head down again, he trudged past the tree without a second look. The rain eased, allowing the squelch of his boots to reach her ears.

He was gone. She counted to a hundred. Then a second hundred. Counting helped her regain control over her panic. She'd take her time getting back behind her gate because she couldn't let him know she'd seen him. Kevin Murdoch frightened her.

chapter
twenty-three

Ruined. All those hours waiting for him to arrive wasted. The one chance ruined. Of course, he would choose a time when nobody would be outside or even look through a window. After midnight. In the middle of a storm.

The cops being gone meant he'd go and check. See what they left. But they're too clever to leave anything. No evidence for him to retrieve. So, the knife in the pocket will be used at last. Teach him. Leave him where he left her. But no flowers for him. When he least expects revenge, it will take every breath from him.

He pushes the police tape aside without respect. Stands over the edge of... of where she'd lain for so long. His foot kicks some soil back in. He lifts a flower and throws it in after the soil. He needs to be ended.

But someone approaches. A narrow beacon of light. Or was it imagination?

Get closer. Take every step with caution so not to give away anything. One chance to do this.

Now, he squats and his fingers dig around in the bottom of the cavity. His attention is on that, not on anyone being out here as well. Anyone who knows what happened. Another few metres. He'll never know. Which is too good for him.

Someone is here.

Her. Always where she doesn't belong. Did she see him from her window?

This ruins it. No way to do this with a spectator.

Lightning so bright it almost blinds. He looks up.

It isn't him!

Step back, step back, step back.

He's leaving. But it is the wrong man. And he passes the place the woman hides so now she knows he was here. And this will confuse everything.

chapter
twenty-four

Charlotte arrived at the police station at the same time Trev parked out the front. She'd walked down in brilliant sunshine, puddles and cool air all that was left of the massive storm of the night.

"You look exhausted, Charlie." Trev met her on the pavement. "Did you sleep at all?"

"A little. But all I could see was his face."

Trev made a humph sound as he pulled keys from a pocket. "We'll talk inside."

As he unlocked the front door and turned off the alarm, Charlotte worried about the nature of the "talk". Her actions last night were dangerous. Why she did things like this without proper forward thought and care was something she didn't understand. It wasn't the first time she'd put herself in danger.

She'd only stepped foot in here once after Sid Browne left, and it was to make another statement about the events earlier in the year around the death of Octavia Morris. With Trev not yet confirmed as his replacement, Bryce and Katrina—the detectives who'd run the investigation—had reluctantly finished their interviews amongst the filth and chaos Sid had created over his time in the job.

Expecting the awful stench of stale cigarettes and body odour, she was surprised by how fresh and clean everything was. She stood near the counter and sniffed the air.

"Better than before?" Trev unlocked the back door and headed to the kettle. "I've requested new paint inside and out, as well as some updated equipment. Appears Sid got funding for a fair bit over the years which went straight into his pocket." He filled the kettle and turned it on.

"It smells normal. The stickiness is gone from the surfaces. And I can see two desks with minimum clutter. Much better than before."

"Grab a seat and I'll bring you a coffee. I will get a machine for in here."

"Not that you spend a lot of time here."

In the middle of taking cups from a cupboard, Trev glanced at her. "No. Seem to spend my time working on a recent crime spree."

Charlotte sat, biting her bottom lip. It was true since her arrival late last year the sleepy town had seen more crime than in its previous ten years. Or twenty. And although none of it was her making, she had a knack of finding a problem where nobody had seen one. She watched Trev make coffee. His appointment as the resident police officer here was a good one. Kingfisher Falls now had genuine law enforcement from a local who understood the community and had solid ethics.

"Why are you looking so pensive, Charlie?" Trev put two cups on coasters and settled into the opposite chair. "Anything you'd like to open with?"

There are two Charlottes and I'm the one who doesn't risk her life?

But there was little point in avoiding the inevitable, one-sided discussion once she began with the details. All Trev knew, so far, was she'd seen Kevin in the clearing. After texting him to see if he was awake at six thirty, he'd phoned.

"You saw him go into the bushland?" Those were his first words on the phone.

"Yes and no. I was—"

"How soon can you be at the station?"

"Oh. Half an hour?"

And here she was. A bit after seven. No breakfast or even a coffee yet. She reached for the cup he'd placed near her, eyes wandering to his. Trev's expression was hard to read. He must expect the worst and she was about to give it to him. Might as well get it over with.

"You'll be cross."

He raised an eyebrow and took a long sip of coffee.

"I couldn't sleep with the storm so sat by the window overlooking the bushland for a while."

"And Kevin Murdoch emerged from the direction of the clearing?"

"Ye...es. A bit later."

"Go on." Trev held his coffee cup between both hands. His eyes never left Charlotte's. Right now she could use some eye aversion. This was about to get ugly.

Stop stalling.

"I saw a person out in the weather. Someone with a long raincoat and wide brimmed hat pulled right down. They were near the entrance to the flower trail one minute, then next flash of lightning, no sign of them. Not anywhere along the main track."

"This was when? Midnight? Later?"

"About then. All I could think was this person must know her... known she was buried there and was compelled to visit what was left of her grave. To mourn or be relieved she was finally found. I wanted to help them."

Trev put his cup down with great care. He turned on the computer, tapping his fingers on the desk as it booted up. Charlotte recognised the intense control he was exerting over himself. He either wanted to tell her off or hold her. Either way, he wasn't moving much and even his shoulders had tensed.

"In a moment I'll take a statement. But tell me this-" he looked straight at Charlotte. "You took yourself out into the middle of a thunderstorm to follow an unknown person to a secluded crime scene. And came across Kevin Murdoch, who has made it clear he doesn't like you. Am I correct in my assumption?"

Charlotte nodded and dropped her eyes, unable to bear the emotion in his. Anger? Disappointment? Either way, her stomach lurched. He'd told her once before of his fear of losing her when she'd kept secrets. This wasn't a secret though. It was a mistake.

All the way through the interview, Trev kept his tone steady and asked her to repeat anything he was unsure of. He typed, questioned, typed. Every so often he drank coffee. Hers went cold. Kevin Murdoch's face haunted her. A flash of light and his face lifted to the sky. Her back hard against the tree. Rain dripping from her hair as she hid. Her heart racing.

It still was racing.

"Charlotte. Charlie, look at me."

With a small gasp, she pulled herself out of the darkness.

Trev's hand covered hers, warm and reassuring. "Where were you just now?"

"I am so sorry." Her voice came out as a whisper. "I followed my heart, Trev. My need to help whoever was in such pain but how was I to know Kevin was the person? And he cannot be in pain over this unless he loved and lost her."

After a quick squeeze he released her hand and sat back, arms crossed.

Without a word, Charlotte stood, collected both cups, and headed for the kettle. The whole time she made coffee she felt Trevor's eyes on her. What she'd done was dangerous and couldn't be repeated. Not if she wanted him in her life. And she did.

"Two coffees." Why she said this she had no idea. Fill the silence.

"Thanks. Sit, please."

Much as her flight instinct urged her to grab her handbag and run, Charlotte managed a smile and sat. "I messed up."

"Messed up. Let's take a closer look. On the up side, you've identified a person trespassing on a marked police site. This gives me a lot to consider about Mr Murdoch and his reasons for being there under such bizarre conditions. And that is the up side."

"Well, it helps. Doesn't it? I mean, what if he killed her?"

"Exactly."

Charlotte didn't understand.

"If he killed whoever was in the grave, does it sound logical he might kill again to keep this a secret?" Trev uncrossed his arms and leaned forward. "Charlotte, if he'd seen you, I might be out there again but this time with *your* body to identify." His eyes bored into hers and then he pushed back his chair and stalked away.

The back door swung shut behind him.

chapter
twenty-five

Trev didn't stop until he reached the back fence behind the police station. His hands were curled into fists and he somehow resisted the urge to hit the timber palings. As it was they were falling down, some hanging by a nail and others bending away from the top. Another thing to fix. He walked alongside the fence, counting the damaged palings until the thunder in his ears subsided. By then he'd reached the corner of what was a large and unkempt yard. Not dissimilar to his station in Rivers End when he'd arrived there.

There was adequate space for a vegetable garden and an idea formed. Something for the community. Unlike Rivers End station, which also had his accommodation on the same land, this was a standalone station. With some nurturing he might turn this into a safe space for locals to have a neighbourhood garden.

The back door opened. Charlotte must think him crazy. Storming off like this. Did she have no sense of danger? No concept of the risk she was in last night? And not the first time she'd acted before thinking around dangerous people.

"Trev?" Her voice held uncertainty. And it should. His return to Kingfisher Falls was as much about being close to her as being home again. He wanted to live his life with Charlotte Dean. But *she* wanted to solve crimes even when there wasn't one to solve. He steeled himself, preparing to deliver some home truths. She had to understand the consequences.

One look at her tear-streaked face and all resolve to keep her at a distance dissolved. He opened his arms and she fell into them. This was where she belonged. Wrapped in his embrace. He could protect her like this. Stop her doing things to put herself at risk. If she stayed here...

He buried his face in her hair. He mustn't cry.

The insistent ringing of a phone was what finally drew them apart. He loosened his arms with an apologetic "sorry," then realised it was her phone. She slid it from a pocket and turned away to answer. Thank goodness. He rubbed his eyes then blinked to clear his vision. At least now the urge to scold her was gone. Going. Equal they might be, but he was only human when it came to wanting her safe.

"Maggie, slow down, I'm struggling to understand." Charlotte caught his eye. Her tone was Doctor Dean. "What's wrong with Mum?"

Foreboding clutched at Trev's gut.

"I see. Okay....yes, I heard. Can you send the number of her specialist please? And a list of what she's on."

Her shoulders slumped as she listened and she nodded every so often.

"Let's see if we can sort it out first." She rolled her eyes. "Yes, I do understand, but until we start to panic, let me review what's going on please."

A moment later she hung up. "Darn. Sorry."

"What's wrong?"

"Mum had a psychotic episode and hurt another patient. They've sedated her and she's safe, so is everyone else."

A message beeped and she glanced at the phone.

"The specialist's number?"

"Yeah. But I can't contact them for another hour or two. Time difference and all that. Darn!"

Two "darns" in one minute. Her face was set, deep in thought. Trev held out a hand. "Come on. Let's get out of here and find a decent coffee."

She hesitated.

"You have time. And I need to eat even if you survive on morsels each day."

"I do not! I eat a lot of food. Just not regularly." But she took his hand and let him guide her past a thorny bush back to the door. "This place is a mess, Trevor."

He grinned, relieved at her normal tone. "Offering to help me do an overhaul?"

"If you believe that, you are clearly over hungry."

———

"Golden latte?"

"Thanks, and the baked eggs please." Charlotte smiled at Vinnie, owner of the café she frequented the most. Being situated on the corner opposite the bookshop, she and Rosie were regular customers.

Vinnie tilted his head at Trev, his expression curious. "And breakfast for you also, young Trevor?"

"Not so young Trevor would love a black coffee and pancakes, thanks."

For the first time this morning, Charlotte stopped worrying. For a few minutes anyway. His rapport with the long-time owner of the café was funny. She'd once teased Trev in a phone conversation about the amazing man who knew she needed coffee just by looking at her. Vinnie was one of those traders who made everyone welcome and remembered what they liked.

"What, please enlighten me, is a golden latte?"

"Really? Hm. I guess you are a black coffee drinker."

"Hey. Is that an insult?"

"Never. Golden latte isn't coffee. Mine has almond milk with turmeric, black pepper, ginger and some other spices. Creamy goodness in a glass."

"There you go. Learn something new every day." Trev's phone buzzed. "Sorry, back in a sec." He stepped outside to answer.

Charlotte sat back in her chair, eyes on him through the window. She had no doubt he was disappointed in her. And frightened she might have died. The reality hadn't sunk in yet but she knew it would when she had less to worry about. Her mother was an issue she couldn't avoid.

Nor can you avoid Trev's feelings.

If he cared less for her, his reaction would be different. When he'd walked out of the station, his body rigid and words left hanging in the air, she'd glimpsed into his heart. All her life she'd avoided being close to anyone who might want more from her. With Trev, she'd even moved hours away from his home. Except it was to work for his mother.

Vinnie returned with their drinks and a raised eyebrow.

"He's on the phone."

"Should be in here. With you." With a wink, Vinnie left her again.

Was everyone in this town a matchmaker? It was funny though, the assumptions of people that she and Trev belonged together.

"Apologies for the interruption." Trev slid into his seat again. "Mm, coffee."

"Do you want to taste mine?"

He contemplated her glass of steaming, bright yellow milk, and shook his head. "Thanks, but coffee is fine for now. That was Katrina. She and Bryce expect a report today regarding the remains. I've mentioned your sighting of Kevin Murdoch and they'll drive down a bit later to meet with me. Might need to take some more of your time."

She nodded and stirred her drink.

"We didn't finish our interview but might leave things as they are until more information comes to light. What I do want to ask is for your opinion of Kevin Murdoch. You don't need to answer now, but think about it. Of the interactions you've had and what you've observed."

After a delicious mouthful of her drink, Charlotte glanced around. It was still early and only one other patron had a table and that was out of earshot. "I'm happy to profile him for you, from a professional angle. Personally, I've kept a distance from him after seeing how ruthless he was about the Woodland family last year. Holding court out in the plaza to drum up outrage over the thefts of the Christmas trees. I got the impression…"

"I'm interested."

"Well, my impression was how orchestrated the meeting was. Him, Jonas. Some random voices in the crowd. A clever attempt to turn attention away from something else—but I've never worked out what that was. And with Sid Browne in the mix, it clouded who was behind it and what the motives were."

"Go on." Trev held his coffee cup, taking occasional sips, his eyes on her.

"After Octavia died and he came to the bookshop, I thought his hostility was misplaced grief. But looking back, I think he picked a time I was alone and used his size to intimidate me. He isn't as pushy as his brother, and defers to

Terrance a lot, but Kevin Murdoch has something simmering under the surface. In my opinion."

Vinnie arrived with a tray. He was careful to use a serving glove to place a steaming stone bowl in front of Charlotte with a solemn, "it is very hot." Then he served Trev's pancakes. "And much colder is our homemade vanilla ice cream on the side."

"Looks wonderful!" Charlotte took her phone out. "I'll tag you on Instagram."

"Enjoy." Vinnie grinned.

"Don't eat yours yet." Charlotte reached for Trev's plate and turned it slightly. "That's better." She snapped away, uploaded both images, and then glanced up. "What?"

Trev shook his head, a smile in his eyes. "May I eat now?"

"I give you permission. Actually, yours looks so yum." Three fluffy pancakes were piled with fresh berries and flaked chocolate, then drizzled with caramel.

"So do your eggs. What's in there with them?"

"Tomato, capsicum, some olives." Charlotte nudged the bowl with a fork. "chilli slices, herbs. I am so hungry."

Both ate in silence. Every mouthful improved Charlotte's mood and when she finished, she sighed in pleasure. Trev's plate was empty and he drained his coffee cup.

"Better?" he asked.

"Much. I'm going to have to go open the shop soon."

"When will you phone the specialist?"

"Once Rosie arrives." Thinking about this lowered her mood again. "Maggie sent the other information I requested so I'll look at that first. If Mum's reaction is from the mix of medication then adjusting it is the first step."

"And if not?"

She shrugged. "Need to speak to her specialist. With a bit of luck this is something I can help with remotely."

"If not? You'll go to see her?"

With a smile forced from somewhere deep inside, Charlotte picked up her phone and stood. "Long way from
considering that. I'll pay."

chapter
twenty-six

Charlotte spent a few minutes doing deep breathing, laying on the floor of the apartment and getting into a better head space. Rosie was in the bookshop, shooing her out as soon as she heard about the call from Maggie. After reviewing the information about her mother's current list of treatments, Charlotte shook her head. Too many. Some there just for the sake of it. Mum had such a range of conditions it was tricky balancing medications.

Once she'd calmed her nerves and thought through the coming conversation, Charlotte stood and stretched. Then, she wrote a few notes on paper and finally, sipped a glass of water as she focused her mind to communicate to a professional peer, and one who may not appreciate her interference.

As it was, the conversation was short and sharp. Mum's specialist was yet another male psychiatrist and one with no interest in discussing his patient, despite Charlotte having power of attorney for Angelica. She hung up, then uttered a rare swear word.

Instead of throwing the phone at the wall, which was what she'd have liked to do, she dialled Lakeview Care.

Calm down before you speak.

Easier said than done.

The phone was answered and she was connected to Maggie. She'd known Maggie since first looking for a suitable place for Angelica to move into. Lakeview Care dealt with long term patients.

"Hello, Doctor Dean. Were you able to speak with Doctor Hicks?"

"Good morning, Maggie. I just got off the phone."

"Was he able to help?"

"He wasn't interested in speaking with me. What happened to Mum's previous psychiatrist? We've discussed keeping to female doctors on more than one occasion."

Keep your tone pleasant, Charlie.

"We have. But it isn't always possible. People move on and sometimes we don't have the choices we'd prefer for our patients. Angelica seemed to like Doctor Hicks. At first, anyway."

"She'll never settle with a male authority figure. Who else is available? I'm happy to make some calls—"

"With all respect, Doctor Dean, we have access to a small pool of professionals. Most of them have private practices also, which means less time for us. We are not able to pay the high fees they receive from their private clients, which I'm sure you would understand."

Was that a dig? Charlotte opened the sliding door. Out on the balcony, fresh air helped her stay calm.

"I appreciate your position, Maggie, and you know I have the highest regard for you and the staff at Lakeview, which is why Mum is with you. My concern is the mix of medications she's on. There is some conflict which may be why this intense paranoia is happening."

"You may be correct, but unless you'd like to see her yourself, in a professional capacity, I am reluctant to change what her current psychiatrist has prescribed. We've tried doing this long distance in the past and it is less than satisfactory."

"Last time we spoke, she was doing well." Charlotte leaned on the balcony, her eyes on the street below. People wandered from shop to shop. A normal day. "Her clarity was a bit off, but overall, it appeared she was more stable than in the past."

Maggie let out a long, deep sigh. "I wish it were true. I've worked with Angelica for a long time now and only see a downward spiral. Less and less good days. And with the violent episode, we are considering her future suitability as a resident. I'm sorry."

The air left Charlotte's lungs. If they wanted to move her mother, where would she go? What other place would take on someone with her needs, yet provide reasonable freedom. Not to leave or roam alone, but come and go from her room without constant supervision. Or was it too late?

"Doctor Dean?"

"Go on."

"One thing Angelica continues to ask is for you to visit her. It has been close to eighteen months and quite frankly, she's lost hope of seeing you again. At the risk of sounding unkind, I'm not prepared to pass on your excuses to her any more. So often you say you will come in a month but never do and she is still aware enough to know you haven't."

Never had Maggie spoken this way. It cut into Charlotte. The truth was there and if she didn't change something, nobody else would.

"I understand. What is Mum's current status?"

"She's been isolated for her own good and that of the other patients. Dr Hick's will see her on Friday and meet with me afterwards to discuss options. You may not like those options, so if you've ever considered visiting again, this Friday is the most critical time to do so."

There was little more to say. Charlotte slumped against the railing once she'd hung up, her head down and eyes closed. The truth hurt. She'd let Angelica believe she'd visit too many times then always had an excuse. Busy working. Busy moving.

Busy not being available for you, Mum.

Charlotte had spent most of her life looking after Angelica, one way or another. Her move to Rivers End last year was an escape. A new beginning. But she'd left unfinished business behind and it was a matter of time before it caught up with her.

She opened her eyes. The sky was brilliant blue. On the hills behind town, deciduous trees changed colour, creating a masterpiece of hues against a backdrop of dark green. How she loved Kingfisher Falls. This place was her home and gave her strength. And she was going to need strength because that unfinished business was knocking on her door.

chapter
twenty-seven

Detective Katrina Mayer sat in Trev's seat in the station, searching on his computer. Coffee was cold beside her and handwritten notes covered a notepad. Trev watched over her shoulder.

"I can't believe how brave Charlie is." She opened a different search.

"Brave wasn't the first word I thought of." Trev had filled Katrina and Bryce in on the events of the early hours. Bryce had thrown his hands in the air and muttered "typical", but Katrina was quiet on the matter. Until now.

She stopped searching and looked up at Trev. They'd been friends for years after going through academy together. Now with a young family, she'd moved to the mountains from her beloved city of Melbourne to raise her children around nature. He admired that in her. She thought about the long term. "What would you call Charlotte, if not brave? Going out in a thunderstorm, which frightens her. Following somebody simply because she believes they need her help?"

"Reckless. Dangerous. Being brave might have got her killed."

Katrina grinned. "Glad I wasn't around when she told you."

"Hm."

"That good. Anyway, back to the issue at hand before Bryce returns with Mr Murdoch." She pointed at her notes. "He has no form at all. Lived here his whole life. Was a partner with his brother in a conveyancing company for twenty years or so. Dabbled in politics then bought the hotel from Glenys Lane. You don't recall anything else of note?"

"Kept my distance from the Murdoch brothers. Both intolerant of anyone who couldn't further their lives and they were never friendly toward my parents." Trev straightened. "I remember Kevin when I was a kid. He yelled at me for interrupting him."

Katrina raised her eyebrows.

"On my paper round. I'd normally leave their paper with the receptionist. Nice lady. One morning she wasn't there and Kevin was screaming at someone on the phone, back to the door. I walked in and he turned on me."

"Charming. What then?"

"Nothing. Always checked he wasn't around before going in. But I never got a sorry and Terrance is little better. They'll be polite and helpful to your face, so be aware of that."

After minimising the search screen, Katrina swivelled in her seat. "Any theories why he was visiting the grave site last night?"

"Curiosity? He's tied up with Jonas Carmichael through Terrance, and Jonas wanted access the other day. I stopped Jonas and then he had a crack at Charlotte when she overheard him running off his mouth to a reporter."

The front door opened.

"Right. Happy for me to lead?" Katrina pushed herself to her feet.

"Pleased if you would."

Kevin Murdoch scowled as he followed Bryce past the counter. Bryce rolled his eyes but the corners of his lips curled up.

"What the heck is this about, Sibbritt?"

Katrina gestured to a chair. "Please, take a seat Mr Murdoch. I'm Detective Senior Constable Katrina Mayer. We met earlier in the year."

"Right. You were on Octavia's murder case and I thank you for finding her killer." Kevin sat as he spoke, but didn't look any happier.

Bryce did his usual thing. Found a spot on the second desk and leaned against it, arms crossed, eyes settling onto Kevin. Trev followed his gaze. Ankle crossed over one knee, Kevin undid the buttons on his jacket. In his sixties, he wore his white hair in a comb over and sported a speckled, pointy beard.

"Well? I have a busy day and coming here was not on my agenda."

Katrina sat opposite, leaning her elbows on the desk and steepling her fingers. Trev remained standing, hands on the back of a chair.

"Just a few questions and you'll be on your way. Where were you this morning, between the hours of midnight and two?"

His already pale complexion ghosted. A muscle twitched along his jaw. "Why?"

Guilty as charged. Or not charged. You were there alright.

"You were seen out in the storm during those hours."

He scoffed. "Seen? That storm was severe and the chance of anyone being out in it, let alone two people, must be slim to none."

"And yet you were identified."

"What if I was out? I'm allowed to walk around my own town. Not afraid of storms or the dark and as a busy publican I have less time than others to exercise. Often finish up at the pub about midnight and take a walk."

"And where did this most recent walk take you?"

Trev's respect for Katrina grew by the minute. She was so calm but missed nothing. He needed to get some interview tips from her later.

With a glance at his watch, Kevin moved as though to stand. "No time for this."

"Perhaps you would explain why you crossed a police cordoned area and inspected a crime scene. During a heavy downpour. In the middle of the night." Now, steel crept into her voice. Kevin flopped back in his seat.

"Fine. I did find myself at that clearing but had no idea it was where the body was found. Not until I stumbled across what looked like a scene from a horror movie. Dirt piled to one side of what was obviously a grave. I was curious."

Bryce adjusted his stance a little. "Why did you stay there once you worked it out? We've been clear about that being a no-go zone."

Kevin shot him a look. "Stay there? I left the minute I realised. Kept heading to the track."

"Which track?" Katrina again. "Tell me exactly where you entered the forest and where you exited it. Please."

For the first time, the man looked puzzled. "Sure. I had walked from the hotel, turned at the roundabout to the northern entrance. The one where all the police and reporters vehicles entered. Then from the clearing I cut along the narrow trail until reaching the track behind the real estate agents and bookshop and stuff. I followed the track behind all the shops to the next street."

Not possible. The reason Charlotte followed you was because she saw you go in.

"Is there anything else? I'm sorry if I wasn't meant to be

there, but most of the police tape was on the ground so I thought you'd finished up."

"Even so, why go to look?" Katrina asked.

"Why not?"

"Do you know who was buried there?" She leaned forward. "Who might it be, Mr Murdoch?"

He stared at her, his face expressionless. Apart from the same small twitch from earlier.

Trev had questions. Why was he lying about the way in? What did he have to hide? But he stayed silent, observing.

With a shrug, Kevin uncrossed his leg. "How would I know? Isn't that your job?"

"Be helpful if you remember anything. Anyone from the past who might have got themselves in trouble. Left town without notice... at least that's what everyone thought. Didn't your sister-in-law do that?"

"Listen here, honey." Kevin lurched forward. Bryce straightened and Trev moved around the chair, but Katrina didn't flinch. "You want to ask about her? You ask Terrance. But if you are insinuating he hurt his wife, then you don't know what you're doing. He loved her."

"People kill for love. Mr Murdoch." Katrina smiled. "We won't keep you any longer, so Bryce will show you out."

Trev had to turn away. The outrage on Kevin's face was comical and laughing at the man would undo Katrina's good work. He heard him stomp out, with Bryce's cheery, "This way."

A moment later the front door closed and one set of foot-steps returned.

Bryce chuckled as Trev shook his head and took a chair. "Didn't know he could move so fast."

"No doubt there'll be a complaint laid against me." Katrina picked up her coffee and grimaced. "How dare I suggest his brother might be involved in this."

Trev took the cup from Katrina and headed to the kettle. "Bryony Murdoch is worth a look. She left town under odd circumstances so it would be good to make sure she's still alive somewhere."

Nobody spoke as he made three coffees. Katrina was writing notes and Bryce tapped on his phone. Raising Terrance's wife had surprised Trev. He'd mentioned her in passing before Bryce left to collect Kevin. More than ever, he wanted to find out who Charlotte had stumbled across that day.

Katrina's phone beeped and she checked it. Her eyebrows raised. "Got an identification on the remains." She looked up. "Strap yourselves in."

chapter
twenty-eight

Rosie had another reading with Harmony booked not long after Charlotte returned. Between customers and a busy phone, they didn't get more than a couple of words in and as Rosie left, she'd told Charlotte she wanted to know all about her mother when she returned.

Charlotte didn't know what she'd tell her. She'd always kept her past private, or as private as possible. The bookshop quietened and she had no pressing jobs to do, so spent time looking at flights to Brisbane. It was doable, but she needed to leave early on Friday morning in order to see her mother before the meeting with Lakeview Care. And it might be for nothing if Angelica wasn't responsive. Her stomach churned.

There must be a way to do this without imploding. Charlotte dug deep. Angelica was her patient in the past and she'd thrived under her daughter's care. For a while. The complex mix of mental diseases made treatment difficult. Some medications worked for a while, or when combined with another. Or one medication would react with another. One on one therapy and a full day of positive activities was without doubt the best treatment. Or was. If her mother had deteriorated so much, then a review was overdue.

First, get rid of Dr Hicks. Angelica regressed with male doctors, always had. Charlotte got her phone. She had a couple of contacts to reach out to. Doctors she respected and had not met her mother. There was no point calling yet, but it eased her mind seeing their numbers in her phone.

As she considered the options, the churning disappeared. If she thought of Angelica as a patient, she could do this. Fly up and see her.

"I'm back, darling!"

Rosie joined her behind the counter, her face brimming with happiness. From her eyes to her lips, she shone. Charlotte smiled in response. "You stopped by to see Lewis."

"Now, are you the psychic?"

"Nope. Just know you. And I'm going to guess you and Lewis are arranging a trip away together."

"We are! I spoke to him about my concerns. He suggested a place set back from the beach. So, if I find it confronting, we can wander around the town or take a drive to some rather nice mineral springs nearby. We've settled on a place down in the Mornington Peninsula."

"Sounds perfect. And you must collect some brochures to bring back so I can visit sometime. If you don't mind me taking a break now and then?"

Rosie blinked over her glasses. "Mind? Never. And you should, because, we need to discuss you taking over the bookshop. When I get back?"

"Oh." A tingle of delight filled Charlotte. "Yes please."

"Good. Harmony told me there's a long and happy future ahead with Lewis. Well, she said with a widower who adores me and I can't think of anyone else. And it is time for me to let go of the past. She saw me spending my days in the garden and singing in the choir and not working at all. Retirement."

Exactly what we've discussed before she came along.

But Charlotte couldn't bring herself to spoil Rosie's moment. "For once I have to agree with her. Anything else she had to say?"

"Well, yes. And it was odd, darling. She mentioned a dark force."

"Sorry?"

The brightness left Rosie's eyes. "Yes. To be wary of unseen danger. Danger that has been here in Kingfisher Falls for decades and now is rising again."

A shiver scuttled up Charlotte's spine as Rosie continued.

"To be wary of those who once planned the land."

"Planned the land?"

"I know. She went into a kind of trance and her voice was all sing-song, like a little child telling a story."

"Did you ask for clarification?" Charlotte said.

"Didn't get a chance. She opened her eyes, released my hands, and said that was all. Oh, Harmony did ask if you would consider a reading. She feels she got off on the wrong foot and wants to make it up. Said she sees in your aura a conflict within yourself."

The shiver strengthened. This was a guess. But Charlotte was intrigued by the warning about those who planned the land. Did she mean local council? Jonas, perhaps.

"Charlie?"

"I might take her up on it."

The look of surprise on Rosie's face almost make Charlotte burst into laughter. "I know, I am against all of this. But I've seen you come away happy each time you see her. Maybe I'll give her a call, unless she already knows when I'm coming. Being psychic and all that."

"Tease. Her card is near your left hand."

"Time to tidy this counter up then. But okay, I'll make a time with her and see if I can discover what this conflict with myself is."

Conflicts called Angelica. And Trev.

"Good, you're both here." Trev strode inside the shop, trailed by Bryce. Out on the pavement, Katrina was on her phone.

"Hello, dear. And Detective Davis." Rosie smiled at both men, giving Charlotte a much-needed moment to compose herself.

Since when did thinking about Trev summon him? Perhaps she had more in common with Harmony than she first thought. Charlotte's Caravan of Chaos. Or caution. She almost giggled. Give Harmony a run for her money as King-fisher Fall's resident clairvoyant.

Bryce and Rosie were swapping small talk. Trev planted himself on the opposite side of the counter to Charlotte.

"Hi," she said.

"I'd love to know what you were thinking then."

"Oh, it was deep. Nobel Peace Prize deep. Have you heard something?"

He nodded. "And we spoke with Kevin."

She held her breath.

"He admits to being in the clearing. Took a bit of prompting from Katrina, but he reckons he was out for a late walk and was curious. And there's more." He paused as Katrina joined them with a quick hello. Rosie and Bryce were listening now. "Kevin insists he only left down the flower trail. Entered the forest from the other side."

"Rubbish. Seeing a person out in the rain is why I ventured out. And they went in that way as well as out."

"Is it possible," Katrina asked, "it was someone else?"

From her window in the dark, rain bucketing down, lightning revealed a person standing near the entrance to the flower trail.

"I saw a wide brimmed hat. A raincoat. Then they were gone. When I reached the clearing, the person near the grave had a wide brimmed hat and long raincoat." Charlotte stood. "From my window I couldn't identify Kevin Murdoch. The attire was similar enough to make me believe I'd seen him all along... but maybe not. I don't know."

"So, two people skulking around in the dead of night. Spooky." Bryce chipped in and everyone laughed.

"But why?" Charlotte couldn't get her head around it. "Unless Jonas was the first one. But then, where did he go? I followed within a minute or two so why didn't he and Kevin run into one another?"

Katrina and Trev traded glances. Whatever that was about, they weren't sharing.

"And what about the poor soul Charlie found?" Rosie asked.

Charlotte knew before the words formed on Trev's lips. She knew it was the same person who'd collected a teddy bear and baby clothes and a wedding dress. Fingers gripped together, she waited.

"Vi Ackerman. Confirmed by dental records. I'm so sorry." Trev gazed at Rosie.

"Quite a shock! Her family was convinced she'd upped and run away with her boyfriend, whoever he was." Tears glistened in Rosie's eyes and Charlotte reached for her hand.

Nobody spoke for a moment. The phone rang and everyone jumped. Rosie grabbed it and wheeled away to talk.

"What now?" Charlotte looked from Trev to Katrina to Bryce. "Will you find her family? Or start looking for her killer."

"Both." Katrina headed for the door as her own phone beeped. "Sorry. I'll see you later, Charlotte."

Bryce leaned on the counter. "Would you object to us looking around the storage room where you found the trunk? It might help us."

"Goodness, no. Go ahead. And it is Rosie you need to ask,

but in this case, I'll answer because she would say yes. And the trunk is upstairs if you want it. Well, you will want it, so should I get my keys?"

Trev came around the counter and put his hands on her shoulders. "Calm down. You were spot on picking who the remains belonged to. I know this is personal, but take a few breaths and settle."

"I am quite settled, thank you, Trevor."

Bryce sniggered and Trev shot him a sour glance.

The warmth of Trev's hands helped. She might say she was fine but inside, turmoil twisted her emotions. That poor girl. So young to have her life taken. Ready for her future.

"Oh. Trev, was she… pregnant?"

His mouth opened and closed again as Bryce interrupted. "Look, we've told you the identification of the remains out of courtesy based on you finding her, and the history of this building once belonging to her family. As yet, we've not located her next of kin so cannot reveal any more about the investigation. And your discretion in this is appreciated. In other words do not tell another person anything. Please."

Charlotte's eyes moved from his to Trev's. He dropped his hands and looked away and her heart sank. There was a lot more to this.

Rosie returned, off the phone again. "What did I miss?"

"We can't mention we know the identity of the remains, Rosie. Nobody else knows yet. Not her next of kin." Charlotte said, forcing her voice to sound normal.

"Of course. Do you know how to find her family?"

"Hoped you might have an idea, Mum."

"I actually found the file your father kept from the purchase of the shop. Although I didn't look all the way through, there were letters from the solicitors and conveyancers who handled the sale so perhaps that might be a starting point?"

Trev nodded. "Worth a look. Would you mind if I go and get the file?"

"Of course. It is on top of the filing cabinet. Remember to tell the cats you are there first."

He grinned. "You know they both love me. But I will. And may I take photos of details to assist the investigation? Without yours and Dad's info on, of course."

Katrina tapped on the window at Bryce. He headed for the door. "Give me a call, Trev once you have that info. Ladies." And he was gone.

Silence fell. Rosie cleaned her glasses. Charlotte took her seat again. Trev wandered to the front of the counter. The detectives' car drove away, breaking the quiet.

"I might head up to the house now. Are you both okay?"

"Well, it is kind of strange." Rosie replaced her glasses and looked at Trev over their top. "To think of that poor young woman murdered, with her family believing her off on her own adventures. She *was* murdered?"

"There's still some information to come through but it looks that way. More to keep to yourselves. We will speak to her family and then the community, as needed. Being so long ago, evidence is going to challenge us." Trev's shoulders dropped. "Anyway, I'm off for now. Are you okay to hang onto the trunk until Katrina and Bryce can get back?"

"Sure." If only she could go through the trunk first. See if there were clues to consider.

"Charlotte."

Her eyes lifted to Trev's. He was laughing at her with those kind eyes of his. He knew what she was thinking and her lips curled up in response. "I'll keep it closed. Promise."

chapter
twenty-nine

"Why make a promise I don't want to keep?" Charlotte muttered as she circled the trunk which was still on her coffee table. She'd refrained from touching it, but the urge to open the books and magazines was hard to ignore.

Opening it would be breaking a trust. And Trev meant too much to risk it, let alone what Bryce would have to say about her interfering with yet another police investigation. Instead, she went to the back bedroom.

Rosie had insisted Charlotte have an earlier day after her long night and now she was at a loose end. From the window, all was quiet in and around the bushland. Dusk was some time away and she could get a sample of the flowers for Rosie without much effort. Taking action was a good idea. She turned to leave the bedroom and the Christmas cards on top of the box from Lakeview Care caught her attention.

"Who are you, Z?" She touched the top one. A sense of sadness crept into her heart. Of loss, but from what? Or where. If she saw Angelica she could ask again. Perhaps take the cards. Yes, take the cards and the photo album and ask her mother what she knew about them.

She'd phone Rosie and ask for Friday and Saturday off.

Then, assuming that was okay, she'd book the flights up and down to Brisbane. And a hire car. Accommodation.

Her breath caught in her throat. The air refused to go further than her neck, it seemed. Her legs tensed, readying to take her away from this madness. Charlotte reached for the stress bracelet no longer on her wrist. She had to run.

Slow... down.

Had Vi Ackerman lived in this bedroom? Would she have gazed through the window for a sign from her forbidden boyfriend to sneak downstairs and meet him in the forest? Had she gone with him one time and never returned?

Charlotte's chest tightened. She burst out of the bedroom, hand outstretched for her phone and keys as she passed the counter.

Somehow, she was at the bottom of the stairs. A hesitation. Gate? No, she rushed along the driveway and turned left, her feet having a mind of their own. The pavement became grass and then the turnoff to the lookout. She followed. Much as she had last year when overwhelmed, sprinting along an unknown path in the dead of night.

These days her feet knew each dip and hollow, every tree root to miss, and each curve of the narrowing track. The lookout was to one side, the place she'd almost died a few months ago on a rainy day.

Still she continued, her pace forced slower by potholes and difficult terrain. The waterfall ducked in and out of view beyond the canopy of trees. Another day she might head for the tower of steps to the top, but at this moment she yearned for the pool at its base. She stumbled to a walk as she reached the final part of the descent.

Her heart raced from adrenalin and panic. But birdsong filtered through the pounding in her ears and bit by bit, the anxiety lessened. On the grass she threw off her shoes and hurried to the edge of the pond. There, she stopped.

Charlotte's toes curled into the soft grass. Water lapped so close she could stretch her foot out and touch it if she wanted. The waterfall cascaded to the far end of the pool, sending ripples her way. Once they neared the shore, they smoothed. She watched them over and over until her pulse was steady and her breathing went all the way to the bottom of the lungs again.

Better. Much better. If she kept her thoughts under control, her body would follow. Charlotte lay on the grass, on her back, making each muscle relax until her spine was flat on the ground. So nice. Above, wispy clouds took their time floating across the darkening blue backdrop.

Her phone buzzed. Reluctant to undo the good work, she felt for it in a pocket and raised it to her eyes with minimal movement. Two missed calls and three messages. Rosie and Trev. Whoops.

Come for dinner, darling? Have one of your favourites ready to cook. R.

She managed a smile.

Have some news. May I drop around?

Trev must have sent that from outside the bookshop as two minutes later was the second message.

Call me, please. Your back door is unlocked.

Charlotte sat up. Ten minutes ago. And the missed phone calls were both his and were in the last few minutes. She dialled. He would be so worried.

Trev's familiar ringtone sounded from near the lookout. The call was rejected and within a minute or two he appeared at a run down the steps, eyes seeking her. She scrambled up. "I'm okay."

Before she could say another word, she was buried in his arms. His heart pounded and his warmth surrounded her. Just as she settled against him, he stepped back, his hands moving to her shoulders to inspect her.

"I'm okay, Trev." She repeated.

"You didn't pick up. And your back door is unlocked. Was unlocked. I locked it. After looking for you."

"Sorry. I was running and didn't hear the phone. I saw the messages a minute ago which is why I was calling—"

His mouth stopped her speaking. His mouth, on hers, as he bundled her back into his embrace and drew her close to kiss her.

As quickly as it began, it finished. "Um… sorry. Should have asked." He stood back again.

Charlotte blinked. Her lips tingled. "I… I didn't mind."

With a squeeze of her shoulders, he released her. "What happened?"

She shrugged and returned to the edge of the pool. He joined her, his arm brushing against hers.

"I have to go to Brisbane."

He was silent and when she looked at him, his eyes were on her, serious and questioning.

"My mother is struggling and Lakeview Care are reviewing her suitability to remain there. They have her with a male doctor again and he is not interested in speaking to me about her."

"When are you going?"

"Friday. But I need to check with Rosie first. I must be there to see Mum before the meeting about her future. To evaluate her. And then I'll be back Sunday. I guess."

Trev put his arms around Charlotte's shoulders. "No wonder you needed a run. A chance to clear your head and I interrupted."

She leaned her head against him. "Can't believe I left the door unlocked. My mind wasn't functioning properly."

"Would you like me to head back? Leave you to reflect on your own?"

"No. I'll come with you. The peacefulness here cleared my

mind. See, there's the kingfisher." Charlotte lowered her voice as though she might scare the tiny bird. She'd seen him a few times now and he appeared as curious about her as she was of him. There was a branch he frequented, and for a moment or two he preened his feathers as they watched, before skimming across the pool so fast he was a blur.

"Never tire of seeing them. Pity they are so few and far between in the region." Trev stretched. "Not a good idea running down from the lookout. Council needs to fix all the holes."

"You've just noticed?" She grinned. "And what about the dangerous missing steps up to the top of the waterfall?"

"Shall we check them?"

"No. I'm happy to leave such exertion for another day." Charlotte started off. "You said you have news for me."

"I do. But it's for Mum also. Come and have dinner."

"Oh, she did ask. I'll text her. Yes of course."

"All good, I told her you'd be there."

Charlotte stopped dead and Trev almost ran into her. He put his hands on her waist. "Warn me if you intend to do that. Anyway, you love her macaroni cheese bake." His breath tickled her neck and she leaned back. "Or you could say no."

"Clearly you are overtired, Trevor. If you think I would insult Rosie by refusing her offer you must not know me very well. So, when we get there, you should take a nap and leave more for me."

"A nap? Tempting. But getting to know you sounds much more enticing. Hey, where are you going?"

With a laugh, Charlotte took off up the path.

chapter
thirty

The moment Charlotte stepped through Rosie's front door, the undeniable aroma of macaroni cheese pasta bake filled her senses. Hunger rose with the tangy smell of mustard and garlic.

She'd gone home for a shower and to change. Trev offered to wait and walk up with her but she told him he needed to make himself presentable for dinner with his mother. He'd laughed, and left her at the end of the driveway with a kiss on the tip of her nose. Her return to the apartment was one in a much happier frame of mind than only an hour or so earlier.

Even the sight of Sid going into the supermarket wasn't enough to do more than irritate her for a moment.

The walk to Rosie's house gave her time to wonder about Trev's news. Had there been a development around the Ackerman family? Or had the killer walked into the station to confess? One could only hope. Whatever it was, she'd be okay. This afternoon she'd learned a bit about herself. She had support and for the first time in her life, she was accepting it. A smile lifted her lips. This was more than a friendship.

"You had me worried, child." Rosie appeared around the doorway from the kitchen as Charlotte followed Mellow from the front door. "Not like you to not respond to a message."

Charlotte dropped a kiss on Rosie's cheek. "I am sorry. Worrying you was the last thing on my mind. I had to get some air and didn't hear the phone at all. Trev could tell you. I missed his messages and calls as well."

Rosie raised both eyebrows. "Messages and calls? Has my son turned into a creepy stalker?"

"Oi. I heard that."

"He's setting the table outside. Meant to be, anyway." Rosie spun the wheelchair and returned to the kitchen, Charlotte following. "Can you toss the salad?"

"At Trevor?"

Rosie shot a horrified look at Charlotte, then burst into laughter.

"What on earth is going on in here?" Trev joined them. "Two seconds alone and chaos ensues."

"We were talking about the effect of gravity on lettuce." Charlotte struggled to keep herself from giggling. "And tomatoes."

"I was about to see what you'd both like to drink, but I will make it water for you."

"Thanks, dear. Gin and tonic." Rosie checked the oven. "Twenty minutes."

"In that case, shall we have a quick talk?" Trev headed for the bar. "I'll do this first."

"Are we going to need a drink?" Charlotte followed him.

In a couple of minutes, everyone was seated in the living room. Mellow predictably climbed onto Rosie's lap and to Charlotte's surprise, Mayhem settled on the back of Trev's armchair. This was not a cat who liked people, as a rule.

"Trevor has had a busy afternoon, Charlie," Rosie said. "Including a return trip to Torquay."

"Isn't that where Concetta Bongiovanni lives?"

"I'm impressed with the pronunciation and your memory. Yes, she does live there, or close by." Trev sipped his drink, holding the glass between his hands. "I couldn't take the dress to show her, but thanks to your photographs, she was able to identify it."

Charlotte sat up straight. "She was?"

He nodded. "Knew the dress. Told me the name of the person who made it—apparently, she had a network of seamstresses who supplied her with handmade wedding gowns. Also, the year she purchased it." Mayhem tapped his shoulder with a paw, and Trev reached back to offer his finger to the cat, who then bit it. Not hard, but enough to make everyone laugh.

"He never changes. But he likes you more than most." Rosie grinned.

"Lucky me. Where was I? Oh, couple of things. She still keeps those chocolates and gave me one. Worth the trip down. And that dress? It was stolen."

There was a collective gasp from Charlotte and Rosie as Trev sipped his drink.

"How? Did she know at the time?" Charlotte frowned. "And was it around the time Vi disappeared?"

"Yes and yes. Never discovered the thief, but she came to work one morning to an open back door. She thought somebody hid in the store when it closed and then stole the dress. There was also a pair of shoes and some other items, which I have note of."

"How curious. Dear, how old was Vi back then?" Rosie asked.

"Seventeen. We've located her parents who are living in South Australia. There are police heading to them as we speak to break the news. Once we can release her name, my work really begins. Door knocking and old records."

"I can help." Charlotte offered. "Good with records."

The dinging of the alarm on the oven stopped Trev from answering as he shot to his feet. "I'll get it."

Over dinner, Rosie told Trev about her plans with Lewis. "He's so sweet to cater to my concerns. And with Harmony's belief that he is the one, then how could I refuse again?"

Charlotte stabbed a piece of macaroni. Not that it looked like Harmony, but it happened to be in the right place. Trev nudged her foot with his and she slid the morsel into her mouth. It was delicious and helped her mood a little.

"So, you and Lewis will stay near the hot springs? I've heard they are special." Trev asked. "How long will you go for?"

"Just the weekend. Being a long weekend gives me a little more time but not until Saturday. Which brings me to ask you, Charlie if you mind being on your own this Saturday?"

"Oh, this weekend?" Charlotte exchanged a glance with Trev as worry rushed through her. His foot pressed against hers in support.

Rosie looked between them both. "What? Are you planning a getaway? In which case then I shall delay mine—"

"Mum!"

"Rosie!"

"No?" She smiled as if pleased with herself. "Nothing is carved in stone, no bookings made, so tell me what's making you look so serious, Charlotte."

In a few sentences, Charlotte explained about her mother and the specific timeframe involved. "I was hoping to fly up on Friday. And be back Sunday, but I can fly back Friday night if that helps?"

"You've never asked for anything, darling. I'll tell you what we'll do. This long weekend is always quiet in the shop.

Without fail, because it is the last chance for people to go away before the cold sets in. So, you go on Friday and then the bookshop can have its own long weekend. I'll close early on Friday and we'll both be back to open for Tuesday."

"Really?" What a wonderful woman Rosie was. "You are so generous."

"No. I'm greedy. If I was still running the shop on my own it is what I would do. But I just thought of one problem." She gazed at Trev. "The cats."

"Not a problem. I might be out and about but have no plans to leave the town for any length of time. I'll drop in during the day and be here at night. Mayhem will have to deal with it."

chapter
thirty-one

For the rest of the evening, Trev struggled to take his eyes off Charlotte. Discovering her door unlocked earlier had sent a cold shock through him. With no response to his text nor a phone call, he'd let himself in. At least the apartment had appeared normal and a cursory glance noted her keys and phone weren't where she often left them. He'd tracked her on the app she'd sent her location on the day she'd found the grave.

She'd phoned as he'd arrived at the lookout. In the couple of minutes it took him to descend to the pool, he'd considered several opening lines, from telling her off for leaving her door unlocked to acting as though nothing happened.

Instead, he'd kissed her. And she'd been fine with it. And now he wanted to kiss her again. Today, something changed between them. Something good was happening.

"Your phone is ringing, dear."

Trev felt for his phone then remembered leaving it near the sink when he'd helped wash up. He got to it in time to answer to Katrina, who sounded exhausted. They spoke for a few minutes as she ran through her news. A child laughed in the background.

"Sh. Mummy's on the phone. Sorry, Trev."

"That is so cute."

"Cute? If only you could see the devastation two small humans create when Mummy takes five minutes for a shower."

"It suits you. The mother thing, not the devastation thing."

"Thanks. You should try it."

"Gotta go now. See you in the morning." Trev hung up. He'd love to try it. Have a family with Charlotte. But there was a giant bridge with a lot of water to cross before that was considered by either of them. Sorting out Angelica was one big step.

"Off the phone, dear? I poured us a nightcap."

"Sorry about the interruption. Thanks." The glass was cool in his fingers as he sank back onto his armchair. Mayhem was on the arm now and growled at him. "Enough of this silliness, cat." He spoke softly. "You love me and you know it."

Charlotte sat opposite, her legs tucked under herself. She was so at home here. It made his heart happy seeing the two women he loved such close friends. Who knew last year when he'd driven up here to Kingfisher Falls with Charlie that this would be the outcome?

"Everything okay?" Charlotte spoke, her eyes missing nothing. He was used to her intensity, her ability to absorb information from a person's tone of voice, body language, or what they didn't say.

"Katrina wanted to update me. The Ackerman's—the parents that is—were informed of Vi's discovery. Will see the full report tomorrow, but the lead officer mentioned both her parents were shocked. His opinion is they truly believed she'd run off with her boyfriend. Her father blames himself for not searching for her."

"How sad." Rosie took off her glasses and folded them in her hands. "To not know your child is deceased. Believe they might one day return."

"Their older child, a son—and I didn't get his name—lives with them. He said nothing during the police visit. Oh, apart from something about it serving her right."

"How awful." Charlotte's face reddened. "His own sister! Why do people think that way?"

Rosie and Trev both looked at her with a long silence.

"Fine. I might be a psychiatrist but I don't understand it. Not really. If you love someone it remains in you. No matter what might happen. Unless he didn't love Vi. But who doesn't love their own sibling?" Her expression changed. Went inwards as if something called her.

"What about her little sister? Any sign of her?" Rosie tickled Mellow's stomach as the cat rolled on her back on her lap. "She was quite a few years younger."

"Not mentioned but will be another thing on my list for morning."

Charlotte looked up. "I need to get going. Thanks, Rosie for another lovely dinner."

"Always a pleasure, darling. Trevor will escort you home."

"No need."

On his feet, Trev checked for his house keys. "Not debating. Too many strange people wandering around late at night in Kingfisher Falls."

"Is he calling me strange?" Charlotte whispered as she kissed Rosie goodnight. "I thought you raised him better than that."

"Go on with you both. Bicker all you want, it's a sign of a healthy relationship."

Trev shook his head and lead the way to the front door. "Back soon, Mum."

"Take your time!"

Charlotte said nothing until they reached the footpath, then she giggled. Music to his ears. "We have permission to bicker, Trevor."

"We do. What would you care to bicker about?"

To his surprise, she slid her hand into his. "Not a thing."

They walked all the way to the bookshop hand in hand. It was after ten and the town was quiet. Mist-shrouded street lamps cast eerie shadows and the air had a chill. But Charlie's hand was warm and Trev wouldn't have cared if they walked through a snow storm.

They turned into the driveway of the bookshop and Charlotte stopped in her tracks.

"Charlie?"

"The automatic light is on." She pointed to the bottom of the stairs. "It activates when I'm halfway along here, not this close to the road."

The hair on Trev's arms rose and he released Charlotte's hand to step in front of her. "Go back to the footpath."

"Um, probably safer with you."

She was.

"Okay. Are you certain about the light?"

Her reply was just a bit tense. "It is activated by motion, Trevor. From here it can't see us move, so yes, I am certain."

"Then where."

"Another four steps. Three of yours."

"How long until the light goes… off." They were plunged into darkness. "Let's light things up again."

She was right. About three of his steps and the light turned on. He took her hand and they reached the bottom of the stairs. These were empty and nobody was at the door. "Stay put for a second, please."

His keyring had a brilliant narrow beamed flashlight

attached and he flicked it on. The garage looked untouched. And the small garden. He rattled the gate which was locked.

"Somebody was here."

Trev jumped at her voice so close. "I told you to stay at the stairs, Charlotte!"

"But—"

"But go back now."

"Fine. But somebody climbed the fence." Charlotte retreated to the stairs.

How do you know?

His flashlight landed on a broken vine. Tendrils clinging to the palings, a long branch was snapped. Beneath in the softer earth of the garden bed was a footprint. A bare foot-print indented at a deep angle toward the toes. He found a spot away from the vine and used the lower crossbeam of the fence to raise him until he could see onto the track.

"They've gone, Trev." Her voice was uncertain. He dropped back down and joined her at the bottom of the steps.

"Agree. Let's get upstairs and check the door."

She nodded and let him go first. The light above the steps was on and there was no sign of any damage. The door was locked.

"Whoever it was had bare feet. There's an imprint in your garden bed."

"We need photos."

"Yes. But I will take care of it. There's no rain forecast tonight but I'll cover the area and get a cast done tomorrow. Would you unlock the door? I want to be certain you're alone in there."

Her lips were straightened and jaw clenched as she turned the key and gestured for him to go first. He wanted to point out this was for her safety but she knew it already. The apartment had no signs of intrusions. Trev opened the window in the third bedroom. Charlotte was in the doorway.

"I'll be here for a short while, downstairs. Feel free to watch from up here, but do me a favour and stay put."

"Can you hold the flashlight and take good quality photos at the same time?" She tilted her head. "Nothing will happen to me when I'm with you."

Her faith poured warmth into his heart and he covered the distance between them, hands outstretched. She took his hands and gazed at him, worry in her eyes.

"Firstly, stop stressing because I can see it. Whoever was in the garden is well and truly gone. And I'm certain it wasn't Kevin or Jonas. Footprint looks too small and narrow. Secondly, I appreciate your offer to help and know your photos are the best, but I'm saying no."

"But, Trev, I—"

"Let me do my job." He squeezed her hands and after a moment, she returned the pressure. "Do you have a large box or something I can cover the footprint with overnight?"

Without hesitating, Charlotte went to the bed and upturned the box, spilling its contents in a pile. "This."

"Thanks. Lock me out and I'll let you know when I'm going."

At the door, he gave her an all-too-quick hug before waiting for the lock to turn. Then, he ran down the stairs.

———

"You should let me help." Charlotte grumbled at the locked door. Trev's footsteps faded and she sighed. He was doing his job and she needed to let him, without making him feel he might hurt her feelings. But she was a better photographer.

She wandered back to the window to watch him take

photos with a flash of the garden bed and the fence. The broken branch upset her. Those vines worked hard to stay alive over years of neglect and deserved better than being snapped because someone used them to climb with. Who on earth was it?

Was the person barefoot to start with? Or did they have shoes unsuitable for climbing so removed them when they knew they were trapped. High heels came to mind, but Veronica—the only person she knew who wore them day and night—was long gone from Kingfisher Falls and awaiting a trial for a range of charges around Octavia's death and more. Unless she was back.

"Do you think it was Veronica?" Charlotte called to Trev.

He straightened. "Doubt it. Can you imagine her clambering over a fence this high in one of those narrow skirts of hers?"

Nope. "Probably not." Tight miniskirts and high fences were not a good combination.

Trev covered the footprint with the upturned box and weighed it down with a rock from the end of the garden. "I'll be back early to deal with this." He moved below the window. "If you hear anything, phone me. Or would you prefer to come back to Mum's for the night?"

"I'm fine here. Thanks though."

"Charlie, whoever we surprised was probably some youngster wandering where they shouldn't. Perhaps curious about looking over the fence at the crime tape or something."

"Oh, I bet it was the reporter. The one who interviewed Jonas. She tried to come through the gate."

"Probably not. But when did she do that?"

"Just before she interviewed him. I'd closed the bookshop and heard the gate being rattled. She even commented it was locked."

Trev made a note in his phone. "Might pay to fingerprint

the latch on both sides. And I'll track down her name and employer in case I feel like having a chat." He put the phone away and smiled up at Charlotte. "I'm going now. So, give the speculating a miss for a while and try to sleep."

"Will you message me once you're home?"

"I will. Then you'll sleep?"

"Yes. Goodnight."

"Goodnight, Charlie." He waved and disappeared into the night. A moment or so later the light outside flicked off.

"Oh, you *are* tired!" Charlotte tapped on her phone to open the app for the security cameras around the building. She leaned on the window as she played back until finding what she wanted, then dialled Trev.

"Not home yet."

"I forgot about the cameras."

"Cameras… oh, shall I double back?"

She smiled. "Nope. Had a look and I think you were right. Couple of teens, by the look of them. Had a bottle of something and were taking swigs from it sitting on the steps. Took off just before we got there and she had heels on. He helped her over the fence and almost fell over it himself."

"Okay. I'll grab the footage tomorrow and still take a cast of the print. I'm going up the path to Mum's house, so goodnight again."

She closed the window and locked it. Her reflection stared at her. She looked as tired as she felt but needed to book her flights before anything else.

On the bed, the contents of the box were a big mess. Apart from the bundles of letters, Christmas cards and photo album, there was a variety of items she'd not yet uncovered. A baby book with her name on the front in her mother's scrawl. She hadn't known it existed. A handful of paperbacks covered in plain paper. How odd. And an address book.

Charlotte couldn't bear to touch any of them. Not yet.

First see Angelica and sort her future care out. Then? She touched the cover of the baby book. So tempting. But it was as likely to be empty. With a shake of her head, she left the bedroom, turning off the light and closing the door with a sharp click.

chapter
thirty-two

"Flight is early, just after six in the morning so I'll have plenty of time to get the hire car and drive to Lakeview Care." Charlotte unlocked the gate as Trev packed up the equipment he'd used to create a cast of the footprint from a rapid-set compound. "I'll leave at half past four to get to the airport in time."

"Happy to drive you." He wished she would let him.

"Again, thanks but I'm better getting myself there so I can focus on the day ahead. Are you leaving that to dry?"

"Yeah. Let's take a quick look at your theory." He grinned as he followed Charlotte through the gate. She'd cut part of the vine back with a few choice words under her breath. The remains were piled on the grass until she worked out what to do with them. Something about starting a compost heap.

When he'd arrived just after dawn, he'd hoped not to disturb Charlotte, but it was only a few minutes before she'd brought him a coffee, and stayed there as he'd worked. There was a deep tiredness about her but her eyes were bright and excited about something she'd remembered from the other night.

"The footprint reminded me. Not at once, but later, after I'd booked the flights. It was what Kevin said."

They followed the main track to the entrance of the flower trail. There, they stopped.

"Okay, run through it with me." Trev peered into the gloom. This was a dark place despite the early sun making some inroads through the canopy.

"Kevin told you he approached the clearing from over there." Charlotte pointed in the general direction of the other vehicle entrance, out of sight from here. "He'd cut across the back of the bushland to reach it. I wonder how many people know there's a path there?"

"Lots of people use this area to walk."

"Nope. Not really. I'd say a dozen, tops, and they tend to be the same walkers, usually with dogs and because of that, they avoid going into the heavy growth. Snakes, perhaps? Anyway, not lots."

He managed to hide his smile. Listening to her reasoning always taught him something. Sometimes about her, often about himself and how to do his own job better.

"I saw somebody here. Well," she moved a few steps, "here. I think."

"And it was raining at the time?"

"Bucketing down. From here, the view is clear." She turned to face the bookshop. Her apartment was easy to see and the window overlooked this area. "Whoever this person was, Kevin or someone else, they stood in this spot or very close."

"You mentioned footprints. Do you think there may be evidence to prove it was him all along?" Trev peered at the ground. It was churned up by the volume of foot traffic over the past few days. There were footprints, but they mingled with other ones.

"Not so much here, but along the trail. I walked in and

ran out. Kevin claims he walked out. And we know one person walked in. It was muddy and slippery underfoot. I had to clean my shoes under a hose the next day."

"We'll take a look. It rained so much that night there may be nothing though."

He led the way, his flashlight out to scan the ground ahead in the dimmer light. As he'd feared, much of the path was a mess of dried mud.

"I stopped at the tree over there." Charlotte slipped past him and stepped into the undergrowth with great care to avoid any fresh ground. "The rain was so heavy and I'd not grabbed a hat, so my hair was drenched and getting in my eyes. I leaned against the trunk for a moment to wring my hair out and get a break from the deluge."

Trev joined her. "Almost clear view of the grave site. Only one tree fern and it still lets you see the mound of dirt."

The police tape was broken in a couple of spots and he made a mental note to lay out a new perimeter. Crime Scene Services were returning for a last sweep today and didn't need anyone else thinking they could use the broken tape as an excuse to nose around.

"Where was he? Kevin?"

"Right beside the grave. He had his hand in it."

"Did he now? I'll mention that to the detectives. Get Crime Scene Services to take a close look when they arrive. Which is in a couple of hours and I need to get some fresh tape out before they do. Anything else before we go back?"

Charlotte stared off to the far side of the grave. "Where did the person I saw go, Trev? If Kevin was telling the truth, why didn't he see them? Most of the bush on either side of the flower trail is dense. Really thick and not the best place to walk during a storm."

"Do you think they saw him and hid?"

Her eyes, when she turned to him, were startled. "Perhaps

I did see someone who was grieving who came to see the grave because they knew who was buried here. And when they saw Kevin, they hid, like I did, until he left."

"You assume this person, the one you followed, is an innocent party."

She nodded.

"If they knew Vi was here, why not tell someone? Even an anonymous tip? It doesn't make sense, Charlie."

"But Henry kept secrets for years, based on fear."

"Henry wasn't here the other night. I've checked and he has a solid alibi."

"Then someone else. Perhaps Vi's boyfriend?"

Trev checked his watch. "Got to get going. One of my jobs today is to find out who this mystery boyfriend was. It might shed some light on this whole case."

"Good! I mean, it will be good to narrow things down." She smiled and picked her way back to the trail. "I need to collect a sample of these flowers if that's okay? I'll do it near the entrance."

"Why?" He caught up with her.

"Identification purposes. Isn't it odd these flowers are only along this path and were on the grave? There has to be a reason."

Yes, there was. He'd let Charlotte do her side-investigation and see if she came up with anything useful. At least she'd stay out of trouble doing that.

———

Charlotte put a small vase at the far end of the counter and tidied the arrangement. Close up, the flowers were simple beauties. If nothing else, she would continue to pick them from the forest for as long as they bloomed and might try transplanting some into a pot for the balcony.

To set off the display she located a variety of gardening books and placed three on top of each other behind the vase. The fourth, a specialist book on flowers and trees from the region, she stood upright, slightly open to prop it with a gorgeous pine tree image facing the door. Then she stood in the doorway and looked at the counter. Eye catching.

The customers agreed. Rosie was starting late after breakfast with Lewis, and by the time she arrived, Charlotte had sold and replaced two of the books already. She needed to think more outside the box with these displays and rotate books more. The counter was a space they'd not experimented with, at least not since she'd worked there. As long as there was room for the customers, it was worth playing around with it. Back at the counter she adjusted a book.

"Ah! Those are a variety of asters, darling." Rosie's eyes were on the flowers. "And there is no way they simply self-sowed. Not if they are lining the path."

"Are they common?"

"Asters grow here in this climate, but aren't found wild. Such a lovely colour, the deep purple. And I love what you've done with the books, clever girl. Coffee?"

Rosie made her way to the other side of the counter and took takeaway coffees from the arm of her wheelchair. "I had the loveliest late breakfast with Lewis. And I think he's enjoying working a few less hours a week. He's talking about selling the business in the future and retiring and I think that sounds perfect."

"Coffee smells wonderful. Thank you." Charlotte was happy to sit for a bit and sip the steaming coffee. "The forensic team are back in the clearing."

"They are? Why?"

"Trev said a final sweep. Guess they want to be certain nothing was overlooked. And now they will look at the grave again seeing as Kevin Murdoch had his hands in it."

"Oh my goodness, is there no end to the appalling behaviour of those men?"

"On a different note, I have flights, hire car and accommodation booked. And I need to thank you again for closing on Saturday."

With a smile, Rosie patted Charlotte's arm. "Will you be okay going on your own? I know it's been a while since you've been home."

No, I'm not, and yes, it has.

"Mum's future depends on this meeting. If resolution can't be reached, I'll need to find another place and it won't be easy. Beds are hard to come by in any form of care, let alone the type she requires."

"I'm only a call away if you need to talk."

"That means a lot. But, you, young lady, are going to be busy. How exciting is your short break?"

The doorbell rang and Harmony appeared carrying Rosie's sunglasses. "You will need these on your holiday."

"Silly me leaving them behind!" Rosie took them from Harmony. "Thanks for bringing them. We were just talking about my weekend away."

Harmony's gaze moved to the end of the counter and her face paled. Her eyes widened and mouth dropped open and then in a blur of red hair and purple skirt, she spun around and ran from the bookshop.

chapter
thirty-three

Rosie's face was as shocked as Charlotte imagined hers was. For a second, their eyes met, then Charlotte was on her feet and chasing after Harmony.

The other woman was at a standstill on the corner of the street, hand over her mouth as her head darted from one side to the other. Charlotte caught up as Harmony took a step forward.

"Harmony, wait."

With a shake of her head, Harmony crossed the road and Charlotte followed.

"What's distressed you?"

"Not distressed."

"You ran out without a word." Charlotte walked beside her. "Did we do something to upset you?"

There was no response. Nothing. Just face forward and fast walking.

"You looked at the end of the counter where I have the display. Was it one of the books?"

Harmony stopped and wrapped her arms around herself. She nodded.

"But they are just gardening books. And the top one is about local plants and trees."

"The picture. The cypress. They're not good trees."

What on earth?

"I don't understand." Charlotte kept her body language open to encourage Harmony to talk to her, arms at her side and head tilted a little.

"You won't understand. Or will scoff at me." Harmony lifted her chin up to stare at Charlotte. She had a pretty face behind the elaborate makeup. Bright, intelligent eyes. "People with education laugh at my powers. My calling. And beliefs."

"I may not believe the same things you do, but I never laugh at people or look down at them. Education has nothing to do with it, Harmony. There are good and bad people from all walks of life."

Something changed in Harmony's expression. Her eyes softened although doubt remained. "Nevertheless, if I tell you a cypress has a negative symbolism for me, are you going to believe it?"

Charlotte couldn't help grinning. "Considering I talk to a baby Christmas tree all the time, who am I to judge anyone's views?"

The corner of Harmony's mouth flickered up. "You do?"

"I do. And have a long running debate with a certain young man about the possibility the tree is part alien. If the book upsets you, I'll replace it."

"No need, but you are kind, Charlotte. It just… took me by surprise."

"While we're doing surprises, Rosie has talked me into having a more open mind and considering booking a time with you. If you still want me to visit. Every time she returns from seeing you, her spirit is lifted, so what can I lose?"

When Harmony looked away, Charlotte thought she was about to refuse. Perhaps she'd been too obvious about her scepticism and made herself unwelcome. And fair enough. In her practice she'd had one or two patients so critical of psychiatry she'd eventually moved them on to see different mental health professionals.

"I am again surprised, but in a pleasant way. Would you care to see me tomorrow?"

"Perhaps next week? With the long weekend I'm taking a few days off. Would Wednesday suit?"

"I'll make a time and call you."

Almost as if nothing untoward happened over the past few minutes, Harmony nodded and resumed walking. Before taking more than a few steps, and before Charlotte had turned, Harmony stopped again. She glanced over her shoulder, her face expressionless. "Charlotte? You won't find her. Not yet."

"Sorry? Find who?"

"Your sister."

"I don't have a sister."

Without another word, Harmony walked away.

Charlotte couldn't move. Her legs were frozen in place as an icicle formed between her shoulder blades. There was no sister. She was an only child, the only one to be at her mother's beck and call and miss out on being young and normal, whatever that was. A sibling would have meant company, someone to share the workload and daily diet of Angelica's bizarre behaviour and demands.

Yet somewhere in the depths of her mind, a memory stirred. The dream she'd had... the one with the brides in the forest. It filled her vision for a second. The bride about to raise her veil and reveal herself.

She gulped. Two words from a stranger. And one who profited from getting inside people's heads and giving them hope.

Like a psychiatrist.

Perhaps she and Harmony weren't so different.

———

"A sister?" Rosie repeated herself for the third time, following Charlotte around the bookshop as she returned the gardening books to their shelves. "Why would she say that?"

"She's fishing."

"Fishing?"

"Seeing if she can glean some information from me by throwing an idea out there. How I reacted no doubt will help her profile me." Charlotte knelt to properly place a book. "What I don't understand is why she even assumed I'd be looking for anyone."

Rosie frowned at the shelf. "What I don't understand is why you dismantled what was a nice display."

"If it upset one customer…"

"Harmony is different. And I need to research her allegations against cypress trees because I adore them. Even if she is bothered by them, I'm still a bit taken back by her reaction."

Charlotte pushed herself upright. "I thought it was the flowers. At first."

"Yes. They do look dangerous."

"You're silly."

They both laughed and returned to the other side of the counter. Charlotte played with the arrangement to make it sit better in the vase. "They are such a vivid colour. They must have drawn Harmony's eye and then the big bad tree loomed behind them."

"She's only been in Kingfisher Falls such a short time so would have no idea about Vi's family or disappearance or anything. Even if she'd heard about the flowers on the grave, there's no reason to be upset by them. Is there?"

"If she's highly sensitive and associated them with gossip about the grave. Perhaps. She talks to dead people, so who knows." Charlotte pulled her hair back and retied her ponytail. Strands had come loose when she ran down the road. 'Can I leave the keys to the bookshop with you? Rather than them sitting in the apartment for a few days."

Rosie grinned. "We should give yours and mine to the resident policeman seeing as neither of us will be here."

Hadn't thought of that.

"Good thinking. And my spare garage keys in case he needs to dig around for more about the Ackerman family in the storeroom."

A customer came in and Charlotte stood with the smile she reserved for first contact in the shop. It disappeared the minute she set eyes on the reporter from the other evening, who offered a wide, if fake, smile. "Doctor Dean, the very person I hoped to find!"

"No comment. You may leave now."

Rosie caught Charlotte's eye with a surprised expression.

"Reporter, Rosie. You know, the one who tried to open my back gate."

"Oh, *that* reporter. Yes, you may leave now, dear." Her tone as sweet as ever, Rosie joined Charlotte near the end of the counter.

"I see you have taken to picking the flowers from the grave." As if nobody had said a thing, the woman pointed at the vase. "Interesting choice, don't you agree?" She leaned on the counter. "We've never been properly introduced. I'm—"

"Leaving?" Rosie suggested.

"As I was saying, I'm Lorraine Masters representing *Live Stream News*. Such a pity we got off on the wrong foot and I must blame Councillor Jonas Carmichael for it. He suggested I open the gate because he told me the resident was interested in joining him for an interview. I would never intrude otherwise."

Yet here you are.

Lorraine paused and glanced around. "What a quaint little bookstore. I could get some lovely shots in here as part of an interview and my viewers would swarm up here to buy books and... stuff."

"Why are you here? I asked you to delete the footage you took the other night—did you?" Charlotte didn't move.

"Did I? Mm. I shall have to check with my cameraman. How about we make a deal, Doctor? You make yourself available for a proper interview and I'll delete the other footage in front of you."

Privacy mattered too much to get in front of a camera on purpose. "I have nothing to discuss so an interview will be a waste of time for us both."

"I disagree. This was once the home of Vi Ackerman." Lorraine turned her attention to Rosie. "You purchased this building from her parents only a short time after she disappeared. Then you renovated it from bakery to bookshop never knowing the young woman was buried in sight of the building. Well, assuming you didn't know. Women do strange things for their husbands."

Rosie drew her breath in.

Charlotte put a hand on Rosie's shoulder. "Please leave."

"Struck a chord? Someone knows what happened to Vi. She had a boyfriend, I hear. What if he wasn't a local boy but a local... man. Maybe married." She straightened. "As I said, interesting choice of flowers because sometimes killers keep souvenirs. And sometimes their families continue the tradition when the killer dies."

Rosie spluttered. "What... what are you implying?"

With a shrug, the reporter headed for the door.

Charlotte grabbed the back of Rosie's chair as she tried to follow, leaning down to whisper, "Let her go. Not worth it."

"Well, if either of you change your mind, I left my card on the counter there." She waltzed out with a wave as if leaving her friends behind.

"Let me go, Charlotte! I'm going to... going to..." Rosie burst into tears.

On her knees in an instant, Charlotte held Rosie tight.

chapter
thirty-four

Trev almost ran into the reporter from the other day... or more accurately, she almost ran in to him as she rushed around the corner tapping on her phone. He stepped out of the way and she didn't even look up.

Should be a law on texting and walking.

He'd finished his stint at the clearing with a couple of young uniforms from Gisborne arriving to watch the area while Crime Scene Services worked. Freed to begin following the lines of enquiry, Trev wanted to see if Charlotte was able to have lunch first. Tonight, she'd be packing and planning and this might be the last chance to see her before she left for the airport.

His feelings were mixed about her trip. This was her first visit home since before the day he'd pulled her car over when she was lost near Rivers End. Back then she was running from recent events around her psychiatry practice as well as her mother's illness, and every decision she'd made was coloured by her past. Even coming here to Kingfisher Falls. But the town, the bookshop, and his mother breathed new confidence into her and Charlotte was changing. All in a good way.

Apart from the sleuthing.

With a grin, Trev stepped into the bookshop and the smile left his face. For the second time in as many days he'd found Rosie in tears and Charlotte comforting her. Except now, the tears were racking sobs and Charlotte was gripping Rosie as though her life depended on it.

Heart pounding, he crossed the distance to his mother and dropped to her level. He extracted a hand from Charlotte's grip and squeezed it. "Mum. Mum, what is it?"

At first, she didn't seem aware he was there, but the sobs lessened until she managed to speak, somewhat muffled by her face being against Charlotte's chest. "I ha...te her."

"Hate? Who, Mum?"

Rosie shook her head and gradually straightened. Trev hurried for the box of tissues always on the counter. "Here you go." He put the box on her lap and she grabbed a handful to soak up the tears.

"I'm right here, Rosie, just standing up." Charlotte kept one hand on Rosie's arm as she stood. Her face was white, drawn, and serious. "She'll be okay, Trev."

He mouthed, 'what happened?' and her lips tightened.

Nobody else was in the bookshop and with the absence of answers, he made a decision. Going to the front door, he turned the sign to "closed" and swung it shut, locking it.

"Dear... I'm fine."

"No. You are not. And now is not the time for customers. Let's head to the kitchen and you can wash your face."

Charlotte's shoulders relaxed and she nodded. "Good idea. Come on, Rosie. I'll put the kettle on while you freshen up." She waited until Rosie turned the wheelchair and followed her, reaching back with a hand for Trev's. He enclosed it with one of his. His heart beat steadied. She was okay. But what was wrong with Mum?

With a bit of encouragement, Rosie disappeared into the

bathroom as Charlotte started to fill the kettle. Her hand visibly shook and Trev took it from her. "Give yourself a moment, Charlie." He filled it and found cups and coffee, tapping at the label. "Never complain about police station coffee again." This extracted a glimmer of a smile from Charlotte. Coffee prepped, he held his arms out and she leaned against him. She still shook and his stomach clenched.

As the bathroom door opened, Charlotte stepped back and busied herself with the coffee. Rosie's face was free of tears but her eye rims were red and she avoided looking at Trev.

Once everyone had a coffee, Trev looked from Charlotte to Rosie. "Tell me what's wrong. Please."

Rosie opened her mouth then shook her head and closed it.

"Mum, are you ill? Is it Lewis?"

"Trev, we had a visit from Lorraine Masters."

"Who is?"

"A cruel and evil woman," Rosie muttered to her coffee cup.

"She's the reporter who taped me talking to and about Jonas."

The one who'd almost run into him.

"I saw her as I headed over. What was she doing here?"

"Telling terrible, evil lies. What a horrible—"

"Shh. Rosie, you're letting her get in your head. Take some long breaths deep into your lungs and I'll explain."

Rosie closed her eyes. Trev took her coffee before it spilt.

"This so-called reporter has decided Vi Ackerman's boyfriend was an older, married man. Which may be true. She kept referencing the flowers I put on the counter and suggested… " Charlotte grimaced, then took Trev's hand. "She said "women do strange things for their husbands", and followed it up with something about killers keeping souvenirs, and their families continuing the tradition if the killer dies."

A truck hit Trev. It felt like a truck. He knew Charlie held his hand but everything else was a blur. A deep rage stirred in his gut. Trev could read between the lines. The woman thought his father... no.

Charlotte leaned close to him, her fingers tight around his. "Now you need to breath. Come on, Trevor, suck the oxygen in as if your life depends on it. Hold it and count to five, then exhale."

Breathing was the last thing on his mind. He was going to chase down that woman and confront her. Arrest her.

For what?

"Trev. Do this for me, please. You're shocked. We all are." She rose on her toes to whisper, "Rosie needs your strength."

Yes. She did. He sucked in some air, holding onto Charlotte's hand as a lifeline. With each breath, the blur sharpened and then he was back in the moment. He leaned down and kissed her cheek.

"I saw that," Rosie said.

"Good. Get used to it. And you too, Charlotte." Seeing Rosie smile helped. "I'm angry. Furious. But I'm going to use Lorraine Master's visit to help find Vi's killer. Not sure how yet, but I will."

"May I have my coffee back? I could use something in it."

Charlotte handed it to her. "Know the feeling."

Trev drank a mouthful and wished he hadn't. "This is dreadful."

"Which is why we buy so much takeaway coffee," Charlotte said. "But I'm not leaving Rosie to go get some right now."

Such a loyal person. So caring and understanding and even practical. But bossy.

"We'll order some coffee machines. One for here and one

for the station. Bulk deal. But first I'm going to catch a killer. And prove the press wrong."

"*We* will." Charlotte gave him one of those looks. The one when she had something in mind and wasn't above keeping it to herself. "But Rosie, you still need to have a break and if anything, spending time with Lewis away from here is the best therapy I can prescribe."

Rosie nodded. "I know. And he will be so upset over these dreadful allegations."

"She's clutching at straws, Mum. She has no idea who the killer is, any more than we do, unfortunately. Whatever she thinks she knows, I'm going to find out. And she won't be bothering either of you again."

Charlotte's lips flicked up for a second. "Sounds ominous, Leading Senior Constable."

"She may not realise my father was a journalist. A decent, and award winning one. Coming after his family raises questions about her own ethics, or lack thereof and there are laws about slander and harassment."

As Rosie's eyes teared up again, Trev shook his head. "Mum, I want you to think about your weekend away with Lewis, not this reporter. Trust me to handle it."

She nodded.

Trev glanced at Charlotte. "You too. No changing your plans or anything silly."

"Well, I can't. Or I would. But I don't believe finding out who Vi's boyfriend was is silly in the least." This time her smile was more a Charlie smile. Genuine and with a hint of mischief. "Forward warning, Officer. If you haven't found who it was by the time I get back, you'll need to leave it to a real detective."

He believed her. She'd probably spend every spare moment of her trip researching Vi and her family anyway.

There was as much chance of stopping Charlotte Dean doing her thing as stop the waterfall cascading into the pool below. As long as she didn't dive into danger.

chapter
thirty-five

Charlotte was good at many things, but navigation was not one of them. Thank goodness she'd allowed extra time to reach the airport because she needed it. Leaving home in the dark was fine and she had planned her route the previous night, but once physically on the road, she second-guessed herself.

There were multiple options to get to Tullamarine Airport from Kingfisher Falls. Once she got onto the Calder Freeway it was a matter of following the road to one of the turn-offs. But which one? The first would lead through the town of Sunbury and along back roads, reputed to be frequented by kangaroos around dawn. The next road was even worse with long curves and a narrow, one-way bridge at the bottom of a steep hill. Or should she go all the way down to the next freeway and double back?

She passed the first exit, too conflicted to commit to it. Trev had suggested the second, despite the narrow bridge. He'd said it was quieter and the road itself was in good repair. As the turn loomed, her fingers gripped the steering wheel until the last minute.

"Darn it."

With a flick of the indicator, she decided. Once on the road, she kept a close eye on the sides of the road ahead for tell-tale signs of kangaroos. They often crossed this region in large mobs. But they were off somewhere else and she made it across the narrow bridge and onto the road to the airport with no dramas.

Once in the airport precinct, she made a wrong turn and wasted ten minutes searching for long-term parking. She could see it, but missed the entrance twice.

Next time Trev can drive you!

But when she'd parked the car, grabbed her bag, and was waiting for the bus to the terminal, Charlotte was proud of herself. As self-sufficient as she'd always been, it was odd little things like driving to a new place which threw her off.

Less than an hour later she was in the air, flying over the Macedon Ranges and peering into the early dawn for a sign of Kingfisher Falls. It was too hard to identify from up here when she was confused anyway about which way she'd come. She settled back in her seat. Good thing she wasn't the pilot.

Last night Trev had dropped in for a few minutes. He'd spent the afternoon with Katrina and Bryce, going through the information they had and setting up the investigation. They'd commandeered the other desk as their own and taken over the station's whiteboard. "You'd love it." He'd grinned. "Maps, lists of residents in the area back then, lines of enquiry."

It did interest her. As did his run down of a conversation he'd had with Lorraine Masters. He'd invited her to the station for a chat and when she arrived with a small crew, he'd let her in and told them to clear off. Nicely.

"Did she say why she said those things?" Charlotte had asked. They'd sat in the living room as the evening was colder than recent nights. "What was her reasoning?"

"She claims she was surprised by the flowers and her mind went into overdrive. Reminded her of a movie where a serial killer's wife continued his gruesome work after he died."

"So, Rosie is now a serial killer. Fantastic."

Trev had sighed. "I don't believe Ms Masters. She wanted to rattle your chain, yours and Mum's, probably to get that interview she's so keen to do."

"Those flowers are a problem. Harmony Montgomery claims a picture of a tree upset her earlier... don't ask. But the flowers were right next to the book in question. What is it with them?"

"We've added them to the whiteboard at the station. There's the matter of the wreath from the grave, so tomorrow we will be about talking to florists among other things."

He left a short time later, after accepting Charlotte's spare keys to the apartment, garage, and bookshop. And reminding her he was only a call or message away. Also to message him once she arrived in Brisbane. Then a kiss. So, she had something nice to think about if she got stressed. She'd locked the door in his wake, smiling at his fussing.

Now, she touched her lips. Today would be stressful. But she had a job to do and wouldn't allow her emotions to get involved. She needed to treat her mother like any other patient. One who needed her because Charlotte was the only ally she had.

Once she landed, she'd collect a hire car. Lakeview Care was on the opposite side of the city from the airport and a fair way beyond. Before she arrived, she'd find somewhere for coffee and to reread her notes. Prepare herself. After seeing Angelica, she had an appointment with Maggie and depending on the outcome, another with the powers-that-be who made decisions about patients.

Whatever happened today, visiting her mother was the right thing to do and long overdue. She refused to harbour guilt over the length of time since seeing her. She was here now. And they had much to discuss.

Who is Z? And where do I look for him or her?

The question burned in her mind.

———

Brisbane was blanketed by rain. The landing was bumpy and the runway slippery. Charlotte only had carry-on luggage and hurried through the terminal, relieved to be back on the ground.

The drive to Lakeview Care was familiar. She'd lived in Brisbane for most of her life, punctuated by a stint in northern New South Wales when her mother decided to embrace a natural living approach. But being isolated from the world wasn't good for Angelica and they'd moved back to the old house in Brisbane before Charlotte had time to settle in her new school.

After a short coffee stop in the town closest to Lakeview Care, Charlotte turned into the carpark outside the main building. Set on a few acres to allow patients fresh air and exercise, the facility sprawled with different buildings for various level of care and security.

The rain was gone as she stepped out of the car. The air here was warm. She'd forgotten about the humidity up here. A security guard headed her way, which she'd expected. As low-key as the place appeared, patient security was paramount. She collected her handbag and locked the car.

———

Angelica sat on a sofa in a sunroom by herself, staring out of the window at the lake in the centre of the property. Even from the doorway, the lines in her face were more pronounced than Charlotte remembered and her mother's once-brown hair was almost fully grey and cut short.

What are you thinking? Where are you?

Her last visit was close to eighteen months ago. A difficult, distressing visit for them both. She'd left when her mother began screaming obscenities and she'd never looked back. But that was then. Charlotte dug deep for her long-practised techniques to cope. Think calm. Speak calm. This is a patient.

"I can see the ducks from here, Charlotte." Angelica's voice was hoarse and she didn't move. "Lots of ducks."

Charlotte moved with purpose. One step at a time until she was beside Angelica. "There are lots of ducks. Hi, Mum."

"Sit and we can watch together."

She perched next to her mother. "It was raining earlier."

"It woke me. I was dreaming and it woke me."

"I flew in this morning and was surprised to see so much rain."

Angelica leaned back and looked at Charlotte. Her eyes were almost expressionless, probably from medication. Close up, her hair was limp and dry. Again, perhaps a side effect of the mix of pills. Or poor nutrition. Angelica had never eaten well. Her preferred diet was bowl after bowl of dry cereal during the day.

Charlotte took her hand. So cold. And almost no return pressure. "I'm staying for a couple of days, so maybe we can go for a walk to the lake later. If you feel up to it."

"They won't let me leave this room. And my room. Just the two. Back and forth, back and forth. I can't remember why."

"I'm having a meeting in a couple of hours with Maggie,

and some of the others. So, I can talk to them about it, if you want me to?"

With a nod, Angelica turned back to the view. They sat for a while. Charlotte had plenty to talk about but knew better than to push her mother. This first visit was about observing and assessing. She'd ask some gentle leading questions soon, once Angelica looked her way again. Until then, she'd sit with her mother and pretend this was normal.

chapter
thirty-six

Trev stared at the whiteboard in the police station. He'd reread the same line three times. Or four. But he might as well not have bothered as the words still hadn't made it to his brain.

Stop worrying about her.

But how?

Charlotte was alone in a place she'd run from. Dealing with issues he still wasn't sure of except its effect on her over the time he'd known her. The deep-seated stress, anxiety attacks, fear of being close to anyone. Even him. Much of this she'd worked hard on to reduce and he saw her blossoming every day into the wonderful, confident woman from beneath a lifetime of doubt. If only he'd gone with her.

"Case won't solve itself, Trev." Bryce didn't look up from a file he'd uncovered from the mess Sid had left behind. "The detective will be expecting results once she returns from her trip."

Trev grinned. "Not wrong there. What are you looking at?"

"Notes about missing people in town. Old notes from a long-gone officer with nothing of substance. Didn't make a report or follow up much." Bryce turned a page. "Example. He wrote... Mr Murdoch's wife abandoned her husband and home on June fourteen, 2002. Mr Murdoch refused to make an official statement but requested I speak to persons who may have assisted her or know of her whereabouts."

Interesting.

"Then he's made comment about speaking with Mrs Bongiovanni who stated she offered to drive Mrs Murdoch to the railway station but was refused as somebody was coming to get her." Bryce glanced up. "Whoever that someone is, there's no mention."

"Anything about Vi Ackerman?" Trev joined Bryce, sinking onto the seat opposite. "There were several years between their disappearances."

"Yeah. Nothing about the family but Vi's friend... Cynthia Reynolds, came to ask for help finding her. This was a week or so after she was last seen by her family. Looks like the officer did speak to her parents but was satisfied nothing was out of place." He closed the file and tossed it onto the desk. "This town of yours has a poor record of policing. I hope you intend to remedy that."

Trev didn't bother answering. "Worth looking up this Cynthia... Reynolds, you said? Don't recall the name but someone will. She might know more about this boyfriend."

Bryce pushed his chair back. "Follow up on that first. I'm meeting Katrina at the council offices." He grinned as he stood. "Bound to stir up those who think this town belongs to them, but we want our hands on more detailed maps of the bushland. And its history. See if we can shake a tree and get some suspects to fall out."

"My understanding is they own the land—council, I mean. There's signs around the place saying as much."

"We'll see."

After he'd gone, Trev wandered back to the whiteboard

and added a new list about the file Bryce read from. He wrote "Cynthia Reynolds" underneath. His mother might know her, or Lewis. A visit to see Lewis was on his schedule anyway, so he might as well begin there. Let him know about the reporter's distressing visit to the bookshop so he was prepared. And to remind him to look after his mother. It wasn't every day she went on holiday with a new man.

––––––

Lewis was busy with customers so Trev headed to the florist instead. He introduced himself to the owner, who'd recently bought the business and was new to the area. They chatted about the weather for a while. His visit was friendly but fruitless as the wreath didn't come from there. He left with a list of other florists in the region, including two who worked from home.

This time Lewis was alone, gift wrapping a teapot with matching cups and saucers. "Looks like something Mum would like."

"No. She prefers yellows and blues. But the pattern is sweet."

How did I not know this?

With a grin, Trev leaned against the counter. "I'll talk to you before her birthday for ideas."

"Good planning. And I have plenty of suggestions." Lewis' eyes twinkled behind his spectacles as he finished wrapping. "There. Ready for collection. Is this a formal visit?"

"Semi. A name came up this morning which might help us in our investigation. A young woman from around the time Vi Ackerman disappeared. A friend."

"I may know. But my time back then was spent driving tourists rather than in town so much. What is the name?"

"Cynthia Reynolds."

"Reynolds. Yes, I know the name. Not Cynthia as such, but I recall the family living out of town on some land. Quiet family. Religious. Same religion from memory as the Ackerman's so that's why the young ladies would know each other I imagine."

Trev took out a notepad. "Out of town, where?"

Lewis provided what he remembered, which wasn't a great deal but might lead Trev in the right direction.

"All set for the weekend?"

"Me? I'm the easy one. You, my young friend, have two cats to concern yourself with."

"They love me."

Lewis looked down at his hands. "I want Rosie to enjoy this little holiday but I'm unsure if the location will be upsetting."

"If Mum said yes, then she'll have considered everything. My advice, if you want it, is to let her lead. I bet she'll get one whiff of sea air and be dragging you to the beach."

"I hope so." Lewis glanced back at Trev. "She's safe with me. I promise I'll take excellent care of her. She is... precious."

Trev wanted to hug Lewis. Instead, he shook his hand. "She is."

Before going to the bookshop, Trev detoured to the café for two coffees. He checked his phone as he waited, relieved there was a message from Charlotte. She'd just arrived at Lakeview Care and would message before she left.

Rosie was finishing with a customer so Trev put her coffee behind the counter. She'd begun packing last night with no less than two suitcases, each half done. When he'd returned from seeing Charlotte, she'd been flustered, taking things back and forward from her bathroom and wardrobe and muttering about not knowing what the weather would do.

"Coffee is always welcome, and so are you." The customer had left and Rosie joined Trev near the window.

"Thought I'd save you from too much of that substance you call coffee in the kitchen."

"Thoughtful. I got a message from Charlie."

"Me too. At least she's safely there." Trev followed Rosie back to the counter. The flowers were gone. "Moved the vase?"

"Charlie put them in the kitchen. Pretty things they are, but they keep upsetting people." She parked behind the counter. "Now, is the coffee just an excuse to check I'm okay, because I am, dear."

"Partly. And a name came up this morning I wanted to run past you. Cynthia Reynolds. Does it sound familiar?"

Rosie tapped the counter as she thought about it. "There's a Reynolds family living up past Darcy's place. Next road I think. They have a bunch of children, well did have. Must be all grown now as I don't see them around. Only the parents from time to time. Secretive folk. Why?"

"Cynthia Reynolds may have been a close friend of Vi Ackerman. Thought it worth finding her for a chat. See if she remembers anything to shed light on the events leading to Vi's disappearance."

"All you can do is visit, I suppose. I've never been to their place but rumour has it they've let it run down. More interested in their cult than maintaining the land."

Matched Lewis' summation. An image of high barbed wire fences and security dogs flashed into Trev's mind.

"Mum? What if I do dinner so you can relax a bit?"

"Relax? Well, that's sweet, dear, but I've still got to finish packing so I could do that. If you're sure? Shall I shop on the way home?"

"No. You go home later and do what you need and I'll make us something while you decide how many outfits a woman needs to go away for a weekend." He grinned and moved fast as Rosie grabbed a ruler and swung it his way. "No assaulting police officers."

―――――

Trev pulled up outside the property, parking on the edge of an overgrown verge along a dirt road. He'd done some research about the Reynolds family since leaving the bookshop. They owned a few acres and grew their own food. Their children had been home-schooled and numbered seven. Cynthia was a middle child and would be a bit over forty now. The same as Vi, had she lived.

The farm gate was closed and had a *no trespassing* sign attached. With a sigh, Trev unhooked the latch and stepped onto the property, thankful of his uniform. The driveway wound past a couple of paddocks with goats. They looked healthy but the fences were barely standing. Surprising the goats hadn't escaped.

He reached the house, where an old man stood at the bottom of the steps, feet planted apart, arms crossed.

"Mr Reynolds?"

No response, only a long glare. A curtain moved behind him.

"Sir, I'm Leading Senior Constable Trevor Sibbritt. Hoping you'd let me ask a couple of questions about—"

"Ya wanna know 'bout me daughter. News travels. Lucky, I thought yar father was a good enough man. For a worlder."

Trev blinked, unsure what a "worlder" was.

"Cynthia left so long ago I can't recall."

"Did you know her friend, Vi Ackerman?"

"Don't remember. Too many years ago. Cynthia knows nothing so don't go looking. Ya hear me?"

Which had the reverse effect on Trev. Finding Cynthia was now top of his to-do list. He took out his notepad.

"When did Cynthia leave home, sir?"

"Long time ago. Not your business."

"I'm investigating the homicide of Vi Ackerman and believe your daughter was her closest friend. I need to ask her some questions."

"She didn't kill the girl."

"Do you know who did?"

This shocked the old man and he dropped his arms. "Didn't know she was dead until yesterday. But it weren't my kid who hurt her."

"Are you aware of Vi being involved with a young man? Someone in your church, perhaps?"

"Don't know much, do ya? Churches are as evil as you worlders."

"Nevertheless, do you know who she went out with?"

The man turned and clomped up the stairs. The curtain fell. "Get off ma property. That girl got what she deserved if she was involved with a worlder."

Charming.

"And your daughter, Mr Reynolds? Where does Cynthia live now?"

"Dunno. Don't care." He opened the front door and slammed it behind himself.

Half-expecting the man to return with a rifle, Trev wasted no time getting back to the patrol car. Wherever Cynthia was, she'd probably left home the minute she was old enough. Or was she also missing? He glanced back along the driveway. Was Vi the only victim or were Cynthia and Bryony also buried somewhere in Kingfisher Falls. Did he have a serial killer on his hands?

chapter
thirty-seven

Charlotte sat in her car outside Lakeview Care and closed her eyes, forcing her breathing into slow, deep inhales until she no longer felt ready to faint. Between not eating since last night—or was it the previous lunchtime—to holding her body so tense her muscles locked up, it was surprising she'd made it back to the car.

The rain was back. Not heavy, nor cold. It increased the humidity and rather than opening a window and risking getting water in the hire care, Charlotte opened her eyes and turned on the air conditioning, sending a whispered 'sorry' to the planet.

She dialled her phone and settled back in her seat.

Please answer. I need to hear your voice.

"Charlie, hi. Give me a moment to pull over."

Where was he going? Or coming back from? Rain streaked the windscreen, blotting out the world.

"I'm here," Trev said.

"Me too."

"You okay?"

"Sure. You said pull over. What's been happening this

morning?" He needed to talk for a while so she could listen and let his voice sooth her nerves.

"Began with Mayhem staring at me until I woke then forcing me out of my own bed. Then a delectable breakfast made by Mum—"

"Okay, enough of food talk. Haven't had time yet. How is Rosie?"

"In good spirits and excited about her trip away. Mind you, she can't decide what to pack so is taking everything."

He updated her on his day so far, as if he sensed she needed some normality. His description of Mr Reynolds both amused and alarmed her.

"Is there another woman missing, Trev? This makes three, all within what… five years?"

"Let's not jump to conclusions. My take on it is the Reynolds children all abandoned their parents once they could. Probably more than ready to leave a controlling life-style, although so many people do stay in those cults. I'd have been interested to have your perspective on the man."

"Happy to consult. Informally that is."

"Where are you?"

Charlotte turned the windscreen wipers on. "In the carpark outside Lakeview Care. I needed a chance to think away from the place."

Trev's voice had a gentle tone she found endearing. "Cars are good like that."

"My mother isn't doing well. Drugged to the eyeballs and not eating properly. Not eating much at all by the look of her. But I am confident she won't repeat her behaviour as long as they keep to my suggested changes of medication. I found a conflict between two prescribed by this Doctor Hicks. How he hadn't picked up the potential for disaster is beyond me."

"Then she'll be able to stay there?"

"We'll see. I met with Maggie earlier and have a meeting with her, Dr Hicks, and two decision makers this afternoon. I'm going to get something to eat and put together a brief."

There was a pause. Charlotte checked her phone to make sure it hadn't dropped out.

"I believe in you, Charlie. Your mother is in safe hands."

Warmth rushed through her. His positivity always surprised her. And she needed his backing more than ever because she didn't quite believe in herself.

"Means a lot. Thank you."

There was an intermittent beep on the line.

"Sorry, Charlie. That's a call for me."

"You go. I'll call later?"

"Anytime. I'm thinking of you."

Then he was gone. She stared at the phone. "Me too."

———

"I'm not comfortable having Ms Dean present during this discussion." Doctor Hicks, a short, stubby man with a comb-over reminding Charlotte of Kevin Murdoch, didn't meet her eyes, directing his statement to Maggie.

Maggie was the head administrator of Lakeview Care and as able to deal with professionals as patients. Charlotte had known her for a long time and trusted her. Now, Maggie took her seat at the long table next to Charlotte. Doctor Hicks and the two board members were opposite.

"I appreciate your comment, but *Doctor* Dean is here in two capacities. She has power of attorney, so has every right to be present during a discussion on her mother's future. And she is Angelica's former psychiatrist."

He made a scoffing sound. "Whatever she might have been, she isn't now. And hardly an appropriate person to be here in an official capacity, given her history."

Charlotte was expecting his attack. She'd checked his background after speaking with Trev, discovering he now had a practice where she once had, before she'd made a terrible error about a client and sent her career and personal life into a downward spiral. The ensuing disciplinary hearings almost destroyed her, but she'd emerged with her licence intact. Some peers thought she deserved to lose it. And this man opposite appeared to be one of them.

She kept her expression and her voice neutral. "Doctor Hicks, this meeting is to discuss Angelica Dean's situation. As her current psychiatrist your *professional* opinions are welcome."

Maggie nodded. "Let's begin."

For the next half hour, Angelica's place at Lakeview Care hung in the balance. Debate over her long-term care, changes to therapy and medication all factored into consideration. Charlotte left Maggie to raise the conflict of medications. As expected, Doctor Hicks was adamant Angelica needed to go to a high security psychiatric ward. He grew angry with questions from the board and flustered when pressed about the medication.

"This is a waste of my time. If you refuse to listen to my years of expertise then clearly my services are no longer appreciated. I will arrange to sever the contract I have here." He pushed his seat back, grabbed his briefcase, and slammed the door on his way out.

All eyes followed him. Then, there was a collective sigh of relief. Maggie patted Charlotte's arm.

"Would you mind waiting in my office whilst we finish the discussion and make a decision? I don't believe we will be long."

It wasn't until Charlotte stood that she realised her hands shook. She let herself into Maggie's office and stood at the window. The small lake was between here and Angelica's room. The rain was gone again and now the sun glared off the water.

Doctor Hicks wasn't a good practitioner. He'd revealed himself as short-tempered and opinionated and if this was how he'd been with Angelica, no wonder she'd regressed. Coupled with medicine working against each other, she'd have reacted more than usual to dealing with a male authority figure. Charlotte sighed. She couldn't stay here in Brisbane and had no idea of how to go about bringing Angelica closer to Kingfisher Falls.

"Charlotte, thank you for waiting." Maggie bustled in and joined her at the window. "Angelica can stay."

"She can?" Charlotte's voice squeaked and she threw her arms around the other woman for a second. "Sorry. But thank you. Thanks to all of you."

Maggie half-smiled and went to her desk, motioning for Charlotte to sit opposite. "Not quite all of us."

"Oh. I am sorry about Doctor Hicks. He won't really leave?"

"He will. And frankly, after his behaviour today I was prepared to terminate his contract. *I* have to apologise, not you. While we don't condone Angelica's outbursts, it is possible we contributed to them by assigning her to an unsuitable therapist. It won't happen again."

Charlotte wanted to cry. Relief was one part but so was a deep sense of sadness for her mother. She'd not asked to have multiple mental diseases. Her fault was not accepting treatment for them until so much damage was done.

To you and to me, Mum.

Maggie continued, unaware of Charlotte's simmering emotions. "How long are you staying in Brisbane?"

"I have a return flight booked on Monday."

"And you'll visit Angelica while you're here? She asks for you daily."

"If you'll allow me to, I'll see her now. And then each day until I go home."

"Home? Then, this time away of yours is permanent?"

"It is. But I promise I'll visit more. At least every few months I'll fly up for a couple of days." This she could do.

There wasn't an immediate response as Maggie gazed at her, as if deciding what to say. The phone rang. "It will go to voicemail. Charlotte, Doctor Dean, you must see your mother is deteriorating. She's losing herself to dementia quite apart from her other illnesses. Every visit there will be less of the person you know, so do consider the timing of those visits."

A cold stone settled in Charlotte's stomach, forcing out all other feelings. She finished her conversation with Maggie in a few minutes and went to find her mother. Time to have that walk around the lake.

chapter
thirty-eight

Trev got off the phone as Katrina and Bryce arrived in the station. He crossed to the whiteboard and ran a line through *Cynthia Reynolds*.

"So, there's not a serial killer at large?" Bryce asked.

"Why, you do sound disappointed." Katrina grinned at him. "You found her, Trev?"

"Alive and well. Living in New Zealand. Happy to talk about being as far away from her parents as she could get. Married and has kids over there. Had a bit of a cry hearing Vi was confirmed as the victim." He returned to his desk. "She had a bit to say though."

The others sat at the second desk and waited as he gathered the notes he'd made.

"Right. Cynthia and Vi were friends. Neither had friends outside their religion on fear of their parents finding out. Vi kept it a secret she had a boyfriend. Except for Cynthia from the sound of it." He glanced up. "Cynthia never met him. Never heard his name. Just that Vi was in love and he was married."

Getting any information from Cynthia was difficult. She was suspicious of Trev, concerned he'd tell her parents where she lived now, and worried she'd somehow be blamed for her friend's death. It took a lot of assurances and calm conversation to draw a small amount of information from her.

"A married man. How much older than this seventeen-year-old kid was this creep?" Bryce hit the desk with the flat of his hand, sending papers flying and making Katrina jump.

"Dude, chill." She tidied the papers. "We're all disgusted but keep that for when we find the killer."

"Who is probably the same person," Bryce said. "Sorry for that."

Trev was impressed. He'd taken a while to warm to the detective who he suspected had a thing for Charlotte, but never once did Bryce overstep in his relationship with her. He might tease her but the respect was there beneath the bluff. Seeing him wound up about Vi Ackerman reinforced his growing admiration of the man.

Katrina leaned forward. "So, no name perhaps, but did Cynthia take a guess at who this man was?"

"Only that he was important. Had money and would whisk her away to a new life once he divorced his wife. Her last memory of Vi was a whispered conversation outside the bakery. Vi was seeing him that night to tell him something very important. She didn't elaborate to Cynthia."

Bryce pushed his seat back and stood. "This kid told her married boyfriend she was pregnant and he killed her." He stalked to the whiteboard and made notes under Vi's name.

"Trev? Did you mention the pregnancy to Cynthia?" Katrina asked.

He shook his head. "I've not told anyone. And I mean anyone. You told me it's a card we need to hold onto and I agree. Not even Vi's family know yet."

Nor does Charlie. She's already said she believes it, but has nothing but her gut to go on.

He wished he had her instincts. The mood in the room

was dark as silence fell. Each in their own thoughts about this latest information. Bryce put the kettle on and made coffee.

"What happened at the council office?" Time for some lighter discussion.

"Not a whole lot." Katrina screwed her face up at the taste of the coffee. She should try the bookshop's and then compare. "Had to make a request for the maps so they'll be ready later today. Jonas Carmichael made himself unavailable. Terrance Murdoch offered us a tour of the building but claimed to know little about the bushland other than it belonging to council and is a fire hazard."

"It doesn't ring true." Trev searched his mind for what bothered him.

"The fire hazard thing? It is overgrown and neglected," Bryce said. "Council should be fined for letting it get that way. For that matter, if they properly maintained it, most likely Vi's grave would have come to light a long time ago."

"Unless someone in council is keeping it that way," Katrina suggested. "A few married men work there. Might be considered wealthy by seventeen-year old kids from reclusive families."

Still puzzling over what he couldn't remember, Trev wrote a few notes on his phone. Key phrases to come back to. *Terrance doesn't know much about bushland. Signs around the area. Go for a walk and check them.* He put the phone down. Both detectives were staring at him. "What?"

"He's texting Charlotte. Thinks she can solve this from Queensland." Bryce stretched his legs out.

"She could solve it from the moon, given enough time," Katrina added.

"And secrecy. She likes keeping things to herself," Bryce continued.

"Knock it off, both of you. I was making notes about the

case before I forgot. And she's stopped with the whole secrecy thing."

"That's what she tells you." Katrina's phone beeped a message. "Maps are ready. Trev, any chance you can collect them? We have interviews soon."

"Anything to escape this assault on my relationship."

"We love Charlotte." Katrina grinned as Trev collected his keys.

"Not you so much," Bryce added.

———

Still smiling at the teasing, Trev drove toward the council offices building. This was tucked away a few streets from the main shopping around the corner from the old garden centre. That had a *For Sale* sign plastered on its front doors.

As he waited for traffic to clear so he could turn into the street, his attention was drawn by a woman walking past, her arms filled with flowers. He might not know a lot about plants but this was lavender. A huge armful of it.

A moment later he parked around the corner and sprinted after her. The long red hair and purple skirt touching the ground were a giveaway.

"Excuse me. Ms Montgomery?"

She glanced over her shoulder with a startled expression but didn't slow down. Her shop was along here and as Trev closed in on Harmony, she pulled keys from a pocket and dropped most of the lavender. By the time he reached her, she was kneeling, trying to scoop the scattered flowers.

"Here, let me help." He leaned down and started picking long stems up.

"No. I'm fine. Leave them."

He'd never spoken to Harmony. His mother liked her and even Charlotte was tolerating her despite her distrust of the woman's occupation. But her sharp tone and reaction interested him.

"Okay. I hadn't intended to startle you. Just want a quick word."

"About what?" She collected the last of the lavender and climbed to her feet. "I have a reading in a few minutes."

"I won't keep you long. My name is Lead—"

"I know who you are. Rosie's son. The policeman home from isolation."

Wouldn't call my posting in Rivers End isolation.

"Trev. And yes, Rosie is my mother and speaks highly of you."

Her mouth relaxed a fraction but her eyes—intense eyes —remained fixed on his. Something wasn't right with her. If she had nothing to hide, she was going the wrong way about proving it.

"I'm curious about the flowers," he said.

"What about them."

"Where did you get them? Such a large amount."

"How can it matter? I have them to make lavender tea. I dry them." Now, she looked down.

"I'm not accusing you of anything. I'm looking for a source of lavender and saw you carrying them. Nothing more."

She shuffled her feet.

"Look, as long as you didn't steal them, I'm not concerned with the details of the transaction. Just where they came from, or who?"

"Is it stealing to cut back a plant at the right time of year from a deceased estate?" Her eyes came back to his and held a trace of something he thought was uncertainty. "Lavender benefits from heavy pruning on occasion and the garden I found them in has nobody caring for it."

Deceased estate? Octavia's?

"From the house up past the garden centre? On the right with silver birches along the driveway?"

Harmony nodded.

"Possibly not the best idea but nothing I'd arrest you over." He offered a smile. "Happy to speak to whoever is looking after the place and see if they mind you being there."

"I have what I wanted. Thank you." She turned to her shop door. "I really have to get things set up for my client."

"Thank you for speaking with me. I'll leave you to it." Trev waited until she was inside, locking the door behind herself, before looking at the shop window. Unlike the bookshop, the display was only a black backdrop and signage with a list of her services.

"What is behind this curtain?" he muttered.

He'd ask his mother next time he saw her. Something about Harmony Montgomery reminded him of a scared animal. On the defensive in case it was attacked. In his experience, people like that had something in their pasts to hide. Whether she was guilty of anything more than stealing some unwanted flowers, Harmony was now in his sights and he mentally added her to his list of people to investigate.

chapter
thirty-nine

It was late afternoon when Charlotte pulled up outside a rundown, white weatherboard house in a Brisbane suburb. At one point she'd thought she'd typically taken the wrong turn as most of the homes along here were modern, two level affairs with new, perfect gardens. But she'd remembered the way and couldn't believe how a street could transform in only a few years. She'd always heard a saying about buying the worst house in the best street if you wanted value and when she put this place on the market, the recent trend in this suburb might get Angelica more than anyone would think possible.

Nothing had changed. If anything, the place was in worse condition than the last time she'd been here. Back then she'd been here only long enough to pack what she'd needed to move Angelica in with her. A year in her home and then her mother disappeared one morning. She'd found her on her way back to this house, looking for Dad. A month's trial of her mother living alone but having social workers and carers visit regularly was unsuccessful.

Poor carers. Angelica turned into her cold, nasty persona

until they refused to visit. Then, she reverted to helpless Angelica and implored Charlotte to move in with her.

"Back here. As if I would."

Charlotte stood on the footpath.

Her fingers twisted her hair. Unease settled in her stomach. This time she had to consider emptying the house. Paying someone to fix it up enough to sell. She glanced either side. The weatherboard and brown brick homes from her childhood were gone as the suburb morphed into one of the on-trend places to live. No point fixing up what would likely be torn down by a developer.

She followed the path with its broken concrete and weeds. Charlotte paid someone to keep the lawns down and check the place every so often. At the bottom of the steps she stopped, reminded of the photograph in the album. Her father once lived here with them. This house was all she had left of him. It was paid in full and transferred to Angelica some years after he walked away. Once sold, this would see her mother's costs covered for the rest of her life instead of from Charlotte's dwindling savings.

The lock was uncooperative until Charlotte rattled the door and pressed the key in further. It turned and she swung the door inwards, recoiling from the rancid odour.

Why didn't I clean the place out properly?

Too late to worry about the past now. It was more a question of whether she could open enough windows to avoid suffocating from holding her breath.

The power was off so Charlotte left the front door open and moved through the house to open windows in each room. Then she locked herself in before opening the back door and going into the yard. Grass. Fences. Clothes line. Nothing else. But why would there be? Why would a child have needed a sandpit or swing, or even a tree to climb and read beneath?

She'd forgotten how large the garden was. In someone else's hands, this might have been filled with vegetable beds, a trampoline, wading pool, and perhaps a dog. No pets for Charlotte. No playtime for Charlotte. No fun for Charlotte.

With a gulp, she hurried inside. The best thing to do was hire a company to clean the place out. Dispose of anything left behind and then put it on the market. She'd never need to return.

One by one she closed the windows again, then locked the back door. The kitchen was how she'd left it after arriving to help move Angelica to Lakeview Care. She'd not come back and had forgotten there were plates in the sink and food in the pantry.

"I can't deal with this right now."

On her way to the front door she paused outside her mother's bedroom where the door was ajar. Angelica had tried to lock herself in there when she'd realised Charlotte was committing her. Her bed was still a mess of blankets piled at the end where she'd wrapped them around herself to hide, such was her belief she could be invisible behind them. There was little else in the bedroom. A few drawers were open in the dressing table and Charlotte closed them one by one. The bottom one wouldn't close and she pulled it right out and peered behind. A large, dirty, white envelope was stuck behind the drawer and she wiggled it out. It was sealed and had her mother's handwriting across the front. *Mine.*

After closing the drawer, Charlotte put the envelope on top of the dressing table and left the house. This envelope would reveal nothing new. Angelica loved hiding things and in Charlotte's experience, they were always useless items. Newspapers. Magazines. Notebooks full of Angelica's bizarre words and drawings. This was nothing more than the same.

Back in the car, she gazed at the house. She'd come back

in the morning. Bring cleaning products and garbage bags and fix the kitchen. Probably the bathroom and laundry as well. One more time inside and then she'd walk away forever.

Like Dad did.

And 'Z'. Whoever that was.

She started the motor. Her hotel wasn't far and she needed a shower. And food, if she could get her stomach to stop churning. Rosie had messaged to check on her and she'd call her a little later. Make sure she was ready for her own adventure which would be a whole lot better than this trip. She pulled out onto the road.

chapter
forty

Trev was behind the bookshop when Charlotte messaged to see if he was free to talk. He rang straight back, longing to hear her voice. She'd already called Rosie and he'd left them to chat and walked down to check the detectives had locked up the garage after going through the storeroom.

"This isn't a bad time?" Her voice held a note of something. Stress?

"Never a bad time. Where are you?"

"At the hotel. I've ordered room service because I can't be bothered to go looking for dinner. Rosie sounds excited."

He grinned and settled onto a step. "She is beside herself. Humming away as she packed and to her credit, Mum managed to fit all into one suitcase and is impressed with herself."

Charlotte laughed and the sound cheered him. "I'm happy for her."

"Me too."

There was a silence. The last he'd heard was a brief text this afternoon. *Mum can stay.*

"I'm sitting on the steps to your apartment."

"Oh. If you're waiting for me, you're likely to get cold. And hungry. I don't really have a portal."

"Funny. I just checked Bryce and Katrina locked up the garage seeing as they were poking around in the storeroom today."

"Find anything?"

"They came back to the station with a couple of boxes but we haven't caught up yet. But some good news. I found Cynthia Reynolds alive and well. Living in New Zealand."

"Thank goodness she wasn't a victim. What did she remember?"

Trev ran through the basics of the conversation. "We're compiling a list of married men living in and around Kingfisher Falls back then."

"It was Terrance," Charlotte declared.

"He's on the list. But why are you so sure?"

"His own wife disappeared and she was younger than him. Lots younger, so he has a track record. And as a councillor he has some say in the maintenance of the land behind the bookshop. Could probably ensure nobody got close to the grave."

Trev got to his feet and wandered to the back gate. "Good logic. Now I have to find evidence."

"Have you located Bryony?"

"Not yet. Katrina's on it but so far, the trail stops at the bridal shop." He unlocked the gate and stepped through. All was quiet under the night sky. "Tell me about your day."

"Basically, Mum can stay at Lakeview Care indefinitely. Some of her medications were working against each other, which, combined with a horrible excuse for a therapist sent her into a spiral which was missed by her carers. A whole lot of issues at one time."

"I've never heard you speak badly of a peer."

"Doctor Hicks is a nasty man. Didn't like treating Mum

and I got the feeling he did so only after finding out she is my mother."

"Not following."

"He works where I had my practice and thinks the worst of me. And was happy to voice his opinion in front of members of the board."

Trev leaned against the fence. "I'm so sorry. You don't deserve that."

Charlotte didn't sound the least bit worried. "Mum didn't deserve it. But he is now out of a contract with Lakeview Care *because* he showed his true colours to the board members today."

He chuckled.

"Wasn't funny then, but I'm relieved he's gone. Mum and I went for a slow walk around the lake and I left her tired but looking a lot more relaxed."

"You sound happier, Charlie. As if some weight lifted off you."

There was a long pause and Trev went back through the gate.

"I guess I am. There's some stuff I need to sort out while I'm here. But Mum's going to improve, at least for a while. And the staff have worked with me on a plan for her." She sighed. "I should have visited a while ago, Maggie kept asking me to do so."

"You're there now. What happens next?"

"Well, once dinner arrives I eat, which is nice. Tomorrow I'll see Mum after lunch for as long as she can tolerate company but, in the morning, I'm cleaning her house."

"Her house?"

"Oh. There's probably a lot you don't know. It's the house I grew up in and when she moved out... for want of a better term, it was left a mess. Quite awful really. But nothing a hazmat suit and long tongs and garbage bags won't fix. Or a flame thrower."

He wasn't sure if she was joking. It sounded appalling.

"Trev?"

"Still here. Do you need help with it? I could fly up and take on some of the workload."

"No. No, thanks but no need. Besides you have an investigation and cats to look after. What would Rosie say if you left them alone?"

Her tone was different. Almost panicked.

Is it so bad you don't want me to see it?

"I was going to suggest you hold off cleaning until Sunday. Mum's back in the afternoon so I'll be freed up then."

Again, the silence.

Trev headed for home, giving her time to think as he walked.

"I'm okay. I really am, Trev. This is just part of making sure my mother has what she needs. The house will sell quickly I think because the suburb is trendy now. That money means her future fees are covered without..."

"Without what, Charlie? Are you paying her costs?"

"Nobody else was going to. There is only me." Her voice was small.

"There *was* only you, sweetheart." His heart went out to her. "Now you have me and Rosie as family. You're not alone."

Through the phone there was a tapping sound.

"Room service is here. I'll be a sec."

Charlotte spoke to whoever had brought her meal and then there was the sound of a door closing. "I'm back and it smells so good. Do you mind if I say goodnight and eat?"

"Enjoy. Sleep well and we can catch up when you're free tomorrow if you like."

"I like. Thank you. Really, thanks, Trev."

He put the phone away. There was a lot more going on up there than Charlie was letting on. Something about the house was upsetting her, more than the mess. But short of jumping on a plane, which she didn't want him to do, he'd have to wait for her to come home.

"And then we'll talk."

The florist's window was lit up and he stopped to gaze at a pretty display of wedding bouquets. Vi's wedding dress was a hopeful—if stolen—dream of an impossible future. She'd probably stolen the teddy and baby clothes as well.

He kept walking. When he'd spoken to Harmony today, her arms filled with lavender, she'd been to Octavia's garden. Were there roses there also? Octavia's ex-husband left town after deciding another woman, another married woman, was more to his liking than his wife. Where was he these days? If he'd not cared about destroying two marriages to get what he wanted, was there more in his past and would he go so far as to kill someone to protect himself?

chapter
forty-one

As hungry as she was, Charlotte hadn't even lifted the lid on her meal ten minutes after it arrived. She stood at the window staring at the familiar yet forgotten skyline of Brisbane. A ride on a catamaran on the river would be so wonderful. Or a stroll along Southbank to the beautiful little swimming area. She loved this city.

Her muscles ached. Too much tension today. And as tired as she was from the early start and big day, she knew she'd not sleep well. Too many scenarios played out in her head and now she had another. Trev's words.

She moved from the window and poured a glass of wine from a bottle she'd bought on the way. Then she sat at the small glass table-for-one and removed the lid from the plate.

Garlic and herbs filled her senses and her stomach rumbled. The simple pasta dish looked pretty and tasted nice, but it wasn't the same as Doug's dishes from Italia. But food was welcome and she finished it before her glass of wine was empty. When she was back in Kingfisher Falls, when this case was over, she'd take Rosie and Trev to dinner at Italia. And then the next night at India Gate House.

She giggled and refilled her glass. Thank goodness those

were her only go-to restaurants otherwise they'd be eating out every night the way she felt this moment. And then there was the dinner on the balcony of the apartment to plan. Trev, Rosie, and Lewis. She'd already worked on some menu ideas and needed to chat to Doug to get some tips on technique. She couldn't wait to host the little dinner party.

"There *was* only you, sweetheart." Trev's endearment had surprised her. "Now you have me and Rosie as family. You're not alone." And this both filled her heart and terrified her.

I'm not alone.

His calm assurance of her place in his family sent her pulse racing. She didn't quite understand or believe it after all her years of solitude.

"More like loneliness, Charlie. Be honest."

She sipped more wine, letting it go to her head. She wanted to drink until the thoughts went away. What on earth got into her? Charlotte put the wine into the bar fridge. Enough.

After calling room service to say her tray was ready, she put it on the floor outside the door and locked herself back in. All the lights off, she curled up on a chair near the window. This was a high floor overlooking the city lights. If she looked hard enough Charlotte could see the building where her office was. Once. Years of her professional life spent there as part of a small but dynamic group of practitioners. She was well paid. Most patients who came to her were from wealthy backgrounds. Politicians. Executives. Elite sports players. Every so often she took on a case free. One with a difference.

And it was one of those free cases which cost her everything.

Charlotte stared out across the city. If she'd refused to take Alison as a patient, she'd still be working there. Closer to Mum. Still well regarded by her peers. She'd made a good life from the shambles of her early years. Educated against the odds. Respected by people she admired. A nice enough place to live and money to save for the future. She'd hoarded the money knowing any future would be alone and she might as well have a decent sum for when she retired and bought a little place by the sea.

I was going to be alone for life.

She retrieved the wine bottle and refilled her glass. This hurt, delving into memories she'd worked hard to bury. The fears lurked like a shark circling beneath the surface.

Not the fear of retribution. That was done and behind her with a board disciplinary hearing that almost took her licence. She'd paid a high price for the mistake she made with Alison financially, professionally, and personally. But it was finished and Alison was out of her life.

The lingering fear was about her future. Some of Angelica's mental illnesses had strong genetic links. Charlotte had a high chance of inheriting them.

Trev changed everything. The moment she'd met him, her eyes red from crying and hair out of control from sleeping in her car, something shifted inside. The calm, assured, and firm police officer took stock of her state and helped her. He might have booked her for driving erratically or with a paper map in her hand but instead he made sure she was up to driving and led her to Palmerston House, the place she'd yet again not managed to find.

Enrol in a map-reading class, Charlie!

She smiled and sipped her wine, leaning back in her seat to stretch tired muscles. The police officer soon became a nuisance. He'd know when she was hiding something or was upset and try his best to help. No matter how many times she'd told herself there was nothing between them, it never rang true and he never believed it. Bit by bit he wore down her defences. Always gentle, respectful, and persistent. His patience was the key. And then Trev sacrificed his own happiness to give Charlotte a fresh start as well as help his mother. Unselfish was his middle name.

And selfish is yours.

Moving to Kingfisher Falls was as much to get distance from the man she was falling for as start over her life in new surroundings. It was time to stop expecting the worst and find out whether she inherited the gene for her mother's illness. One test and she'd have a better idea of her future.

Clouds scuttled across the sky and a flash of thunder startled Charlotte. There was so much to stop fearing. Storms. Tests. Commitment. Love.

———

She woke refreshed to a clear blue sky much later than usual. Whether it was the wine or the resolve to take the test, she'd slept well. There was a lingering memory of a dream. The bride in the clearing about to raise her veil. This time though the atmosphere was different. Not about a lost soul. Charlotte couldn't define it yet. The bride wasn't the victim. It was more personal.

A long shower and breakfast in the hotel restaurant kept her spirits high. As she ate eggs and toast, she made a list to buy and do today.

Rubbish bags

Gloves

Disinfectant

Clean out kitchen

Clean out bathroom

Check house for any paperwork or valuables

Charlotte laughed aloud at the last comment. Valuables were the last thing she expected to find. Angelica had always squandered every cent that came into the house and sold anything of value. She had no idea of what was important, collecting pebbles rather than money for them to eat and pay bills with. Charlotte found jobs while underage and often asked charities for help.

She tapped her fingertips on the table, then noticed and stopped. Getting worked up wasn't the object. There was a lot to do today and sitting here moping about the past was unhelpful. Rather than getting a second coffee, Charlotte took her list and went shopping.

The house was as bad as she remembered. With every window and the back door open, some of the awful odours lessened but she sprayed copious amounts of air freshener around before working in each room. She dug out a wheelie bin from behind the garage and left it at the back door, its lid open to throw things in as she went. Charlotte remembered paying a cleaner to go through the house a few days after her mother was committed but they'd not emptied the pantry or fridge, instead just turning it off and leaving food inside.

It took several attempts to clean everything out. She double-gloved her hands but still could barely touch what was once food. Throwing the whole fridge away would have been a better idea. After gagging twice, she found a clean cloth and wrapped it around her nose and mouth as a makeshift mask. The contents of the fridge in the bin, she sprayed vinegar throughout and wiped the shelves to get the worst of the mess off.

After such trauma, the pantry was less offensive and emptied in minutes. On a roll, Charlotte sped through the remainder of the kitchen then moved onto the laundry and bathroom. These were riddled with mould and after emptying the cupboards, she closed the door on each. She'd talk to a real estate agent and if they thought it worth marketing it to a family, Charlotte would pay a professional cleaner to come through.

She wheeled the bin to the kerb at the end of the driveway. Who knew when garbage pick-up was? Another problem to add to the list, along with finding someone to wheel it back in. With all these new homes along the street she didn't know anyone. The neighbours would probably rejoice to see the place demolished.

Another hour and Charlotte had sorted the rest of the house. None of the furniture was worth keeping. She'd packed old clothes into garbage bags and would drop them into charity bins. They were clean and in good condition but Angelica had dropped so much weight they'd not fit anymore. Shoes and just about all other items were only suitable for the bin. About to start on the remaining rooms she checked the time and groaned. She'd have to come back later to finish.

chapter
forty-two

Trev's morning was nothing short of busy. Up earlier than
planned thanks to the complaints from Mayhem that he was
neglected and dissatisfied with the new arrangements, he'd
let both cats out before making coffee. The quiet house
overnight was odd. After living alone for fifteen or so years,
he'd settled back into the routine at home as if he'd never
left. Having his mother around was nice. They were close
and he'd missed her more than he'd realised during his time
in Rivers End.

Over an indulgent breakfast of mushroom omelette with
toast and more coffee, he scrolled through emails from
Katrina. She had found relatives of Bryony Murdoch but not
managed to make contact yet. This was her first job today. A
second email put him on notice to be available for a talk with
Terrance once she'd got further information. A third email
went over some of the discussions she'd had with Bryce on
the way back to Kyneton. And a fourth to apologise for all
the emails made him grin.

In preparation for interviewing Terrance, he did a search
on him. He already knew the man was free of any criminal

charges from a recent background check. Now he was interested in filling in some information and sometimes the
internet was the best place to look.

His observations of Terrance over time revealed an ambitious and rude man, one who'd treated Trev's parents with
disrespect more than once. His conveyancing firm sponsored
the local cricket club where Graeme was active in coaching
so there'd been occasions where their paths had crossed.
Terrance wanted a trophy named after himself once and
Graeme stopped the committee from being brow-beaten
into complying.

"Probably never forgave you, Dad."

He made notes as he searched. Born in 1953. Married at
the age of forty-six. When did he divorce Bryony? Trev
frowned. He couldn't locate anything on Terrance's current
marital status. This was a red flag. One he'd check at the
station on the police database.

Terrance had run for mayor twice. He'd never got there
but stayed in the wings. He'd sold the conveyancing firm he
owned with Kevin a few years ago. From the look of it, he'd
spent most if not all his life in Kingfisher Falls, not even
leaving for higher education. He must have commuted to get
whatever qualifications a conveyancer needs.

Trev searched for images and more came up than he
expected. Headshots from various professional positions,
casual images at sporting events, an awards night with his
brother. The same photo was in the bookshop. He scrolled
down until only the occasional repeat of a photo appeared.
At the bottom, something made him click to the next page.

He didn't believe what he was seeing and enlarged the
image. A wedding. Terrance and Bryony. Not a brilliant
photograph but the first time he'd seen the missing woman.

So young. She was like a deer in headlights. Her arm was

gripped by Terrance as they stood on the top step of a church he recognised. Bryony was pretty with long dark hair in a mass of curls. He knew little about wedding dresses but hers was not unlike the one in the trunk. He made a note to speak to Concetta Bongiovanni again to see if this was one of her originals.

After printing out the image and saving the source, Trev washed up and made sure both cats were safely indoors again. Mayhem wanted to sit in the sun outside and objected to being picked up, hissing as his tail switched from side to side.

"Keep telling you, cat. You love me. You love Charlie too. Not just Mum."

Mayhem wasn't interested and took himself into Rosie's bedroom to sulk on her bed. Mellow followed Trev around until he left, purring with her tail high. Two different personalities but both adored their owner.

He walked to the station, preferring to leave his patrol car there most nights. Once he had his own place he'd revert to keeping it close, but it was a five-minute walk and gave his brain time to switch to work mode. Today they'd get closer. Katrina and Bryce were on the ball, hardworking detectives determined to solve the crime of Vi's murder. Evidence was starting to make an appearance thanks to their work and his.

If he didn't do anything else today, he would speak with Terrance Murdoch. Charlotte's unwavering belief in the man's guilt backed him. Her instincts were solid. Most likely a mix of her keen intellect and training combined to pick up little cues.

Last night he'd almost booked a flight to Brisbane. There was a lot more going on with Charlie than she admitted and he wanted to help her face whatever was upsetting her. He'd always sensed a dark history from her childhood. Her reluctance to discuss her mother was understandable if she was ashamed of Angelica's situation, but she wasn't that sort of woman. It ran deeper. The way she'd spoken of the family home told him as much.

His musings were put on hold as he unlocked the station. Katrina and Bryce arrived a moment later, in the middle of a heated discussion as they used the back door to come in.

"Jumping the gun will not help us with a conviction, Bryce. You know better."

"The man is a monster." Bryce followed Katrina in and slammed the door behind himself. "You know he's guilty of something so a proper interrogation—"

"Whatever you think it means, an interrogation does not include mishandling a suspect, Detective." Katrina dropped an armful of files onto the desk. "No more talk of it."

Bryce dropped into a chair, his face red. He crossed his arms and glared at the ceiling.

Trev ignored them both, filling the kettle and finding cups. He wasn't about to get in between partners disagreeing. Katrina might be senior, but Bryce was a lot older and used to doing things his way.

There was no more talk from the others until Trev placed coffee on their desk. "Morning."

Katrina glanced up from her files with a smile. "Morning, Trev. Have you got anything new?"

"Found a wedding photograph." He turned his computer on before picking up the printed image. "Raised some questions for me."

Bryce still wasn't talking but couldn't hide his curiosity at the photograph when Trev put it on their desk.

"Bryony!" Katrina peered at it. "Where did you find this?"

"Good old internet. Was searching Terrance Murdoch and this popped up. Going to ring Concetta and see if she sold her the dress. Looks like one of hers."

Now, Bryce turned to Trev, eyebrows raised. "Bit of a wedding dress connoisseur?"

"Hardly. Just observant. Anyway, I couldn't find anything about a divorce, so will check our database."

Trev returned to his desk. The computer was awake and he began a search which gave him nothing. "Can't find a divorce."

"Told you. He's a monster, Katrina. Terrance killed his under-age girlfriend then his wife. And I never said I'd hurt him."

From his tone, Bryce was both angry at Terrance and irritated Katrina thought badly of him, or at least that's how it sounded to Trev. Bryce probably blew off steam on the way down and she'd taken him seriously.

Katrina levelled a gaze at Trev. "Would you locate Mr Murdoch and request he attend an interview?" Then she looked at Bryce. "Will you lead the interview, please?"

For a moment, Trev thought Bryce might fall off his chair. But he nodded as his body relaxed. "Sure, boss."

With a small smile, Katrina stood and went to the whiteboard. "While you're collecting Terrance, Trev, we'll go over what we know and formulate some questions. Time to put the fear of God into this... man."

———

Like his brother, Terrance was not happy about being asked to attend the station. He complained all the way there, insisting there was nothing to discuss and pondering aloud whether to call his lawyer. Trev said little but took in the other man's nervous tapping of fingers on his leg and constant checking of his watch. Once they arrived, Terrance stalled at the door.

"You're sure this is necessary?"

"Best to have a chat, don't you think? Saves us getting warrants and the like." Trev opened the door. "Please, go ahead."

Terrance scuttled inside and Trev closed and locked the door. If anyone needed him, there was a bell and phone number. He didn't want anyone walking in on this.

"Mr Murdoch, thanks for helping us out." Bryce held out a hand, which Terrance ignored. The corner of Bryce's mouth twitched upwards. Whatever Katrina had said in Trev's absence, Bryce was back to normal. "Please, take a seat." He gestured to a chair in front of the whiteboard, which had been turned to present a blank side. Three other chairs faced the whiteboard. Interesting.

With a grunt, Terrance settled onto the chair. Katrina sat in the middle chair, Trev assumed he was meant to take the one on the left, and Bryce stood behind the one on the right.

"Don't have a lot of time." Terrance glared from one to the other.

"Council business?" Bryce asked. "Saturday usually a busy day?"

"Family things."

"Of course. No intention to keep you from your family. You have one brother. Kevin?"

"Yes."

"Sisters?"

"Nope."

"Parents alive?"

"Course not. I'm almost seventy."

"Right." Bryce kept his voice friendly. "Children? Grand-children?"

"Never had them."

"Wife?"

The word hung in the air. A twitch began near Terrance's

left eye. His mouth opened, closed, and opened again as he folded his arms.

"Once."

Bryce dropped onto his seat, legs apart, elbows on knees so he leaned toward Terrance. He waited. There was no response from the other man.

This could take a while.

The twitch got faster.

"Are you divorced or widowed, Mr Murdoch?" Katrina asked.

He started, his eyes shifting to her face.

"Divorced."

"Oh, Terrance." Bryce kept his tone friendly. "There's no record of a divorce being initiated nor completed. Can you explain this? Or are you lying?"

Terrance uncrossed his arms and rested his hands on his knees. "Of course not. Misunderstood. I'm separated. Have been for more than a decade. Think of myself as divorced."

"We need the contact details for your wife. Bryony."

"I wouldn't know where to start looking for that ungrateful little—"

"That's quite enough, Mr Murdoch." Katrina cut him off. "Relatives? Last known address. Mobile phone number. Bank account details. Anything at all will assist."

Terrance pushed himself to his feet. "Ask my lawyer. He tried to find her to begin divorce proceedings."

"Sit, mate." Bryce hadn't moved. He looked ready to spring into action but didn't have to when Terrance sank back on his seat. "Thanks. We'll speak to your lawyer. Tell us about the day Bryony left."

"What good is it to bring up the past? I loved my wife, treated her like a queen. Talking about it won't bring her back." His face was red.

Trev considered getting him some water but thought

better of it. If Bryce had intended to stir the man up, he was doing a good job.

"Did you know she planned on leaving that day?" Bryce continued.

"No. Was a shock to come home and find a note."

"Which said what?"

"I don't remember. Something about needing to find herself. Thought she'd come back one day once she grew up."

From the corner of his eye Trev saw Bryce's hands ball into fists. "Why marry someone so much younger than you? Someone you've just said wasn't grown up."

Terrance straightened his back as a sneer lifted one side of his mouth. "My preferences in women are nothing to do with you. She was of legal age."

"And what about Vi Ackerman. She was under age."

With a hiss, Terrance stood, his chair falling backwards. "How dare you!"

Bryce was on his feet and Trev followed, taking a step forward in case he needed to get between them. But Katrina, who remained seated, caught his eye with a small smile as though she knew Bryce was in control. Trev planted his feet and watched.

"Mr Murdoch, your wife left you with no explanation or forwarding details. You've never seen or heard from her again. Why have you not reported her as missing?"

"Look, Officer whatever, I'm well regarded in this town and don't need to answer to you. What happened back then was private and is over. She wanted to go. I let her. End of story. And as for the Ackerman girl. Why would I be involved with her when I was already married to a beautiful young woman?" He straightened his jacket. "Are you arresting me?"

Katrina rose and opened the door. "Leading Senior Constable Sibbritt, would you drive Mr Murdoch home and obtain the details of his lawyer? That way we will follow up on any contact details for Mrs Murdoch."

"Mr Murdoch, this way." Trev went through the door first so he could unlock the front door. He glanced back. Bryce was in Terrance's face. "We're not arresting you. Not yet."

Terrance reddened even more and hurried to catch Trev. This would be an interesting drive.

chapter
forty-three

As it was, Terrance said nothing on the short drive to his house. He lived in a large two-level house on an acre in a leafy street a block or two behind Octavia Morris' home.

Trev nosed the patrol car down a long driveway. "How long have you lived here? Beautiful place."

"Ask the clairvoyant."

"It wasn't a leading question. Haven't been up this area for a long time and was admiring the trees out the front."

Terrance undid his seat belt as Trev stopped. "More than ten years. Couldn't bear being in the other place without Bryony if you must know." He dropped a business card on the seat as he dragged himself out of the car and slammed the door.

"Bye," Trev said aloud.

There was a car parked in front of the garage. Kevin's car. Trev turned the patrol car around, keeping an eye in his rear vision mirror as he took his time. Terrance was greeted at the front door by Kevin and they stood watching Trev. Something was wrong here. Something was being kept hidden and these two brothers were colluding.

Back at the station he walked in on another argument but

this was one sided and not between the detectives. Mr Reynolds was on the public side of the counter, arms and voice raised at Katrina, who took notes, her face impassive.

"Him. It was him did it." Mr Reynolds pointed at Trev as he went through the second door, latching it behind himself.

"Mr Reynolds. What's wrong?"

"He's making a complaint about you." The corners of Katrina's mouth lifted a fraction.

"Sir? I thought we parted on good terms."

"Ya know nothing. Where's ma daughter?"

Katrina motioned for Trev to leave them. "Mr Reynolds, as we discussed, Leading Senior Constable Sibbritt enquired with you about Cynthia's whereabouts as part of an investigation."

Mr Reynolds voice was audible in the station office. Bryce was pouring coffee, grinning. "You bad police officer. Upsetting such a sweet old man. Welcome to the club."

A few minutes later, the noise stopped and Katrina returned. "Coffee. Double thanks."

Trev made her one. "What's his problem?"

"He wants to know where Cynthia is. Figured we'd look for her and wants to contact her again. I made it clear that isn't happening so now he is going to take it further."

"Media?"

"Nah. Phoning the commissioner's office. Considering he began the conversation by saying police are the foot soldiers of Satan, I'm surprised he'd bother." Katrina took her seat now that the chairs were back in their usual places.

"Any comments from Murdoch?" Bryce asked.

"Silence until we got to his place. I asked how long he'd lived there and he made some smart comment before saying more than ten years and something about not bearing his old place with Bryony gone. Kevin was waiting for him." Trev sat at his own desk, pleased with the relative quiet. "They stood there watching me leave. Creepy."

The whiteboard was back to normal. Bryce underlined Bryony's name. "The only next of kin we've located haven't seen or heard from Bryony since before she left Terrance. Unless his lawyer has some other way to find her, we need to treat her as a missing person."

Trev held up the card. "Want me to call him? I know him. Pretty easy going considering the company he keeps."

"Probably not working today." Katrina said.

He reached for the phone. "Got a mobile number."

Ten minutes later he hung up and took his notepad across to the other desk. Katrina and Bryce had a map open between them covering the bushland behind Charlotte's home. They looked up.

"Right. So, he'd already heard from Terrance and gave me what he knows. Which isn't a lot. Bryony left no forwarding address and her mobile phone stayed at the house. He sent a letter to her next of kin, same ones we have. No response. She had no bank account in her name to his knowledge and from the day she left withdrew no funds from the joint account." He glanced at his notes. "What he did provide was the name of the hotel she worked at when she and Terrance met. Long shot but I'll follow it up."

Bryce and Katrina exchanged a glance before she spoke. "Thinking about taking a look around the area of the grave. Getting the dog squad out if nothing jumps out at us. Two missing young women is not a coincidence, not when you consider what we know."

Trev nodded. "Now?"

"Might grab lunch and drive up there. These maps are detailed enough to point to a couple of suitable locations." Bryce's face was grim. "Suitable for graves."

A chill went down Trev's spine.

———

Angelica was brighter today. She'd applied makeup and brushed her hair, and even smiled when Charlotte arrived.

"Mum, you look nice!" Charlotte kissed her cheek and sat opposite at the small table. There was half a sandwich on the plate, pushed away by Angelica. "Not hungry?"

"Hate bread. Makes me ill."

"Oh, dear, that's no good. What kind of lunches would you prefer?"

"A salad. Or soup. And nothing for breakfast. Can't stomach food in the morning which you know quite well so stop offering it to me."

"Mum, I don't make your food now, remember? But I'll mention it to Maggie and see what lovely options she can come up with. What about a smoothie for breakfast? Some fruit and yoghurt all whizzed up?" With the medication, Angelica needed something in the morning.

Charlotte reached across the table and took her mother's hand. "Would you like another walk around the lake?"

A few minutes later, they wandered along the short path to the water's edge. Charlotte had her arm through her mother's and for a while, it was like any other mother and daughter walking together. They followed a track along the lake, commenting on the birdlife and pleasant weather this afternoon. On the opposite side were timber benches, and they stopped for a rest.

The lake was pretty under a clear sky. A group of ducks swam their way.

"I might have a swim." Angelica announced.

"Sounds nice. But not in the lake, Mum. It is muddy and the ducks wouldn't like it at all."

Angelica laughed and Charlotte joined in. When her mother was calm and coherent, she was the sweetest person to be around. In the months she'd cared for her at her own place, she'd seen a funny and thoughtful side of her mother. Not at all like the woman who'd raised her, if one could call it raising.

But the laughter died away and Angelica pointed toward the buildings opposite. "What are those?"

Charlotte sighed inside. One step forward. "We're at Lakeview. This is where you live now. Think about the lovely people who also live here. Maggie. Who else do you know there?"

"Nobody. I don't live here, Charlotte. I live in my house. With you, and Dad, and Zoe."

Zoe?

Something flashed in Charlotte's mind. Some deep, long buried memory just out of reach.

A smile. But no face.

A cuddle. But no arms.

"I want to go there now."

Charlotte blinked. "Mum? Who is Zoe?"

Angelica played with her wedding ring, spinning it around and round. She hummed something tuneless.

Zoe. Z. Why did the name sound familiar yet there were no real memories to draw on? Charlotte must have been too young. The Christmas cards began when she was two. The photograph in the album showed her as a toddler. The photo album…

From her handbag, Charlotte dug it out. Her mother was off in her own world, but Charlotte found the photograph of Angelica holding her on the steps of the house. She held it in front of her mother. "Mum? Look at this. You look so pretty here."

After a moment, Angelica turned her eyes to the photograph and a smile formed. "Yes. My house. And Dad. And my girls."

"Girls?"

"You were so little and so cute. And Zoe didn't like having her photo taken so she always took the camera. Such a pity though. I don't remember what she looks like now."

Charlotte dropped the album. Her hands shook as she picked it up and the strangest sensation filled her. She struggled to identify it as it raged from her face to her toes, draining the blood away. Charlotte stared at her hands holding the album. They were white. The chattering of her teeth alerted her to shock. She had to get a grip. Not caring if anyone saw, she lay on the grass and stared at the sky.

"One, two, breath. One, two, slower. Breath."

Over and over she chanted the mantra until the panic subsided and control returned. She sat up. Angelica stared at her.

"Mum. Tell me now. Who is Zoe?"

"You know who she is. Stop playing games."

"No. I don't remember." Her voice went up. "Who is Zoe?"

With a roll of her eyes, Angelica stood. "Oh my goodness, Charlotte. She's your sister."

chapter
forty-four

Sister.

Sister.

Sister...

Charlotte had waited only until she saw the orderly hurrying toward them after phoning to say she had to leave urgently. Once he was close enough, she sprinted away. Her mother called after her but she had to run. Find her car. Drive away. Her heartbeat thundered in her ears as she wound her way back to the carpark.

She couldn't remember which part of the key opened the hire car. Her handbag fell to the ground spewing the contents everywhere and she threw herself onto her knees to collect everything. The key fell under the car and she reached beneath, grasping for it as tears flooded her eyes. Her fingertips touched metal and she sank further, dropping her forehead onto the tarmac and letting the tears turn to sobs.

It might have been one minute or ten until she forced herself to move. She couldn't be found out here like this. Charlotte checked she had everything back in her bag, clicked every button on the key until the car lights flashed, then hauled herself up.

Inside the car she put her seatbelt on and started the motor, brushing tears away so she could see the dashboard enough to drive. Taking it slow, she eased the car along the driveway and out onto the road. Within a moment she knew she was putting herself and others at risk and found a wide shoulder to pull over. Car safely parked, she turned off the ignition and let the sobs wrack her body.

The ringing of her phone eventually broke through the tears. She couldn't talk to anyone. What if it was Trev? He couldn't know she'd fallen apart. But the interruption was enough for her to find her way out of the distress. Ignoring the phone as it began again, Charlotte leaned back in her seat and focused on breathing until the tears stopped. She waited for her heartbeat to slow and the shaking to leave her hands before reaching for a packet of tissues in her bag. The phone wasn't ringing but there were two missed call messages from Lakeview Heights. Maggie's direct number.

Not certain she was ready to speak, she hesitated. Maggie must wonder what happened. Keeping communication lines open was in Angelica's best interests so Charlotte steeled herself and returned the call.

"Doctor Dean, are you alright?" Maggie answered. "We're all so concerned."

"Sorry. Mum told me...um, she dropped a bombshell on me. I need to sort it in my head before talking about it."

"Of course. Oh my goodness, it must have been a shock for you to leave so quickly."

Shock is an understatement.

"Is Mum okay?" Charlotte wasn't sure she cared. How could her own mother keep something so important from her for so long?

"She did ask if you were going to get your father. It never changes, I'm afraid."

Where is he? Is Zoe with him?

Charlotte had never heard from her father since he left. Not directly. Only comments made by Angelica when he paid for the house and signed it over. And her undying belief he would be back.

"Charlotte? Do you want to come and talk to me, or I can find you a quiet room with some coffee?"

Put me away. That's what will happen if I have it. Her disease.

She shook her head to dispel the negative thoughts. "I can't. But thank you. Such a kind offer."

"Will you be back? Before you go home, that is."

"Of course. I have to finish up at the house so I can put it on the market but will drive back out tomorrow. Thanks for everything. I have to go."

She hung up before she could take back what was probably a lie. Charlotte never wanted to see her mother again.

———

Back at the hotel, Charlotte headed for the shower. Her face was streaked from tears and her eyes were red and puffy. The water on her head was good and as the steam rose around her, she built a mental box. One for the shock and pain and loss all churning inside. Bit by bit, as water poured down her face and body, she filed all the hurt away for another time. When she was home, in a better place emotionally, then she'd open the box and deal with the complicated mix of feelings.

Once she was dry again and dressed, she made coffee and opened her laptop. She had the rest of today and a full day tomorrow in Brisbane.

A simple search of the name Zoe Dean returned hundreds of images which Charlotte scoured, narrowing it to women in their late forties. She figured Zoe must have been at least seventeen to leave home which made her around fifteen years older. Mum must have been in her teens. It occurred to Charlotte she didn't know when her parents married.

So many missing pieces.

Knowing her family history had never been a priority. Dad left when she was a pre-teen. She remembered him, or at least, flashes about him. His leaving calmed the house. The yelling stopped. And the door slamming and people coming and going in the middle of the night. For a short time, Angelica had showered Charlotte with love and gifts to make up for his absence. It didn't last long.

The images blurred together. Had she even seen Zoe after she left? She was unlikely to have any strong memories of a sibling if the last interaction was as a two-year-old. But there were feelings bubbling beneath the surface. The smile with no face.

This wasn't going to work. Perhaps something was left in the house with some clues. Even in the box she had at home.

Charlotte shut the laptop and stood. Why had she never opened any of the letters in the box on the bed at home? They might be from Zoe or reference her, or be about Dad.

She paced the room.

When she'd received the box late last year from Lakeview Care, she'd left it untouched for months, apart from returning time and again to the Christmas cards. She'd thought it was more of Angelica's nonsensical collection of random items. But there was a handful of sealed, addressed, stamped envelopes. She had to wait now.

At the window Charlotte halted, leaning her head against the glass. If she went to the house she'd run out of daylight before finishing the job. Without the power on it was best left until morning. She'd go through every drawer and cupboard and make sure nothing important was overlooked. Angelica's habit of hiding everything made this harder than it needed to be.

Something played at the back of her mind, a vague thought about the house. She shook her head. She'd missed lunch, again. Her stomach needed filling and she needed fresh air. An early dinner along the river was the most appealing idea she'd had in ages.

chapter
forty-five

Trev waded across a shallow part of the river, boots in hand and pants rolled up. The water was cold and the rocks underfoot not the most pleasant to walk on. He'd spent the past hour or so on the opposite side from where it snaked behind the bushland to near the top of the falls.

Bryce stood with his arms crossed watching Trev. Katrina was on the phone a little further away.

"Isn't there a bridge somewhere?" Bryce asked with a grin. "Or do you like splashing around like a kid."

With a glare as an answer, Trev climbed onto the bank and wiped his feet on the grass.

Katrina hung up and joined them as he forced still-wet feet into socks. "Right. First light we'll have the dog squad here for a decent look around."

Several hours searching hadn't uncovered another grave, but Bryce carried a collection of items they'd found, each in their own evidence bag. With dusk closing in, there was nothing more to do now than examine these back at the station and make plans for tomorrow.

Trev's boots back on, he led the way along the river until turning onto the track to cut back through the bush.

"Wouldn't want to be out here alone at night." Bryce commented.

"Scared of the dark?" Katrina asked.

"Seems a lot of evil goes on out here."

Trev glanced back at Bryce. "Growing up none of us would wander around here whether night or day. I didn't think much of it until Charlie said it gave her the shivers. And from personal experience, it isn't the nicest place to spend a night."

At a fork, a small sign was almost obscured by branches of large tree fern. On a tall, narrow pole, it blended in with the foliage with a green background and faded white writing. Trev swept the fronds to one side. "Anyone got a torch? Bit hard to read."

Katrina flashed the one from her phone onto it, squinting at the letters. "No trespassing. Um…think then it says private property, yes."

"Private? Doesn't council own it?" Bryce peered over Katrina's shoulder. "Phone number at the bottom. I'll take a pic." He did so and Trev replaced the frond. "Hmm. Mobile. Shall we call it?" Without waiting for consensus, he dialled, putting the call onto speaker mode.

It rang a few times then went to voicemail. "You've reached Kevin Murdoch. Leave a message."

Katrina shook her head and Bryce disconnected. They all stared at the phone.

"Let me get this straight," Trev said. "We've been told this is council land. In our interview with Kevin he said nothing about owning the land, assuming it is the case."

"What else would it be?" Katrina turned the light off her phone.

"He and Terrance were conveyancers. Perhaps they acted on behalf of the land owners. Regardless, even the council office said nothing to make us suspect it was privately owned." Trev glanced at the sky, which was hard to see through the canopy but looked almost dark. He got going again. "Can I take a look at the map you had earlier?"

———

"I reckon only some of it is private." Trev poured over the map. "See this line here?" He traced a faint, broken marker. "Almost goes through the middle of the forest. Everything back of it, including the other side of the river, looks like council property. But forward, as far as the fence line behind the bookshop, might be someone else's."

Katrina nodded. "How odd though. If you own land, why not fence or otherwise make it obvious it is private?"

Bryce's phone rang. "Detective Senior Constable Davis." One side of his mouth lifted. "Ah. Mr Murdoch."

Trev and Katrina exchanged a glance.

"Yes, yes I did call your number." He perched on the edge of the desk. "No. I didn't leave a message."

You're enjoying this.

Kevin's voice was raised on the other end as Bryce held the phone away from his ear. When there was silence, he put it back. "Done? Excellent. Such a nice afternoon, I went for a walk." He pulled the phone from his ear with a wide grin and mouthed, "he's a bit cross".

Katrina held her hand for the phone but Bryce ignored it. "Dude. Kev. Conversations go two ways. So, I was out walking with my friends not far from where the grave was found and came across a sign with your phone number on it. Didn't know it was your number, so it looks like we'll need another chat with—hello?"

"Making friends, Bryce?" Katrina laughed.

"Thought so. He was irate I didn't leave a message. And doesn't seem inclined to drop by."

"Time to go home anyway." Katrina reached for her coat. "Trev, thanks for the help. Do you want to meet us at the entrance to the flower trail at seven?"

"Who calls it a flower trail?" Bryce collected his keys and wallet from the desk.

"Charlie does. See you tomorrow."

"I'll be there." Trev locked the back door after them. He needed to shop for dinner and then, if she was around, he'd catch up with Charlotte for a phone call.

————

An hour later, he'd fed the cats and put his own dinner in the oven. He'd messaged Charlie and got a reply.

Having dinner in the city. Can I call a bit later?

He'd sent back a thumbs up. Good on her going out tonight.

Laptop open on the dining table, he grabbed a beer and resumed his search for more information on Bryony. Earlier he'd phoned the hotel where she'd once worked, but nobody there could help. They suggested he email the information through and they'd go back through their employment records. He did this first and sent it.

He took his notepad out and flicked back a few pages to the notes about the day Bryony disappeared. Fourteenth of June 2002. Mid-afternoon. She'd said goodbye to Concetta and left to wait for someone to take her to the railway station. It was out of town and up a steep hill past the sports grounds.

"So, you walk from your house-" Where was it? He made a note to look it up tomorrow. "To the bridal shop. Then where. Did you go to someone's home who drove you to the station? But who?"

Did she rush to pack and leave?

Trev searched for the weather on the day. Although most of the month was warm enough, the day in question was cold. Not icy, but cold enough for a coat. Next, he looked for a train timetable. This was a dead end so he made another note, this time to contact VLine for their old records.

The timer buzzed on the oven. He'd made a pizza, or at least, topped a premade base. Nothing as wonderful as the one Charlie made the other day, but easy and quick.

The cats followed him from the kitchen back to the dining table, the one indoors as a chill had fallen with night. "None of this is for either of you, so stop staring."

After eating he closed the laptop with a sigh. Not much more information was forthcoming. He washed up and made a coffee, glancing at his watch. Did Charlie think he might already be asleep? Unless she was. He texted her to say he was up for a chat no matter how late, then yawned.

A message beeped.

Sorry. Really tired. Can we talk tomorrow?

He wanted to hear her voice, even for a moment, to say goodnight. Instead, he replied.

Sure thing. Early start anyway. Sleep tight.

"What's going on, sweetheart?" He turned off the lights and headed to bed.

chapter
forty-six

The police tape is finally gone but imprints of their boots remain.

Around the resting place, soil is still displaced. How dare they touch this?

Now it must be mended. Even if it takes all night until this is complete.

Why were those cops intruding on the bush? This must stop, the endless assault on this land. Although...they found some of what was lost. If this leads them to him, then so be it. But revenge is not their job. They can have him. Later.

The soil is level again. And now the flowers to replace those cast aside with no thought for their meaning. The seedlings must grow fast. They must, despite the season. Winter is so close but my love will help them flower.

She has gone away. Charlotte.

He hasn't begun to suffer enough. It must begin before Charlotte returns. Before she sees through her pain to mine.

Done.

The sacred place is restored.

One final touch.

A new wreath.

chapter
forty-seven

Charlotte stared at her phone after sending the text message. She'd been back in the hotel room for a while but couldn't bring herself to call Trev. He'd wonder what was wrong, but how could she hear his warm and caring voice and not fall into a heap again? He'd want to help and was too far away.

Perhaps she could phone anyway. Just to ask where the investigation was going. And how Mayhem and Mellow were. And had he heard from Rosie yet. Not that Rosie should be doing anything other than enjoying her time with Lewis.

She turned the phone off to reduce the temptation. In the morning she'd talk to him. Her walk along the river had turned into a sprint when rain appeared from nowhere. Dinner was nothing more than a bucket of chips from a street vendor after not being able to settle on a place to eat. Her mind kept going back to Zoe and she'd returned to the hotel soaked and sad.

After drying off and wrapping herself in the fluffy hotel dressing gown, she'd curled up on the chair near the window and made a list.

1. *Search for info on Dad*
2. *Check house for any hiding places for documents etc*
3. *Finish cleaning*
4. *Depending on #2, follow leads or go to Lakeview Care*

Beyond that she had no idea. She had to see Angelica again. And do it without the emotion. She'd write down questions and go through them with her. Then say goodbye and leave. Whatever she discovered between now and then would help her decide if she ever returned.

Some things are too hard to forgive.

She pushed herself to her feet. Forgiving wasn't the real issue. It was working out why both her parents, and her sister, kept her in the dark. And that's what really hurt.

———

Charlotte followed the bride along the flower trail. Long, red hair beneath a veil was a beacon through the trees as the path twisted and turned.

The bride was at the clearing when Charlotte caught up, her hand in the empty grave. Like Kevin's had been that night. In her other hand she held a bouquet. The same purple flowers from the trail.

"Let me help." Charlotte reached out a hand and the bride drifted away. "Wait... wait for me."

Stumbling through the forest, over logs and around bushes, Charlotte lost sight of the bride.

She looked down. Flowers. Then more. She followed until reaching the entrance to the path. The light was on in the bedroom of the apartment overlooking the bush.

Someone stood there. The bride. She raised her veil.

Charlotte sat bolt upright, covers falling away and eyes wide.

"Harmony?"

Her heart pounded. There was nothing frightening about the dream, if you weren't scared of brides floating around in dark bushland near a grave and being in your home, but it left Charlotte unsettled. She climbed out of bed, reaching for the dressing gown from its end.

It was light outside. Early morning over Brisbane with no sign of last night's clouds. She filled the kettle and turned it on, then drank a glass of water. By now the panic was gone but the clarity remained.

Why was Harmony the bride? Perhaps because of her odd comment the other day about Charlotte and her sister.

"What do you know about me?"

It had to be a guess. Unless Harmony had some connection with her family, how would she know what Charlotte didn't.

Her fingers loosened and the glass almost fell. Harmony wasn't... Zoe? Tears welled as the reality set in. Harmony was about Charlotte's age. Not fifteen or so years older. And they looked nothing alike. Even hair colour aside, their features were not similar in any way.

With a sigh, Charlotte poured a coffee and took it to the window. The city was waking as the sun rose higher. She needed to call Trev.

Her phone was still off and she turned it back on. Sipping her coffee, she screwed her nose up at the bitter taste. She'd get ready for the day then have breakfast downstairs where the coffee was decent.

A message beeped. Trev, wishing her good morning. He'd sent it an hour ago. There was a second message.

Off to meet the dog squad. Will have phone but may be tied up.

Dog squad? Something must have happened yesterday for the police to take such a big step. Charlotte made a beeline for the shower.

Breakfast was a welcome interruption to thoughts racing around her head. The coffee was nice and she had two cups as she went over her plans for the day. Rather than spending time on her laptop searching for information about her father, she'd decided to take care of the house first. Get it done and then she'd never have to step foot in there again.

She unclenched her hands. This had to stop, all the stress and reactive responses. There was a lot to mentally unpack but it must wait. Get done what was essential. Go home. Back to Kingfisher Falls and the life she loved.

———

The house was as unwelcoming as ever but now, with her mind set on discovery, Charlotte ignored the assault on her emotions when she opened the front door. The first hour was spent on completing the cleaning. At least, the best she could. The bin was full now and she left the cleaning items in the laundry.

She opened a bottle of water she'd bought on the way here and sipped. The house wasn't large with two bedrooms, living room and small dining room. She'd already checked the bathroom, kitchen, and laundry, even standing on a chair to look on top of the cabinets.

The living room had nothing to offer. Nor did the dining room. Her bedroom was empty. She knew she'd left nothing behind in there because she'd moved out long ago. But she still checked under the bed and in the cupboard in case Angelica had decided to use the room. A waste of time.

As soon as she walked into her mother's bedroom, she remembered what had nagged away at her. The large envelope left on the dressing table from the other day. Charlotte sat on the bed and got straight up. The mattress smelled awful. Back in the dining room, she perched on a chair and opened the envelope. It belonged to Angelica, as the word *Mine* scrawled on the front reminded her, but for once Charlotte had no scruples about looking.

She tipped the contents onto the table. There were several pages cut from a magazine, folded into a messy square. A handful of shiny pebbles. The stub of a ticket from a movie or something. Old as anything. A worn paperback novel. A western. Inside, Angelica's handwriting in red over every page. One word here, a paragraph there, all negative statements about the story.

There was a photocopy of a doctor's report discussing Angelica's genetic mental illnesses.

This could be about you soon.

And a crumpled-up sheet of thin, faded cream writing paper. Charlotte flattened it. Not Angelica's handwriting. No address or date.

Ange,

Stop contacting me.

You have everything now. The house is yours. Paid for.

I've signed your lawyer's papers about Charlotte and I'll abide by their terms although it breaks my heart.

You've said you'll get help and you'd better. That little girl deserves more than a life looking after a crazy woman even if she loves you like a mother.

I'm moving again and this time you won't find me. I got a new life and refuse to let you ruin yet another day of it.

Glen.

Hands shaking so much the words on the paper blurred, Charlotte gulped. She released the letter and it floated to the floor. It was dark in the room. Darker than she'd realised. The air was thick and hard to breath.

How odd.

She reached for the letter. Her hand was a long way away.

I'm going to faint.

As a roar filled her ears, Charlotte grasped the table to control the slide onto the floor and laid on her side. Dad had left her, knowing Angelica was not suited to parenting. He'd abandoned her and signed away his rights.

chapter
forty-eight

Charlotte sat on the front step. She was still shaky and wanted to finish her water before attempting to reach the car. The house was locked up. What she wanted to take with her was in her backpack.

What you need to take. Not want.

The letter. She was going to ask her mother about it. She had to get more information if she was to find her father. And she wanted to with every fibre of her being. But why would he leave her with Angelica? Why not take her as well? He must have taken Zoe… but it made no sense. Zoe left when she was two. Dad left much later. Years later.

"Excuse me. Are you moving in?"

A woman smiled at Charlotte from the end of the path. She carried a baby and a bundle of mail.

"Oh. Hello, no. Just cleaning it up in there."

"Thank goodness. It really needs some attention."

"I'm so sorry." Charlotte stood, careful to take it slow. No spinning head this time. She followed the path to the woman. "My mother owns the house. I've been away for a long time."

"You are Charlotte?"

"I am. Hello, sweetie." The baby's hand was waving up and down. "I can't believe how much the street has changed."

"So, what will you do? Are you moving back?"

"No. My life is a long way from here and my mother won't be returning. I'll put it on the market."

"My brother is in real estate so I can give you his number. He found our place and sold a few of the others along here."

"That sounds wonderful, thank you. How do you know my name... sorry... ?"

The woman smiled again. "I'm Mel. Someone was looking for you a few months ago. My husband talked to them and took their number."

Zoe? Dad?

"Do you know who?"

Mel shook her head. "If I give you my number can you send me a message? Phone's inside somewhere. I'll get my husband to locate the details and let you know. And send you my brother's number."

Mel spent a few more minutes talking, then offered to return the bin to the back garden after it was emptied, which Charlotte accepted with thanks. It was a better way to finish the visit than she'd expected. Mel's baby was cute and laughed at Charlotte which left her with a tug of emotion she couldn't quite explain.

Back in her car, she checked her phone, hands still a little shaky. Two missed calls from Trev. What was she to do now? The doctor's report was a stark reminder of her possible future. Probable. She knew the odds of inheriting it and they weren't in her favour. All this time in Kingfisher Falls she'd forced the truth away. In the warmth of Trev's devotion, she'd lost sight of the shadows which surrounded her.

No future. No children to pass this onto. No relationships. Not ones involving love and commitment. A bitter taste filled Charlotte's mouth and she drank the rest of her bottled water to force it down.

She tapped out a text message.

Sorry, tied up with Mum for the day. Talk later.

With all her heart, Charlotte wished she'd never come back to Brisbane.

———

"That's the fiftieth time you've checked your phone today." Bryce patted Trev on the shoulder as he passed. "Gotta love a romance."

"Very funny. I have a community to watch out for and my phone is currently the only way they can reach me."

"Yeah. Community called Charlotte."

Trev didn't bother responding. The dog squad were wrapping up their search after hours of criss-crossing bush-land and working around the grave site.

Once again the clearing was surrounded by police tape after the curious discovery of newly planted flowers and a fresh wreath. Katrina was there now with forensics.

After the dogs were returned to their respective vans, Bryce consulted with their handlers. A message beeped on Trev's phone and relief filled him seeing Charlie's name come up. His heart sunk a little seeing the message but she needed this time to work through issues up there. Tonight, they'd talk. He missed her.

He pocketed the phone and headed to where Bryce was. The dog squad vehicles were parked along the fence behind the bookshop and the handlers, with Bryce, were gazing in the direction of the far exit. Three men approached down the middle of the track. Terrance, Kevin, and Jonas. This should prove interesting.

"Ignore them." Bryce said to the other officers as Trev walked by. "Let Trev sort them out."

Happy to oblige, Trev went to meet them.

"Gentlemen. How can I assist?" He planted himself between the two groups.

"You're trespassing." Jonas gestured at the dog squad. "If they've been in the forest, they should have got permission."

"From whom exactly?"

Terrance and Kevin shared a glance.

Jonas pushed out his chest. "From council. You can't keep digging around there without us supervising. And dogs? Come on, who knows what parasites they'll leave there."

"Parasites?"

"Flea-ridden mongrels."

The expression on Terrance's face as he looked in the direction of the vehicles told Trev they were about to be joined by the handlers of said flea-ridden mongrels. The alarm in his eyes was almost comical as he stepped behind his brother.

"Want to say that again?" One of the handlers, a lean but muscular man towered over Jonas, close but not touching him. "Those dogs are members of the police force and deserve your respect and thanks."

Jonas glared up at him but kept his mouth shut.

Bryce joined them. "What are you really concerned about?" He addressed this to Terrance, who shrank back even more. "That grave is on your land, right? Not council property at all but yours and your brother's."

"What if it is?" Kevin spoke up. "Not illegal to own land."

"Why not come forward at the time. Show some compassion for the young woman buried there and help us instead of putting up roadblocks." Trev had so many questions. "For that matter, what are you all doing here? This is an active crime scene."

Jonas and Kevin exchanged a confused look but Terrance dropped his head. He was a coward, in Trev's opinion, and was his candidate as killer.

"How is it still active, Trevor? Didn't your people finish up and remove the tape the other day, along with the... remains." Kevin asked.

"There's been new information and new activity around the grave site. We'll have uniformed officers here shortly and this area will remain closed to you and anyone else for the foreseeable future."

"We'll see about that." Kevin didn't sound upset or worried. If anything, his expression was cocky, in keeping with his tone of voice. "My legal team may have something to say about it."

Are you a sociopath?

Trev made a mental note to talk to Charlotte about the possibility once she was home. These brothers were opposites. Both full of bluff, but that was where it ended. Overconfidence from one and fearfulness from the other. Made for interesting observations.

Katrina emerged from the flower trail and caught Trev's eye.

"We'd appreciate your co-operation in keeping this area available for our investigation and without the media being involved. This is to help our community, Jonas. Your future constituents." Trev said, wanting this wrapped up.

Jonas' mouth tightened but he nodded. He turned and headed back the way he'd come, Terrance on his heels. Kevin shook his head but followed.

"More chance of finding fleas on him than—" The handler began.

"Walk away." Bryce grinned to soften the words. "That person has been seen at night near the grave site so if he returns, it might be to encounter a canine arrest."

Trev left them to it and caught up with Katrina, who'd gone back down the trail. "Sorry. Thought we might have a small issue there."

"Noticed a little angst from the handlers," she said.

"What do you need?"

Katrina stopped to face Trev and gestured toward the clearing. "I'm worried. There's more going on here than meets the eye."

He agreed. "We need to find out where the flowers are coming from. If I'm right, that wreath was made of lavender and roses, same as the first one."

"And the seedlings are the same species as those along here. These." She leaned down to pick a flower. "Or pretty similar. Too soon to tell if the colour is identical and I'm no botanist, but it looks the same."

"Want me to chase it up?"

"Please." Katrina's forehead was creased. "I had decided to put uniforms out here to stop unwanted visitors, but I'm wondering if a stakeout would be better. I'd like to know who is tending that grave site."

chapter
forty-nine

Charlotte had sat in her car outside Lakeview Care for an hour. She'd written questions and torn them up. Reread the letter from her father a dozen times. Even gone through the novel with its red scrawl to see if there was some cryptic message in there. Nothing. She had the photo album and went through every photograph but only the one on the front steps of the house made any sense. The park was a random image. Her mother's was a nice picture but she was so young. Before family. And the remaining photos were all landscape shots from around Queensland. No people to check out.

She looked at the time and sighed. It was now or leave it until tomorrow. Although Maggie would let her visit almost any time, it wasn't fair to put everyone's routines out. Charlotte gathered herself.

Be calm, Charlie. Get what you need and stay above the emotion.

Easier said than done. The act of walking to Angelica's room was enough to send her heart rate soaring.

"Is that you, Charlotte?" Her mother's voice had a frail quality that tugged at Charlotte despite everything.

She pushed the door open. "Hi, Mum. How are you doing today?"

Angelica sat in an armchair near the window. The room was large enough for a small table for two, a couple of armchairs, the bed, and a set of drawers. A flat screen TV was on one wall. There was a small kitchen. The window, like most windows here, overlooked the lake and afternoon sunlight warmed the room. Charlotte took the other armchair, placing her backpack on the floor beside it.

"I am very tired. Where did you go?" Angelica said.

"Back to my hotel. I'm sorry you are feeling tired."

"Do you want a cup of tea?"

Did she not remember talking about Zoe and upsetting me?

"Sure, but I'll make it. You enjoy the nice sunshine."

Charlotte made them tea. The kitchen was little more than a sink, fridge, kettle, and cooktop. One of those induction stoves which prevented fires and accidental burns. Lakeview Care had different levels of facilities for the changing needs of their patients. She found a little tin of biscuits and took those with her, placing them and then the cups on a side table.

"Who sent the biscuits? They look nice."

"Why don't you ask what you really want to." Angelica's eyes were clear, sharp, and her stare unnerved Charlotte.

I need to find out. I deserve the truth.

After a sip of tea to calm her nerves, Charlotte nodded. "I do have some questions, Mum. Yesterday was the first time you've ever talked about Zoe being my sister. I mean, I must have known at some point but I was so little when she left."

If the comment bothered Angelica it didn't show. She bit into a biscuit.

Charlotte continued. "I'd like to find her. Would you know where I can start looking?"

Angelica raised her eyebrows and finished her mouthful. Charlotte's hands were shaking so she put the cup down.

"You want to see Zoe after all this time and expect me to know where to find her? Let me tell you, that girl packed a bag one day when I was out and left a note. She'd found herself a man and was leaving to marry him without so much as an introduction let alone invitation to the wedding."

"She was old enough?"

"Zoe was almost eighteen. She was born when I was sixteen and I raised her alone for the first few years. Didn't know that, did you?" Angelica's face reddened. "But she took herself off without even a thank you for everything I did for her. Never forgot you though, her precious little sister. Christmas cards for years and I kept them all."

Until I was eleven.

"Mum, I have the cards. Well, I have cards until I was eleven so were there more?"

"Stopped. We moved, don't you remember? Down to New South Wales in the horrible place with the vegetable gardens and fruit trees."

Yes. Charlotte remembered. Near the sea, the place was overgrown but so wonderful. Always something to pluck from the ground or off a tree to eat. Hiding places where she could daydream. They'd lived there such a short time and Charlotte never wanted to leave. But back to the weatherboard house they'd gone.

"I do remember. Did you never hear from her again? Even the name of her husband?"

Lips tight, Angelica turned her head to look out of the window. Or at her reflection. Charlotte knew the signs. Enough of that subject. Push too hard and the shutters would come down.

"I've got a little vegetable garden where I live now, Mum. And some herbs growing on my balcony."

"Why would I care? You left me. Everyone does. Zoe did. And your father."

"But you kept in touch with him. He paid off the house and gave it to you, and before you get cross with me, I know this because you told me, ages ago. And I've got all the legal papers because—"

Angelica's head swung back. "Because you control my life! Isn't that right, Miss clever doctor? I raised you and fed you and gave you everything so you could pursue your dreams which include putting me away for life. Putting your own mother away!"

Nausea gripped Charlotte and her fingers circled her wrist feeling for the bracelet she used to wear. Not finding it reminded her she didn't need it. She was stronger than this. Her mother's eyes darted from side to side and her hands tapped her legs and her stomach. Charlotte leaned over and took her hands.

"Mum. Stop it. We're just talking."

"I want your father. When is he picking me up?"

Charlotte saw something in Angelica's eyes. She was making this up, this response. Falling back on the manipulation. Well, not today. "He isn't. But it would mean a lot to me to know where he is. How I can locate him."

"Now you want to see him as well as Zoe. Not content with getting rid of me. Now you want them back."

"I didn't get rid of you, Mum. We tried all kinds of ways for you to manage on your own in the house. You have a better life here. Maggie and her team look after you."

With sudden strength, Angelica pushed Charlotte's hands away and stood. "I want to leave. I want to go home. Make it happen, Charlotte, if you care at all for me."

On her feet as well, Charlotte tried to put her hand on Angelica's arm but it was shrugged off. "Zoe, and Dad. Please tell me how to find them."

With a sneer, Angelica grabbed Charlotte's shoulder. "I will never tell you. And one day soon, you'll be like me. This will be you in a prison with nobody to love you and nobody to care. Go back to your precious new life and stay there. Until you lose your mind."

Charlotte stumbled back with a gasp, freeing herself from her mother's grip. She scooped up her backpack and made for the door, unable to breath or speak.

"You don't deserve to be happy." Angelica hissed.

Door open, she glanced back. Angelica was slumped in her chair, head in her hands. Charlotte closed the door and fled.

chapter
fifty

What is going on, Charlie?

Trev's attempt to reach her before nightfall was a fail. Just voicemail, where he left a message. She'd not replied to an earlier text message when he'd been at the house feeding the cats so he'd waited until heading off to take the first shift at the clearing to ring. He'd called as he drove down.

Once parked, he tapped on his phone again.

Hope all is okay with your mother. Am doing a stakeout so phone is on silent but message if you feel like it.

Hopefully, she wasn't getting tired of his messages. But they'd not spoken since yesterday morning and that wasn't like her at all.

Katrina's idea of keeping an eye on the area was a good one, but not easy to facilitate. A shortage of local police made it a one person at a time job. There wasn't an ideal place to watch from. If he stayed in the car he'd be obvious. Had Charlotte been home, he might have used her third bedroom with its great aspect. As it was, he chose the tree Charlotte showed him the other day and settled against the trunk. This gave a perfect view of the clearing but offered little protection from the elements.

He'd spent much of the afternoon trying to find out where the wreath originated. Not one florist within half an hour's drive knew anything about it. He'd phoned and then sent a photograph to each. The consensus was the wreath was a professional quality arrangement with a unique combination of flowers. One florist pointed out the roses were not ones used by them as they were short stemmed and a hard to find, old variety.

This made him revisit the idea of looking closer to home.

Harmony's House of Mystique was closed. It always was. At least, every time he'd walked past. He knew Rosie had been inside at least a few times, so perhaps Harmony only allowed people in by appointment.

Trev tapped on the door. Unless she was charging a lot of money for each appointment, or seeing far more people than he'd heard about, how was she managing to stay open. Or not open. She'd offered free first consultations to anyone who stood still long enough, so maybe that translated into return business. He tapped again.

The black curtain drew back and then the door unlocked. Harmony stepped outside and pulled the door closed. "The sign says closed."

"I know. But I'm not here as a client, Miss Montgomery."

"Then why. I am busy."

"I'm interested in your lavender. The armful you had the other day."

Her eyes widened.

"Do you remember if there was more left in the garden?"

"I don't."

"What about roses?"

"What about them?"

Was she always so difficult?

"Did you notice roses in Octavia's garden whilst you were misappropriating the lavender?"

"Are you trying to trap me into admitting a crime?"

"Have you committed one?"

Her chin lifted. "There are things I understand and you should know about. Men with motives to hide their crimes. Cowardice and bravado. A patriarchal conspiracy of silence."

Terrance and Kevin fitted the bill.

"Anyone in particular?"

Harmony opened the door and stepped inside. "If you find the roses, you will be led to the right one."

"Harmony, wait please."

But the door closed and the lock turned.

Now, as Trev shoved cold hands into pockets, he wished he'd had more time to pursue the roses. Terrance owned a large property with lots of plants and would have access to Octavia's garden if need be. One way or another, tomorrow he'd find out where these roses came from. One step closer to an arrest.

———

Charlotte shivered. She'd shivered for most of the afternoon since leaving Lakeview Care and it didn't matter that she was inside a plane. Even the coffee she nestled in her hands gave little warm. It was a cold from within. Deep within.

She didn't quite remember how she got from Lakeview Care to the hotel, but once back there opened her laptop to find a flight home. Being in Brisbane any longer was not possible. No more visits to her mother or the house. No walk through the city. She would never return. Not ever.

She managed to book a flight and wasted no time getting to the airport. She would lose money over the abrupt departure from the hotel and cancelled flight tomorrow, as well as one day less for the car hire, but nothing mattered except getting back to Kingfisher Falls. And once she got there?

That question was still unanswered after she'd boarded the plane which was now an hour away from Melbourne.

Go back to your precious new life and stay there. Until you lose your mind. You don't deserve to be happy.

She clenched her hands around the coffee cup. Angelica's words wouldn't leave her in peace. Did Charlotte have the right to continue her relationship with Trev? As unspoken as their connection was, there was nothing pretend about it. The feelings grew every day and she'd allowed herself to get too close. Even believe they might be together. Marry.

Charlotte pushed the cup away and closed her eyes. Her heart was breaking. The little town was her home like no other in her life. The security of friends and community held her in its arms. But she had to leave.

No. You need to be tested, Charlie.

Her eyes opened as turbulence rocked the plane.

You need the truth.

The doctor's report on her mother discussed the high risk of genetic influence on one of her conditions. And there was something Charlotte had never seen before. Mention of Angelica's mother and sister also having the same diseases. Although Charlotte was not a specialist in the genetics of mental health, she knew there were multiple causes and multiple genes involved. There wasn't a simple blood test to prove she had the factors, more a series of tests to look for possible markers.

With her mother, grandmother and aunt affected, what chance did she have of being free of the genes? Her anxiety already worried her, as so many diseases crossed over. But she also knew that her environment—her awful childhood and ongoing issues with her mother—were part of that.

She gripped the armrests as the turbulence increased. If she wasn't on a plane she'd be running. Her flight instinct was in full force and her mind raced. This wasn't the time to make decisions. See what is in the box at home. Look for any reasons to stay.

Even just one.

chapter
fifty-one

Trev wanted nothing more than a hot shower and coffee. Another couple of hours and Bryce would take over. Moonlight filtered through the trees onto the grave but apart from the odd rabbit, nothing else moved. Well, the trees were as the wind picked up. The air felt as though rain might be heading this way.

In between everything else today, he'd catalogued the items found in the forest yesterday when he, Bryce, and Katrina searched.

Most of them offered little to be interested about. An old watch, not working. An empty purse, the kind a child would carry. Assorted bits and pieces more rubbish than of value. There were two unusual finds. One was an earring. It was distinctive being the clip-on type rather than for pierced ears. Trev had spotted it almost at the river's edge, its vivid purple stone attracting his attention despite being partly in the ground. It looked cheap, as if from a discount store, but was tarnished from the weather. The other was a medallion of sorts. Bryce found it by stepping on it and a quick clean didn't show much of the engraving.

Something about the medallion nagged at Trev. He'd seen

it before, or one similar. It reminded him of the cricket club awards given out each year but the size was different. Most though, the earring played on his mind. If Vi Ackerman was part of a strict religion, she may have been forbidden pierced ears and used only clip-on ones when out with her friends. Or her boyfriend. He'd taken photos and measurements of it before dusting for prints. A partial on the clip surprised him. Now the wait for a match.

He took a good look around. Still nothing. Risking the light being seen, he checked his phone. No messages. No missed calls.

———

Getting her car out of the carpark at the airport was easier than getting it in there. Charlotte went through the motions of following the signs and taking extra care on the dark road to Sunbury, wary of kangaroos. She was focused, but felt hollow.

The freeway was quiet but it was late now. Over to the west, clouds loomed with occasional glimpses of the moon. It was so cold here compared to Brisbane and there was rain in the air. Sleep called but she had much to do first. And as tired as her body was, sleep might be impossible with so much going around her brain.

As she'd waited at the airport for the bus to the carpark, she'd checked her phone. Another message from Trev. She should respond. Tell him she was home early. But then he'd want to see her or talk on the phone and she could do neither.

Tonight, she had one job to do. Go through the box in the back bedroom. Pull it apart properly, open every envelope, look for anything which might change her mind.

And if you find nothing?

It hurt too much to consider. At least she hadn't bought the bookshop yet. Rosie would find someone else to take it over. Someone with commitment and courage.

Driving down the hill to the town was the first good thing to happen today. The streets were deserted and the shops looked pretty with their windows lit. Except the bookshop. Rosie must have left the lights off seeing as nobody would be checking in for a few days. Charlotte turned into the driveway with a sense of relief. After locking it into the garage, she took her suitcase and backpack up the steps. Now, the dread was setting in.

―――――

Trev's phone vibrated and he grabbed it out, less careful than before. It was only Bryce, waiting at the edge of the bushland to swap over. He made his way to him, pleased to stretch cramped muscles. Bed sounded nice.

The clouds were heavy as he emerged from the canopy.

"Gonna rain, Trev." Bryce didn't look dressed for a night in the open. "We'll do this another time. Come better prepared."

"Charlie will be home tomorrow so we can ask if she minds us taking over that back bedroom. Won't give us full view, but more than on the ground."

"Yeah. Might work. I'll take a walk around anyway before the rain. Make sure nobody was waiting for you to leave." He trudged into the depths of the forest. "Send a search party if you don't see me tomorrow."

With a grin, Trev turned the other way. He'd parked up past the bookshop, over a rise so nobody would see the patrol car close to the bushland and get put off. And he'd come through Charlotte's gate, leaving it unlocked. She'd given the police permission to access the garage so he still had keys to that and the gate.

Tomorrow he'd bring her flowers. Something to show her he understood how hard this weekend was for her and how proud he was. Just not roses or lavender.

Halfway across the track behind the fence he stopped. The light was on in the apartment. In the back bedroom. No movement. No sign of anything other than the light. Surely it hadn't been on all these days? Wouldn't he have noticed it? The hairs went up on the back of his arms. In a moment he was through the gate, locking it and pocketing the keys. Still no movement up there. He phoned Charlotte's number despite the late hour. It rang until going to voicemail.

"Charlie, when you get this please ring me back. No matter the time. There's something important I need to ask."

As he stepped forward the motion sensor floodlight came on. There was nothing out of place. The garden seemed okay. The steps were empty. Nevertheless, he was going to check this wasn't a break in.

———

Charlotte's hand hovered over the phone as it rang. She sat on the floor of the bedroom sorting the contents of the box. She'd forgotten she'd emptied it onto the bed the other day to give Trev the box. She needed to do this now, without interruption. The ringing stopped and she opened yet another envelope.

So far, she'd found three letters from her father to her mother. Stuff she didn't need or want to know about their personal lives. Some shocked her with candid descriptions of intimacy. They've been separated. A trial separation. But clearly not ready to divorce. She tried to put them in date order but some envelopes were hard to read the stamp. The only mention of Zoe so far was a comment about her changing her mind about the marriage.

Another letter. This time from her mother to her father. More recent and in an unaddressed enveloped. It talked about Charlotte being at university. Complaining she never saw her daughter because all she did was work and study.

"What else could I do?"

The remainder of the letter deteriorated into name calling and accusations. Charlotte's heart was heavy. This was the mental illness talking. What she might have ahead of her. Even with treatment, it wasn't fair or right to inflict upon another human. Trev's message came through and she turned the phone off.

———

A look in the garage surprised Trev. Charlotte wasn't due home until late tomorrow, yet here was her car. Something was wrong on a grand scale. She'd arrived back while he was out on surveillance. Why wouldn't she answer his calls or messages? Had the visit to her mother been so bad she'd shut down? He knew so little of her past but enough about Charlie to see through her efforts to hide the deep-seated pain.

He ran up the steps and knocked.

She must be sleeping. Left a light on and fallen asleep. It was after midnight and if her day was stressful plus the flight and then the drive… he should let her be tonight.

Trev tapped again. She'd ignored him before when under pressure, not wanting to bring her problems to him.

But we're past that now.

Were they?

He dialled again.

———

Charlotte opened another envelope. She'd heard Trev knock but wasn't going to open the door. Not yet. Not until she knew what to do. Her heart ached to tell him everything but her mind refused to let him close. The need to protect him was overwhelming.

This letter was different. It took her a moment to absorb that this was a legal document to her parents. From an adoption agency.

She scanned it, her jaw dropping.

This couldn't be right.

Her name…theirs.

It couldn't be right.

———

Trev got to the bottom of the steps and put his phone away. The rain was here. Fitting. Charlotte's phone was off or she was ignoring him. Either way, he wasn't wanted here tonight. Maybe forever.

He headed along the driveway. Her life in Brisbane was where she'd had her practice. Had being back there reminded her of what she'd walked away from? Was she back to pack and leave?

Don't run again, Charlie.

She'd left Rivers End when their relationship showed signs of heating up. He'd enabled it, but if he'd not introduced her to the town and his mother then the past few months would never have happened.

Hair plastered to his head, he wiped rain from his eyes as he reached the street. If her mother needed her then she had to tell him so. He'd get a transfer. He'd go anywhere for her. Anywhere, anytime.

I love you.

Words never whispered to her and possibly never to be said aloud.

Rain trickled down his neck beneath the jacket. Get home. Shower. Sleep. Think it through tomorrow. But what if she left again? What if she left tonight?

Trev stopped at the top of the rise and turned around.

There was a figure near the bookshop. No. Running toward him, long hair swinging in a ponytail. He blinked to clear the rain from his eyes.

"Trev, wait!"

Her voice reached him through the downpour and now, his legs had a mind of their own.

Charlotte wore a short-sleeved shirt and pants and was soaking wet but she didn't seem aware as she ran toward him.

He opened his arms and she threw herself against him.

Safe. I've got you.

Where were his words? He couldn't say anything.

She was speaking to his chest and he loosened his arms so she could repeat it. The smile on her face filled her eyes and his heart with a love he'd never imagined.

"It's okay. It's okay." Her words tumbled out and he leaned down to hear her better. "I'm not her. I'm not going to be her. Trev. Oh, Trev. I'm adopted."

chapter
fifty-two

Charlotte took the first shower at Trev's insistence, then wrapped in her dressing gown, laughed, and commanded him to go and have his. She threw on fresh clothes and started coffee.

Overcome with happiness, she ran to the middle of the living room and spun around. Nothing would take this moment away. The future was clear for whatever she wanted to make of it.

"Charlie."

Trev was in the doorway, drying his hair. He'd brought the patrol car down to the apartment and grabbed the overnight bag he kept in it. Now he wore a T-shirt and jeans and bare feet. For some reason, that made Charlotte even happier and she twirled around again.

In an instant he was with her, the towel tossed over the back of the sofa. He wrapped her in his arms and she was no longer cold. No longer afraid. A bubble of joy had eradicated the stone of sadness she was used to living with. She turned her face up to his and lifted herself on her toes to kiss him.

The coffee machine interrupted them and she danced

away with a grin. "I haven't had a decent coffee in days. And you've been on a stakeout."

"So, you do read my messages?"

"Sorry." Her hands dropped to her sides. "I really am. I—"

"You are making coffee, not apologising. I was teasing." Trev picked up the towel. "Back in a min."

She poured two cups and then he was back, taking them both and leading to the sofa. "Trev, I thought I'd lost everything good in my life."

"Which is why we talk. Communicate." He handed her one cup and joined her. "Didn't psychiatry school teach you that?"

"Well, yes. But when it is your own world crumbling…" She stared at the coffee.

"Drink. You are clearly caffeine deprived. And once you've had your cup, you can climb into bed and get some overdue sleep."

Charlotte gazed at him. There were worry lines around his eyes. Did she cause them?

He smiled. "There are two cats waiting for me and one in particular will make my life unbearable if he doesn't get what he wants."

"There's so much to say. And so much to catch up on."

"Over breakfast if you feel up to coming to the house. That's if you'd like me to cook for you."

Charlotte burst into tears. She had no idea where they'd come from or why. Her coffee cup vanished from her hand and was replaced with Trev's fingers.

"Shh… it's okay, sweetheart." He reached for a tissue from the box on the coffee table and dabbed at her eyes. "I promise my cooking isn't bad."

"No… that isn't…" Her words wouldn't work so she gave in and let him dry her face as the tears slowed.

He handed her back her cup. "Okay?"

"Thank you. Those were… happy tears."

"Glad it wasn't the breakfast. Tell me why being adopted has changed everything." He settled back but kept one of her hands in his. "I was sure you were about to tell me you'd decided to move back to Brisbane."

She shook her head. "Never. I never want to go back. And I will tell you why but not tonight." No more negativity tonight. Not one bit. "Being adopted means I no longer have a mother, grandmother and aunt with certain diseases linked by genes. Rather than making every decision based on a metaphorical swinging axe over my head, I am suddenly free. And I'm not saying there might not be other issues instead, but I am free of the ones I fear the most." She gripped his hand. "I am free, Trev."

He lifted her hand and kissed her fingers. "You always were, Charlie. None of us know what lies ahead which makes living every day to the fullest the best gift we can give ourselves."

Trev was right. And she was on a new path and it included living her life in ways she'd never believed possible.

———

The power of this freedom flowed into a deep sleep. Charlotte woke as dawn broke through the last of the rain clouds. Her heart beat in steady rhythm to her breathing. Physical tiredness lingered after such a late night, yet her mind burst with plans and a need for action. As she dressed, she caught sight of herself in the mirror. Smiling.

She walked to Rosie's house after Trev messaged to say he was about to cook pancakes. The way her stomach was growling, she hoped he made lots. The sun warmed her back and she touched the leaves of a glistening tree as she passed, laughing as rain droplets filled her palm. Everything was fresh and new and… good. Until she'd read that decree last night, Charlotte had no idea of the weight she'd carried for so long.

Mellow met her at the front door, which was ajar. Charlotte tapped. "I hope there's a handsome police officer in here, not a burglar."

"No burglars today." Trev's voice was rich with warmth from the direction of the kitchen.

How could one piece of paper make such a difference?

She closed the door and followed Mellow to the kitchen. Trev wore an apron over his uniform. A steaming plate of pancakes was on the counter and he was putting finishing touches to a platter.

He grinned at her and washed his hands. Before he could dry them, she slipped against his chest, her arms winding around his neck and on her toes to kiss him. His lips were soft and firm all at once. A moment or two later, she released him. "Hi."

Trev blinked. "Anytime you want, you may greet me this way."

She went to the other side of the counter. "Even at the station?"

"Yup."

"Even if you are arresting a bad guy?"

"Might be a little trickier but we can give it a go. Would you care to take those to the outdoor table? Too nice a morning to be inside."

He followed with the platter. "Coffee on its way so you start."

She would wait. But it didn't stop her taking photos of the delectable array of offerings. Sliced fresh peaches, berries, and kiwifruit. Three small bowls. One had crushed chocolate, another whipped cream, and the third maple syrup. If he was about to propose then she was saying yes!

"So… meets your approval?"

"Yes!" Charlotte giggled, then forced her face to be serious. "Sorry, I think I need food."

"Then eat, woman. Photos are nice but they don't fill your stomach."

Over the meal, Trev updated Charlotte on recent events. Dog squad. The ownership of the bushland. The items discovered. And the grave.

"Someone refilled the grave with the pile of dirt, then planted seedlings of the same flowers along the trail, and left a fresh wreath?"

He nodded and speared the last blueberry on his plate.

"We need to find who it is," she said.

"Would love to. Hence the attempted stakeout."

"I think you're wasting your time, but go ahead and use the apartment window if you think it will help."

"Why are we wasting our time?" He picked up his coffee cup. "You saw Kevin out there."

"But Kevin isn't doing this. It is too personal. A serial killer might act this way, but so might a loved one. A family member. I know you haven't found Bryony yet but nor is there evidence she's a victim of whoever killed Vi."

"If it is a family member, then who? Her parents and brother are in South Australia."

"Wasn't there a little sister?"

"Much younger. I'd have to check with Katrina as she followed up on the Ackerman's with further questions."

"How much younger?"

Trev shook his head. "Can't remember, sorry. Why?"

"If she was very young, she may not even remember Vi." A stab of loss touched Charlotte. Where was Zoe?

"Charlotte?" Trev put his hand over hers. His eyes were serious, worried.

"All good. Part of what we will talk about another time."

"Hm. Had enough to eat? More coffee?" He stood and began clearing plates and Charlotte helped.

"Not one more morsel. But seriously, I had no idea…"

"What? That a man can cook?"

"No."

"That a police officer can cook?"

"Stop teasing."

"Never." He carried his collection back to the kitchen. "I like hearing you laugh."

So did Charlotte. She liked it a lot.

———

"What's different, mate? Did you win the lottery?" Bryce sat opposite Trev with a take away coffee. Where he'd found it on the Monday of a long weekend was anyone's guess, but he'd thought to bring another for Trev.

"Better."

"Charlotte's back?"

"No comment." Trev grinned. He couldn't help himself. Since that moment in the rain when she'd chased after him, Trev's heart was singing. And he wanted to dance, as Charlie had in the living room, spinning around with her arms wide open and her eyes alight.

"Good. Now we can get her onto the case with us. Get some answers."

Trev felt his mouth drop open. Bryce was steadfast in his refusal to allow anyone other than a sanctioned party help on any investigation.

"What?" Bryce said. "She's still a psychiatrist so let's put her to work. Get some insight into whoever is revisiting that grave."

"Speaking of insight, do you remember if Katrina tracked down Vi's sister?"

Bryce raised both eyebrows. "Does this have anything to do with the grave. Ah. You've already discussed this with Detective Charlotte."

Not about to admit to anything, Trev sipped some coffee. Much nicer than the station stuff.

"Fine. We'll pretend you didn't. The sister, according to her parents, moved to Europe about ten years ago to be part of some missionary arm of their religion. Heard from her a year ago but that's about it."

Another dead end.

"I'm keen to find the roses from the wreath." Trev had already told Bryce about the outcome of his talk to different florists. "Thought I'd look around Octavia Morris' garden seeing as nobody is living there right now. And Terrance's place."

"Good luck with that."

"Was thinking about his previous home. The one where he and Bryony lived."

Bryce sat back. "What do you know about it?"

"Turns out he still owns it. Rents it out but empty for the past year or so. Wants too much for it up here, I'd guess. Interesting he hasn't sold it rather than leave it vacant."

"Which makes me very interested in having a look around. Not sure he'll go along with it though."

The station phone rang and Bryce took the call. He stared at Trev as he listened, then wrote an address. "So, breaking glass and a flashlight from inside. Just before daylight. And what are your contact details? Name—hello?" He replaced the receiver, his expression disbelieving.

"Know this address?" He held up the notepad.

"The house we just discussed. Terrance's."

Bryce pushed back his chair. "Lady heard breaking glass from it as she walked her dog past this morning. Saw a light inside."

"Didn't think to call then?" Trev picked up his keys. "No idea who called?"

"None at all. But now we magically have our reason to visit his property without a warrant."

chapter fifty-three

Charlotte hung out the last of her washing and gazed at her garden. How much she loved the vegetables and herbs growing alongside flowers. Why had Angelica been so against the place they moved to for those few months, where a family could live an almost fully self-sustainable life? And yet nothing in their garden at the weatherboard house. Just lawn and a couple of scrawny bushes. It made no sense.

And it doesn't matter.

Angelica's problems were no longer Charlotte's. She'd still consult on her care if required and take on the job of selling the house and setting up finances so Angelica had no future expenses to worry about, but the lifetime of connection through blood was severed.

She had a lot to work through. Finding her own therapist was on her new to-do list. Hopefully she could find one close by and able to help her come to terms with the past. Emotions were tricky beasts.

Back upstairs, she spent some time cleaning the apartment. Windows and sliding door open, she let the fresh air in to clear out a slight mustiness for it being shut up for a few days. If the police were planning to use the back bedroom tonight to watch the forest, she wanted everything as nice as possible. Clean towels in the bathroom. The back bedroom tidied up so only the furniture was in there. She'd already moved the contents of the box to the second bedroom and would revisit it later.

As lunch time approached, she checked the fridge and screwed up her face. Next to nothing as usual. Whether there was company tonight or not, she had to remedy this. Collecting some shopping bags, Charlotte headed out.

On her way home, laden with shopping, she came across Harmony. The other woman stood outside the bookshop, moving from foot to foot as though impatient. When she saw Charlotte, something like relief crossed her face.

"Hello, Harmony. You okay?"

"I knew you'd return early from your trip."

"Just like you knew I wouldn't find a sister I didn't know I had. I'm anxious to discuss that more." Charlotte put the shopping bags down.

"This is important, you being here now."

"Why?"

"To help find the killer. Before he kills again."

A chill swept through Charlotte. Harmony's eyes were serious. "Would you like to come upstairs? I can make some coffee and—"

"No. No I can't." Harmony grabbed Charlotte's arms. "Listen to me. The killer is a man with two homes. A man whose own wife disappeared. And he keeps the wedding veil of his first victim as a trophy."

"Let me call Trev. Please, he'll want to speak to you about this."

Harmony shook her head. "Look for the veil and you'll find the killer." She released Charlotte, spun around, and ran toward the town.

"Wait, Harmony…"

The woman wasn't turning back.

How does she know this? Or even guess at it?

Charlotte picked up the shopping bags and took them upstairs. She sent a message to Trev for him to call when he could and unpacked as she waited. Harmony stumped her. Second sight, clairvoyance, however it was categorised, didn't exist. Yet Harmony knew Charlotte had a sister before she did.

What if it did exist?

Charlotte was sensitive to the environment, she'd always been. Her reaction to the bushland long before finding the grave was unexplainable. A sense of foreboding with no basis. Was it possible some people were even more connected to the world around them? To the point of knowing things they couldn't?

She jumped as the phone rang and shook her head at herself as she answered. "Hi. Thanks for calling back so fast."

"Everything okay?" Trev said. He sounded as though he was outdoors.

"I just had an interesting, well, weird, conversation with Harmony."

"Harmony?"

Charlotte wandered to the back bedroom. "Apart from some other odd things, she said she's glad I'm home to help stop the killer before he kills again. That he has two homes and his wife disappeared. It sounds as though she knows something about Terrance."

There was a long exhale on the other end of the phone.

"Trev, the thing that really got me is she said he kept the veil as a trophy."

"What veil?"

"Presumably, one matching the wedding dress." There'd been a veil in her dreams. "Can you call Concetta and ask?"

"I will. Are you at home?"

"Just unpacked some shopping. Will there be a stakeout tonight?"

"Not sure. We have a lead. Can I pick you up and get some professional advice at the station? Bryce's idea."

Charlotte grinned. "Well, if Bryce asked…"

"I'll be there in ten."

"I'll be waiting."

———

Bryce unlocked a floor safe and extracted a series of large envelopes. "Enjoy the break from all this intrigue, Charlotte?"

"Nope. Nothing beats a good mystery." Her eyes had gone straight to the whiteboard when Trev ushered her in but she wasn't quite confident enough to make her interest obvious, so sat at his desk. A few names had jumped out at her. Vi Ackerman. Terrance Murdoch. Bryony Murdoch.

"Trev and I thought we'd get your opinion on a couple of things, if it isn't an imposition." Bryce pulled up a chair at the end of the desk so that the three of them formed a triangle. He opened the first envelope. "As long as you're comfortable with it."

"I'll do my best."

He slid out a sealed evidence bag. "Crime Scene Services can't get here until tomorrow and anyway, I'd like fresh eyes. And your expert opinion on a person of interest."

Charlotte glanced at Trev, who winked.

Bryce put the bag in front of her. "You can handle the bag but not open it."

She picked it up. "Cheap earring. Pretty colour. Clip on. Oh. You know, some of the fringe religions forbid pierced ears. Look at the pattern though. A flower. Bit like a daisy. Only one?"

Trev cleared his voice as his eyes met Bryce's. She'd nailed something.

"Found this near the river."

"The river?"

"About a hundred metres from the clearing. Where it runs behind the bulk of the bushland before winding to the hills."

Charlotte peered at it, holding it up to see better. "Did you clean it?"

"No. All I did was dust it and got a partial."

"It looks oldish, like nineties oldish. And the style. Why?"

Bryce reached for the bag and put it back in the envelope. "We found this a couple of days ago, before getting the dog squad in." He opened another envelope and passed Charlotte the evidence bag from it. "This one was found this morning."

It was the matching earring. Or something very close, although soil clung to it.

"Charlie, this one was in a garden bed beneath a rose bush." Trev leaned forward. "Both wreaths included a rose variety which several florists have assured me is not common. Some sort of heirloom type. Bryce and I had reason to visit a property earlier and spotted the rose bed. An empty rose bed. Petals and some foliage were scattered about but what looked like five plants were pulled out of the ground. Roots and all."

"How awful. But what does that have to do with this?"

"Lots of displaced soil. This must have been under the roses and lifted with their roots."

One earring discovered close to the grave of a young woman who fitted the profile to wear it. Its partner buried for years beneath a rose whose flowers may have formed a recent wreath on the grave.

"Whose property?" Charlotte knew. She was certain. "Is it Terrance's?" She passed the bag to Bryce. "Did he know about the wreath?"

"The media managed to get a photo of the first one so yeah, he may have seen it. And we were investigating a report of suspicious activity on Terrance's property. The one where he lived with Bryony."

"The killer is a man with two homes."

Bryce's eyes widened. "Sorry?"

"I saw Harmony earlier and she said that. And that his wife disappeared."

"Specific. Who is this Harmony Montgomery?" Bryce took his chair back to his own desk. "What else?"

"That he keeps the wedding veil of his victim as a trophy."

"Trev, chase up the bridal shop lady please."

"On it."

Charlotte got up and headed to the whiteboard. Neither man stopped her. She read everything. Where there were dead-ends. Where people were accounted for. Question marks next to names. Bryony's name.

"Could Harmony be Bryony? I think she's too young but she wears so much exotic makeup."

"Why though?" Bryce asked.

"Revenge. Setting up Terrance if she knew something about his past. Didn't she leave him after receiving a phone call about something he did?" Charlotte swung around. "What if she found out about Vi?"

Trev and Bryce looked at her.

"Imagine it. You are much younger than your husband. Things aren't what you expected and you are isolated from your family. No car. No personal bank account." Charlotte wrapped her arms around herself. "One day you get a phone call that scares you. Your husband was involved with another woman the very same year he married you. A woman who is missing." Her eyes went to Trev and she swallowed as her emotions bubbled up. "What would you do?"

"What I'm going to do is say to not make this personal,

Charlie." Trev was with her in a couple of strides. "I can hear the stress in your voice."

"Part of the package." She managed a smile. If he hugged her, she'd cry.

"Are you okay?" Trev spoke quietly, his eyes intense. "I need to call Concetta."

"I'm fine so go and call. The sooner we find the veil, the sooner we find the killer."

The words were stuck in her head. Did Harmony know something or was this all an elaborate game to get new customers?

chapter
fifty-four

The seedlings weren't faring well. Charlotte was in the clearing with Trev after Bryce had asked her opinion on Terrance.

"But you need to remember I'm not a profiler, and this is my opinion only." She'd reminded them. "What would be helpful is a look at the grave area."

So here they were. There was a uniformed officer keeping an eye on the taped area, and Trev told him to take a lunch break.

"Whoever planted the seedlings took great care, but I think it's the wrong time of the year to plant asters. Certainly with next to no sunshine in this area. And don't give me that look, Trevor. I've been reading up on them since finding the flower trail."

He ran his finger across his lips like a zip but his eyes sparkled.

Back to work, Charlotte stared at the grave site. "Where is the wreath?"

"CSS took it. It was laid in the same spot as the previous one. Looked almost the same."

"Was there lavender growing in Terrance's garden? His old place?"

"None. But we haven't got onto his current residence yet. There is some in Octavia's garden though."

"Can we go there next?"

"Can't really just wander in without a reason."

"We should at least drive there and see if a reason presents itself," Charlotte suggested. "As far as Terrance and this grave goes… I don't believe he did this. Even though the seedlings aren't thriving, they are planted to grow into the same perfect covering of purple of their predecessors. Somebody took great care with this. Replacing the soil for a start. Nothing left on the ground of the rich black dirt dug up by police."

"Some killers create shrines."

"True. If it is Terrance, then you'd find traces of the soil on his clothes, surely. He'd need to kneel to do this."

Trev had a thoughtful expression on his face. Charlotte let him ponder. She got her phone out and searched for information about asters. As she'd thought, the little plants would struggle to take hold unless they got some sunlight and warmer days.

A message popped up on her phone. It was from a private number and had a photo attached.

"We need a reason to search Terrance's properties," Trev said. "A random earring in the ground doesn't tie him to Vi Ackerman."

"You sure about that?" Charlotte turned the phone for him to see the image. It was a colour photograph of a young woman with long brown hair tied back in a ponytail and a big smile on a pretty face. "I've never seen what she looked like, so maybe I'm wrong, but I think this is Vi. And look at her ears, Trev." She zoomed in on a set of daisy shaped purple earrings. "Will this help?"

———

Trev had left a reluctant Charlotte at her apartment, although he did manage to kiss her several times to apologise for not letting her be part of the next step. The photo had changed everything and Bryce was arranging an emergency warrant to search both properties.

Katrina was on her way, along with a couple more uniformed officers from Kyneton, called in on their day off. Waiting to search wasn't an option. Not if Terrance Murdoch was the killer. Trev met Bryce up the road from Terrance's residence, parking the patrol car out of sight and joining Bryce in his unmarked vehicle to watch from a distance.

"I got you lunch. Man, I look after you, Trev." Bryce grinned and bit into a roll. This was the most excited Trev had ever seen him.

"Thanks. Any movement? Do you know if he's home?"

Bryce swallowed. "He is. Saw Kevin drive in a few minutes ago. Sending someone to watch the other place. For all we know, they are in this together and I can't have Kevin or anyone else go to remove evidence."

Trev took a bite. The afternoon would be long. He'd promised Charlie he'd keep her informed if possible, but much would depend on the nature of their findings. If anything. So much was still circumstantial. They'd confirmed the photograph was Vi Ackerman based on one of the school yearbooks in the trunk which was now in the hands of Crime Scene Services. The earrings were yet to be confirmed to belong to her and unless they found a match to the fingerprint from the first one, might remain circumstantial.

Kevin drove out. One less to worry about. A few minutes later, Katrina arrived. She parked behind Bryce and slid into the back seat. "The warrant is approved. Fastest I remember seeing one. Have a patrol car with two officers about ten minutes away and another going to the other property. They can start there once we give the go ahead."

"Can we trace the message Charlie got? We need to find who sent the photo." This worried Trev. Why send it to Charlotte? She'd been the recipient of anonymous hate mail before, mostly from Sid Browne, but it wasn't Sid sending this.

"I've already put that into motion. Didn't that reporter want to stir up trouble? Perhaps she thinks Charlotte will investigate on her own and get caught up in something." Katrina checked her watch. "We might get ready because I want to be at the front door the minute the patrol car arrives."

Terrance Murdoch was furious. He slammed the door on them when Katrina told him the reason for their visit. "I'm calling my lawyer!"

"Go right ahead but first, I would suggest you give us access to avoid the front door being broken. The warrant should be on your phone now." She turned to Bryce and Trev with a small smile. "Do you think ten seconds is enough?"

The door flung open and Terrance filled the space. "This is preposterous! Harassment. You have no grounds to search this house."

"We do, or the warrant wouldn't have been granted. Please step aside, Mr Murdoch."

He did, tapping at his phone. "I'll sue you all. Any damages will be paid for. Why is that officer going into the garden? I don't keep bodies out..." As if his brain caught up with his mouth, he stopped talking.

"Where do you keep them?" Bryce tried to help out. "Is it underneath rose bushes?"

Terrance stalked away to speak, presumably, to his lawyer.

"Right, follow the plan, people." Katrina glanced at Trev. "Shall we start upstairs?"

———

Partway through the search, Katrina got a call from the other house. Trev straightened from his search beneath a bed as she talked. She put her phone away with a nod. "Five rose bushes underneath a pile of branches. Looked ready to light as a bonfire. Appears they match the roses in the wreath."

He got down again and reached for a suitcase under the bed. This was the last of six bedrooms in the massive house. Each was fully furnished even though Terrance lived alone. This room was the smallest. They'd found suitcases under every bed, either empty or with men's clothes. This was heavy and he dragged it out to open. It was locked and he muttered a swear word under his breath.

"I have never heard you say such a thing!" Katrina laughed. "Bit frustrated?"

"Sorry about that. You have no objection to me prying this open?"

"Pry away. Flat head screwdriver should do it."

A few minutes later the clips were undone, if damaged. Trev opened the lid, expecting more men's clothes.

"Boss."

"That sounded official. Oh." Katrina looked over his shoulder. "Let me take some pics."

A wedding dress was pushed into the suitcase. Not folded or in tissue, just shoved in. Trev had seen it before. "Bryony's. I think, not being an expert, but it looks a lot like the one in the photo coming out of the church. Got it on my phone somewhere."

"Can you lift it up?"

As Trev carefully extracted the dress, something soft and white fell to the ground. A veil. Once Katrina finished photographing the dress, Trev laid it on the bed and picked up the light fabric. "It's a different material from the dress. Look at the pattern of the lace around the edges compared to the dress."

Katrina stared at Trev as if seeing him for the first time. "You've missed your calling, dude."

"Katrina, look at it."

She smiled to herself and took more photos, then had Trev lay the veil beside the dress and took more. "You are right. And the quality is incomparable. The veil is so light and perfect whereas the dress is… well, probably off the rack, rather than custom made. Do me a favour and send a pic of the veil to your bridal shop lady. Let's see if this is the stolen one."

While Trev did that, Katrina lifted the last item from the suitcase. A wedding album. She turned a few pages and closed it as Trev's phone beeped.

"She says yes. Needs to see it to be certain, but thinks it is hers."

chapter
fifty-five

Charlotte peered over the balcony yet again. She'd been in and out for the past half hour, waiting for Trev. For news. He'd messaged to say he'd be there but still wasn't. Since he'd told her about the search warrant, her mind had come up with all kinds of outcomes. To keep herself busy, she'd made pasta from scratch. Gnocchi the way Doug taught her during her lessons on Italian cooking. There was enough for a whole department of police should the stakeout be on tonight.

Or I'll be eating gnocchi for weeks.

Rosie had called earlier to say they were spending another night and would Charlotte mind looking after the shop on her own tomorrow. This made Charlotte smile. The little holiday must be agreeing with Rosie.

She'd put beer and white wine in the fridge and was considering pouring herself a glass. Twilight was approaching fast. Charlotte went to check the back bedroom was tidy for the tenth time.

Earlier she'd seen the police officer leave the forest area. Either they needed the man power or they'd found evidence. The window was open so she closed it.

Kevin Murdoch stood on the other side of the track.

Watching her. He was motionless, his arms crossed and legs braced apart.

She stared back, curious. What odd behaviour. He must know his brother's houses were being searched and if he had any inkling of the killer in his own family, it mustn't bother him. Blood being thicker than water was true for some people. Did he blame her?

Ever since moving to Kingfisher Falls, four men viewed her with suspicion. Sid was now out of the police force and not involved with the corruption around town. Not overtly, anyway. But he was still around. Jonas tried to play mind games with her. Terrance considered her an interloper. And Kevin? He'd attempted to intimidate her after Octavia died. All four had the local council in common one way or another.

Well, she wasn't intimidated. She waved. Kevin scowled and walked away in the direction of the far exit.

Back in the kitchen she took the wine from the fridge and almost dropped it when there was a knock on the door. Still holding it, she opened it. Trev was in jeans and jumper and carrying a bottle of wine. They both held theirs up and tapped them together with a joint "cheers".

"Come on in. Particularly bringing gifts." Charlotte put her bottle away and collected two glasses. "I take it things went well."

Trev followed her into the kitchen and took the glasses. After placing them on the counter, he put his arms around her. "First, I need to hold you." He did, his heartbeat steady against her ear. "That feels better."

He kissed her and released her.

"Are you staying for dinner? I made gnocchi."

"Love to. Thanks. And no stakeout tonight." Trev poured two glasses. "The sliding door is open. Want to sit out for a bit?"

Once they were settled on the balcony, he offered a toast. "To catching the bad guy."

"Terrance."

"Arrested and spending the night in a cell in Melbourne. No doubt his lawyer will get him bail but we'll fight to keep him in."

"What did you find on him?"

"A suitcase with a wedding dress. Bryony's."

Charlotte gasped. "He kept her dress?"

"And a veil. Thing is, we have photos from her wedding and she didn't have a veil."

"Vi's." Dreams of brides with veils. Harmony's words about a veil. "Some kind of trophy?"

He shrugged. "He claims he's never seen it before. Admits to the dress because it belonged to Bryony, but maintains the veil was planted."

"Could it have been?"

"Anything's possible. The detectives are determined to build a case strong enough to stand any scrutiny."

"He denies being involved with Vi Ackerman?"

"Claims he and Bryony were on holiday when Vi disappeared. Hard to prove either way. He says he has no proof and can't remember where they stayed apart from being somewhere in country New South Wales. But there's so much evidence now. Pretty sure we can see it through."

Trev's phone rang. "This is via the station. Sorry." He answered. "Leading Senior Constable Sibbritt speaking."

Charlotte headed inside to give him some privacy but stopped and turned around at his change of tone.

"Would you repeat your name?" He listened and his eyes caught Charlotte's. "Please stay there. I'll be less than five minutes." He hung up and strode inside. "Grab a jacket. You'll want to be there."

"Trev? Who was it?"

"You're not going to believe this. Bryony Murdoch is waiting at the station."

————

On first glance, nobody was outside the station, but as Trev led the way in the near-dark, a shadow by the door stepped out. A slight figure wrapped in a thick overcoat.

"Bryony? It is Trev Sibbritt. We just spoke."

"Is it safe here? Is she police too?" Her voice was wary.

"This is Doctor Charlotte Dean. She's consulting in our investigation."

The woman nodded. Trev unlocked the door, turned off the alarm, and ushered everyone inside before relocking the door. Charlotte found the lights.

"Please, let's go and sit at the first desk. Would you like some water, or coffee?" Please not coffee. Poor woman had been through enough.

Without removing her coat, Bryony shook her head and sat. Despite the years between her wedding photo and today, Trev would have recognised her. Same curls and pretty face, although stress lines furrowed her forehead.

He sat opposite and Charlotte pulled over one of the other chairs to sit at the end. She hadn't taken her eyes off Bryony.

"I'm very pleased to see you, Mrs Murdoch."

"Bryony. I don't use that surname now. I changed it to protect myself. Being here is a risk." She glanced around. "Everything is locked?"

"I won't let anything happen to you. Please, tell us why you're here."

Trev opened his notepad and smiled what he hoped was some encouragement. Bryony shifted in her seat then nodded as if to herself.

"I swore I'd never return. But that poor girl... she needs to rest easy at last."

"I'm listening."

"Terrance was a lot of things. Controlling. Mean spirited. Greedy. And he was a cheater of the worst kind." There were tears in Bryony's eyes. "She was only seventeen when he seduced her. All for a bit of fun because of her strict religion. When he married me the same year, I think he stopped seeing her but who knows. I didn't."

Charlotte found a box of tissues and slid them closer to Bryony, who took one.

"When did you find out about his... relationship with Vi Ackerman?" Trev kept his voice low. Bryony looked ready to run at any minute.

"The day I left. All that time with him and I never knew."

"I've spoken with Concetta Bongiovanni."

A small smile flickered on Bryony's face. "She was a friend. My only one, really. I told her about the phone call I received and said goodbye to her. I miss her though."

"I'll give you her number. She misses you also. Would you tell us about the phone call please? We only know second hand."

"Terrance was off somewhere for the day. Out of town. The phone rang and it was a girl. A teen. She told me Terrance had killed Violet and buried her out in the forest. I asked her why she said such a thing and she told me she'd seen Violet go to meet him to talk about their wedding. That Violet had a wedding dress and b... baby clothes."

"Take your time."

"I'm fine. Anyway, I knew he hadn't done any such thing because I remembered when Violet disappeared, he and I were on holiday. A late honeymoon. There was talk about her leaving home because her parents disapproved of her boyfriend and then everyone forgot about her. But this girl was insistent. She claimed she'd seen Violet meet him many times at the end of a little path leading to a clearing. They'd go there. And one evening she saw Violet go down the path and never return."

Tears streamed down Charlotte's face. Trev couldn't give her his attention. So many questions burned in his mind. But Bryony kept talking, her eyes on his face.

"I asked why she'd not told anyone and she said she had. Her parents didn't believe her. She was just a little girl."

A dull thud of understanding hit Trev. Vi's little sister had seen something and remembered.

"Even though I knew Terrance wasn't responsible for Violet's disappearance, something snapped inside of me. I couldn't be with someone who'd treated a girl that way. He's a monster. I took a suitcase and left."

"Did you walk to the train station? It's a long walk."

"No. Kevin drove me. I didn't say why I was leaving, not being about his brother and all. But he'd never agreed with our marriage so was happy to make sure I was gone. He always fixed up Terrance's mistakes." She grabbed a handful of tissues and pushed the box to Charlotte. "Why are you crying? I know you're not Daisy."

"Daisy?" Charlotte asked, taking tissues.

"Daisy Ackerman. Violet's little sister. She'd be about your age."

chapter
fifty-six

Trev was on the phone to Katrina in another room. Charlotte took a bottle of water to Bryony and sat beside her. "You're brave. Leaving when you did. But why not divorce Terrance?"

Bryony shook her head. "He'd have found me and I never wanted to see him again. But maybe now I will. I'm stronger."

"You always were. Is there anything else you remember about the phone call from Daisy?"

"She was angry. Told me Terrance deserved to die for what he did. And the strangest comment ever, right at the end. It made no sense so I forgot about it until now."

Nothing was going to sound strange after tonight.

"Strange, how?"

"It was personal. Everything else was about Terrance and Violet. She said I'd never be free until I faced my greatest fear and it would set her sister free as well. And I do feel free for the first time." Bryony gave a short laugh. "She was all of fourteen or something and sounded like an oracle."

Charlotte felt her mouth drop open and closed it. She looked up as Trev returned, seeking his eyes, and trying to convey the message that they needed to talk. He just looked a bit confused by her expression.

"Bryony, there will be other police here soon to take you out of town, as you've asked. They may want to ask some more questions in Kyneton station, if you are okay with that. Then they'll arrange a motel room for tonight. Nice and safe."

Minutes dragged like hours as Charlotte's mind raced. Terrance wasn't the killer which meant somebody else was. Somebody who met Vi instead. There was an answer in there somewhere. It hid out of Charlotte's reach but she could almost see the connections.

Bryony asked to use the bathroom and Charlotte grabbed Trev's hand to drag him to the other end of the building.

"Um… timing?" He teased.

"No, listen. Never considered Vi was short for Violet. Daisy, now what kind of flower is an aster? A daisy. And those in the forest are purple. Violet daisies." The words tumbled out. She pulled her phone out and tapped a query in. "Look. The Michaelmas Daisy, which is the purple aster, has a meaning… departure. Goodbye. This is all about symbolism."

"What are you thinking, Charlie?"

"Not quite sure. Do you mind if I go home now? I'll get dinner underway and try to puzzle this all out."

Trev kissed the top of her head. "Be quick and careful. Straight home, please. And message me once you are inside."

A moment later and she was sprinting in the direction of Harmony's shop. She'd said a quick goodbye to Bryony, wishing her well and thanking her. Now she was doing the opposite of Trev's instructions.

It was a small detour. And might mean nothing. Charlotte mulled over the last half hour. Violet and Daisy. A purple aster… well, lots of flowers most likely, but in this instance, the flower trail leading to Violet's grave was planted with purple asters. And the grave. Whoever did it had an intense personal relationship with Violet. Either her killer, or someone who loved her.

Like a sister would.

Daisy was supposed to be in Europe, according to a family who cared little when their middle child vanished without a word. A family who'd not seen their youngest child for more than ten years. What if Europe was yet another lie?

The clip-on earrings were purple daisies. Harmony had run from the bookshop after seeing purple asters on the counter. The flower trail and grave were planted with purple asters, not once, but twice. The person who'd lovingly tended the grave was still here.

Charlotte stopped at the corner to Harmony's shop, panting. Night was here. The side streets were quiet. Dark and deserted. But Charlotte needed to see her. Daisy was around her age. So was Harmony who knew a lot about the town for a complete stranger. And Daisy had spoken to Bryony in a manner reminiscent of Harmony's predictions.

A movement down the street caught Charlotte's attention. She took off toward it, trying to see what was going on. A car was parked near the small block of shops where Harmony lived and worked. There was a door open and a man, pushing something… someone… into the car. A scream and the door slammed.

The car did a U-turn and sped past Charlotte. All she saw was a mop of red hair in the back seat.

Charlotte gave chase. Never had she run as fast. The car turned without indicating at the corner and she was there in seconds. By now it was far away but she knew where it was heading. She had to get there in time.

Trev spoke to Katrina by phone as Bryony left in the back of a patrol car. Katrina and Bryce had sent a uniformed officer to collect her after hearing Terrance might have an alibi.

"There's more. That partial print off the earring matches Kevin Murdoch. He has no form but we have his prints from past break-ins at the pub." Katrina sounded frustrated.

"Kevin drove Bryony to the train station the day she left. She said something about him fixing up Terrance's mistakes. Perhaps he fixed up his brother's so-called mistake with Violet Ackerman. And there's the issue of where is Daisy Ackerman?"

A beep on the line signalled another call.

"Can I get this call and I'll ring back."

"We're heading over to Kevin's house to pick him up so meet you at the station." Katrina hung up and Trev answered, seeing Charlotte's name flash up.

"Are you home?"

"No... Trev need you to go to... falls."

He struggled to make out the words. Was Charlie running?

"Slow down. Where are you?"

"Kevin... has Harmony."

Trev unlocked his patrol car and slid behind the wheel. "Where are you."

"Cutting across to the falls." She must have stopped. "I saw him push her... into his car." Charlotte was sucking in air. "He drove toward the bush. Can't see him now."

He turned on the siren and lights and floored it. "Charlotte don't follow any more. I'm on my way. Stay on the line." In a minute he was talking to dispatch. He stopped at the roundabout and checked Charlotte's location. "Still there?"

"I can see them. He's dragging her along."

"Go back to the apartment and lock yourself in. I'm not joking."

Her voice was so quiet he barely heard them. "Trev... I think he's going to push her over the falls."

"Charlie, help is coming. Charlie?"

chapter
fifty-seven

Charlotte dropped her phone as she tripped over a root. She sank to the ground to find it among the dense low branches, finally curling her fingers around it in the dark. The call to Trev was disconnected and she muted the phone. If she got close to Kevin she didn't want him to hear her phone ring.

Back on her feet, she peered through the trees. She was deep in the forest with little light. Somewhere ahead, Kevin was forcing Harmony along the side of the river. She'd thought he was taking her to the clearing but he'd veered around it. Harmony was struggling the whole time, her feet leaving indentations in the ground. But she was gagged and her hands looked tied together from the distant glimpses Charlotte got.

She moved closer to the river and sped up again. He couldn't hurt Harmony. Trev would be here and other police. They'd stop Kevin.

Why hadn't she seen it? Kevin was the one in control of everything in the town. Even Sid Browne said as much. "He's the one pulling all the strings." He'd told her at the lookout when the subject of the dirty antics of council came up earlier this year.

The puppet master.

But what did he want with Harmony? How would he know she was really Daisy Ackerman and even so, why would he care? She'd been a small child when he'd taken her sister. She hadn't even seen who Violet met that evening.

But he might think she did.

The roar of the falls grew louder. As the canopy opened up, it was a bit easier to see the figures ahead. They were almost at the edge. Charlotte wanted to cry out to get Kevin's attention but she was still too far away to help. Instead, she flew along the edge of the river.

Kevin had stopped and Harmony was on the ground in a heap. Charlotte skirted around a cluster of large rocks until in ear shot.

Both appeared exhausted and why wouldn't they be? He'd dragged a struggling woman into a car and then across difficult terrain. And she'd fought him all the way. Kevin pulled the gag off Harmony's mouth and she gasped for air. He stepped back, loosely pointing a gun her way.

Charlotte texted Trev.

At top of falls. Kevin has a gun and Harmony is tied up. Hurry.

How long would it take for help to arrive? She couldn't guess the time it took her to get here but Trev wouldn't care about making a noise. Charlotte crept closer, alarmed by the proximity of Harmony to the edge. She took one photo, afraid her camera might attract attention.

"Not so clever now?" Kevin spat. "Thought you could see the future."

"You killed my sister." Harmony's hands were tied in front of her. She pushed herself up enough to look at him. "Would you have let your own brother go to jail?"

"Once you're gone, the cops will find a note from you. About how you planted evidence to blame an innocent man, someone you disliked because he wouldn't back your application for the stupid mind and spirit festival you wanted to run."

Charlotte had heard nothing of a festival but was appalled by the lengths this man was going to. How long had he planned this?

"You'll pay."

"Yeah, yeah. In a minute you'll be joining your sister on the other side and you can haunt me all you want. Shouldn't have looked out of the window all those times." He glanced over the side. "It'll be quick."

There was no sound of sirens. No lights through the trees. Kevin was going to kill Harmony and Charlotte couldn't let it happen. She stepped out from behind the rock.

"Kevin, stop it."

He started and swung the gun to point directly at her.

"Two for the price of one. Get over here."

"The police are on their way. Trevor knows you have Harmony so all of this is pointless. It's over."

Fury turned his face red. He waved the gun at Charlotte. "I'm not giving up everything I worked for. I've protected my brother all these years from stupid girls and gambling debts and I won't lose it all now."

Harmony adjusted her position, forming a solid base on her knees. Charlotte kept her eyes on Kevin. He had to look at her, not Harmony.

Over the roar of the water came a siren, and another. Headlights cut through the dark on the other side of the river where there were wider tracks. They were closing in fast.

Kevin's head shot toward the lights then back to Charlotte. "No. With you both dead there'll be no proof."

He aimed at Charlotte's head and began to squeeze the trigger.

Harmony slammed her hands against his stomach and his

arms flew up, a shot firing into the sky. His foot slid off the edge and then with a scream, he was gone.

Charlotte threw herself across the distance to grab Harmony before the momentum took her over after him. She pulled her away from the edge and untied her wrists with shaking hands.

"Charlotte! Oh my God, Charlotte!" Trev was a long way away, his voice tortured.

"We're okay!" Charlotte hoped he heard her call back.

Her arms were around Harmony. "You did good, Daisy. You really did."

Harmony's body shuddered. "I just killed him. And he deserved it."

"It wasn't your fault."

"They won't believe you." Harmony got to her feet and Charlotte stood. "I wasn't going to let him hurt you as well, Charlie."

Flashlights criss-crossed the ground as help closed in. Too late. But not for Harmony, or Daisy. It wasn't too late for her life to begin at last.

"I'm your witness and they will believe me."

Harmony smiled. "Your future has changed. All I see is happiness for you." She leaned close and kissed Charlotte's cheek before turning and running into the dark.

———

Trev's heart almost exploded from his chest at the sound of a gunshot. He'd driven as far as he could along tracks not meant for normal vehicles. As he'd run along the river, three people were silhouetted at the edge of the cliff. One on the ground, two standing. Charlotte should never have even been there.

When the unmistakable sound of the shot came, he was

cast back in time to Rivers End. Charlotte taken by a deranged ex-patient, captive in a cave. He was halfway down the cliff and thought she'd been shot.

"Charlotte! Oh my God, Charlotte!" The cry escaped his throat as he returned to this moment.

Words drifted his way. He thought they were hers. Prayed they were.

He came out of the trees on the far side of the river. Harmony ran into the bushland the opposite way. Charlotte stared over the edge of the cliff and then, as though sensing he was there, stepped back to safety.

———

"If you insist on finding trouble, would you do it in daytime, during the week, or when I'm on leave?" Bryce grumbled as he finished taking Charlotte's statement. Trev and Katrina were still at the falls with a recovery crew.

Charlotte yawned. Her muscles ached and she needed water. Lots of water.

"Are we done? Are you going to find Harmony... Daisy?"

"We are done. And we'll find her."

"She did nothing wrong. If anything, she saved my life." Charlotte stood, moaning a little.

"Come on, I'll drive you home."

"I'll walk."

Bryce burst into laughter. He kept laughing as he collected his keys and gestured for Charlotte to leave first.

"What?"

"I can just imagine the conversation between me and your boyfriend." Bryce locked the door. "Charlotte decided to walk home. Oh, sure, not a problem, Bryce. It isn't like she'll get herself into any trouble."

"You have a point. But not my fault that Kevin decided to kidnap Harmony as I walked past."

"Sure. You walked past." He opened the car door. "I'll leave that conversation for you and Trevor."

"He's not my boyfriend." Charlotte needed to point this out as she slid into the car.

Once again, Bryce burst into laughter.

———

Showered and wrapped in her dressing gown against shivers that worsened the more she thought about the night's events, Charlotte opened the door on Trev's first knock.

He came straight in and enveloped her in his arms. His strength and warmth and scent filled her senses until the shivering was gone and she felt safe again. Then, he lifted her chin and gazed into her eyes. "Tonight was the second time I thought you'd been shot. Never again, Charlie. If I ask you to do something, as a police officer and as the man who loves you, then no more detours or thinking you'll go off on your own investigation. Agree?"

He'd lost her on the bit about being the man who loves her. Charlotte leaned back against his arms. "What did you say?"

"Charlotte!" There was frustration there. "I said no more—"

"The earlier bit. Did you say you…" She bit her lip. Maybe she misheard.

His eyes twinkled. "Love you? Did I say that?"

"You're teasing me."

He tightened his arms and then his lips were on hers, teasing her in a whole different way. If she hadn't heard it with his words, she got the message now. He loved her.

Despite her sometimes-reckless actions and occasional poor judgement, Trev loved her.

————

Dinner might have been much later than planned, but it tasted wonderful and was eaten on the sofa with a shared bottle of wine.

"Will Harmony be in trouble?" Charlotte ventured. "I'm worrying about her."

"Not for me to decide but as far as Kevin is concerned, she was defending her life and yours, and for that I am grateful. Whatever else is involved with her actions over the past few months we may not unravel for some time. But we're looking for her to help us, not to penalise her for tonight."

"She said something. That my future is changed."

Trev gave her a sideways look.

"Nothing bad. If anything… well, she said all she saw for me was happiness. And for the first time in my life, my whole life, I feel it is true."

And she did. There was a lot to work out though. Zoe. Her dad. Angelica. But nothing would stop her doing so. She'd been through a lifetime of difficulties and heartache and here, now, it stopped.

Charlotte put down her wine glass and reached for Trev's hands. His eyes held a question and for the first time, she knew the answer.

"Trevor? I love you too."

chapter
fifty-eight

Rosie sat on the balcony, her eyes alight with delight as she gazed around. "You are amazing, darling. You did all this on your own and turned it into an oasis."

Charlotte grinned and joined her at the table. It was set for four and looked beautiful with candles and a small bouquet of asters in the middle. There were no other lights on out here, so the candles cast interesting shadows and the scent of fresh herbs in their pots made her hungry.

Trev and Lewis were making cocktails inside and their laughter made Rosie and Charlotte smile.

"I'm so glad they get on so well." Rosie hadn't stopped smiling since returning from her holiday. Well, they had for a short time when she'd heard about the events while she was away, but then her happiness bubbled up again. "Lewis likes Trev a lot. And you too, Charlie."

"And I like him a lot. Besides, who else would I ask for advice on buying you presents?"

"He does know my tastes well. And now he knows I really can't be far from the sea after all. We spent every day visiting the beach and it was silly of me to stop for so long."

Charlotte squeezed her hand. "We've both learned to face our fears recently. Good for us, I say."

"Sounds like time for a toast." Lewis, followed by Trev, carried four glasses of delicious-looking drinks out. "Our own recipe. So, pretend to like it, even if you don't."

Once everyone was around the table, Trev made the first toast. "To Mum. You inspire me every day and make me the proudest son alive."

Rosie's eyes glistened as everyone raised their glasses to her.

Lewis added his own toast. "To Rosie. A beautiful woman on the outside as well as in her heart."

Now, a tear escaped and trailed down Rosie's cheek. Lewis put down his glass, found a handkerchief in his pocket, and dabbed the tear dry. "Shall we tell them?"

Charlotte stole a look at Trev. He was smiling at Rosie and Lewis. Whatever they were about to say, she knew he was fine with it. He loved his dad and would never forget him, but was all about living now, not in the past.

Rosie nodded and took Lewis' hand. "Trev, Charlie, this wonderful gentleman has proposed marriage and I have accepted." She turned her eyes to Trev.

He put his glass down and leaned over to hug her. "I am so happy for you both." He shook Lewis's hand while Charlotte rushed around to hug Rosie.

Much later, over dessert, Rosie explained their plans. "Lewis will sell his house and buy a small place near the sea. A holiday home. And we will spend some time there and some here. With our family. My son, and the woman who is like a daughter to me."

Charlotte blinked away tears that suddenly threatened. There'd been enough crying, both happy and sad, to last a lifetime. She smiled. "I love you lots, Rosie."

Rosie lifted her glass. "And my son loves you and I know

you love him, so don't either of you deny it. My toast is to Trev and Charlie. You belong together and one day, I hope you find the same happiness Lewis has brought me."

Over their glasses, Charlotte's eyes met Trev's. In those kind, warm eyes of his she saw her reflection. She might sometimes follow a different path, particularly where a mystery was involved, but he would always be there for her.

And she would always be there for him.

next in the series

PLANS FOR MURDER IN KINGFISHER FALLS

A happy life. A bright future. A past which is catching up...

Charlotte Dean is finally living the life she wants. Happy in her small town of Kingfisher Falls with a great job and loving boyfriend, everything is perfect.

But after a terrible accident rocks the community, Charlotte suspects there is more to it. Much more. When someone comes forward to point their finger at a beloved member of the community, Charlotte isn't about to allow history to repeat itself. As she begins to do her own investigation, a chance sighting of someone from her old life sends Charlotte's world into a tailspin, forcing her to doubt her relationship with Rosie, and future in Kingfisher Falls.

But is there a common link behind everything, and who is really behind the planned shopping mall near the bookshop?

In a shocking series of events, Charlotte comes face to face with the past and will have to risk everything, even her life, to overcome the most dangerous situation yet.

NOTE: This book was previously titled Deadly Past.

about the author

Phillipa lives just outside a beautiful town in country Victoria, Australia. She also lives in the many worlds of her imagination and stockpiles stories beside her laptop.

She writes from the heart about love, dreams, secrets, discovery, the sea, the world as she knows it... or wishes it could be. She loves happy endings, heart-pounding suspense, and characters who stay with you long after the final page.

With a passion for music, the ocean, animals, nature, reading, and writing, she is often found in the vegetable garden pondering a new story.

Phillipa's website is www.phillipaclark.com

also by phillipa nefri clark

Detective Liz Moorland

Gripping Australian Police Procedurals

Rivers End Romantic Women's Fiction

Temple River Romantic Women's Fiction

Charlotte Dean Mysteries

Daphne Jones Mysteries

Bindarra Creek Rural Fiction

Maple Gardens Matchmakers

Sweet Contemporary Romances

Doctor Grok's Peculiar Shop Short Stories

Feel-good short fantasies

Simple Words for Troubled Times

Short non-fiction happiness and comfort book